TWO MARRIAGES.

BY THE AUTHOR OF

"JOHN HALIFAX, GENTLEMAN," "CHRISTIAN'S MISTAKE,"
"A NOBLE LIFE," "A LIFE FOR A LIFE,"
"FAIRY BOOK," &c.

"Hearken, son:
I'll tell thee of two fathers."

NEW YORK:
HARPER & BROTHERS, PUBLISHERS,
FRANKLIN SQUARE.
1867.

INSCRIBED TO

A. M. M.,

FRIEND, READER, AND CRITIC,

WITH OUR LOVE.

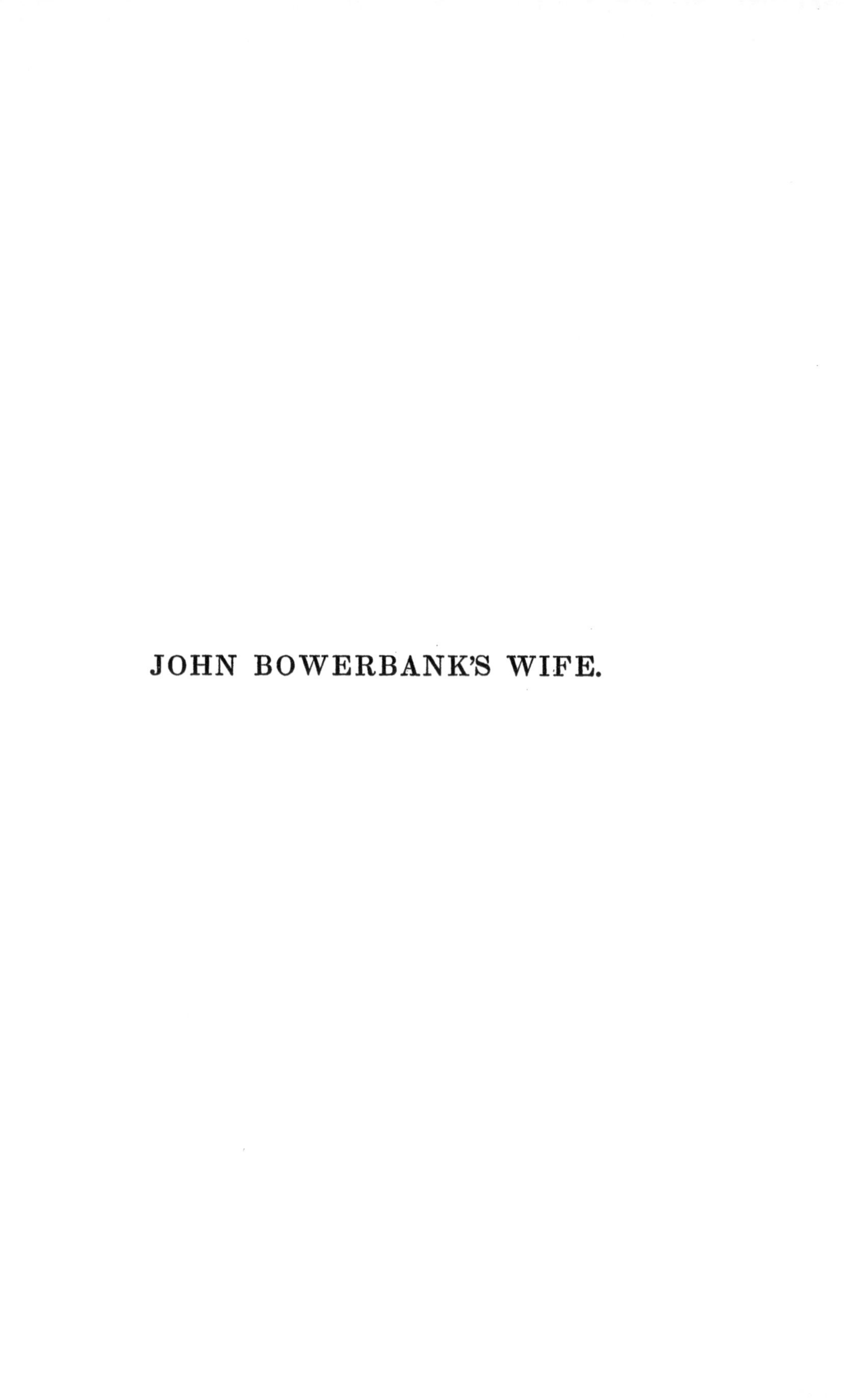

JOHN BOWERBANK'S WIFE.

JOHN BOWERBANK'S WIFE.

CHAPTER I.

"WELL, I am glad it has come off at last, for never was there a wedding so talked about," said Mrs. Smiles.

"It hasn't come off yet," replied Mrs. Knowle, shaking her head mysteriously. "And, for my part, even though we sit here, in the very church, with the clerk arranging the cushions, and poor John Bowerbank—he looks nervous, doesn't he? even though he's an elderly man and a widower—walking up and down the aisle before our very eyes—I say, Mrs. Smiles, I shall never believe, till I see the ring on her finger, that they are really married. How strange it seems! Poor Emily Kendal—John Bowerbank's wife!"

"Why do you say 'poor Emily Kendal,' 'poor John Bowerbank,' when it is such a suitable match—except in years perhaps; but a man's age is of no consequence. And then Miss Kendal looks so much older than she really is, and is such a grave, sedate sort of person—grown old-maidish already. I'm sure, when I looked at her at their farewell dinner-party last week in Queen Anne Street—I could hardly believe it was only two years since the ball there, when she came of age. Such a splendid affair! Do you remember it?"

"Indeed I do!" said abruptly the other lady, who had not been paying much attention to Mrs. Smiles's conversation. Her broad, honest, regular-featured Lancashire face—she had been one of the fair "Lancashire witches" till she developed into coarseness of color and size—was fixed earnestly upon the church door, where John Bowerbank had just entered, and where his wife to be was expected every moment to enter. But Mrs. Knowle carefully hid herself—the good woman! who was usually not at all given to surreptitious proceedings—behind the curtains of the pew, which was in that gloomy old church, so noted for fashionable weddings—St. George's, Hanover Square. By the number and style of the guests, this was evidently a fashionable wedding too; and Mrs. Smiles—a bright, dapper, shallow little Londoner—evidently longing to see more of the fine dresses, proposed that they should change their places, and get a little nearer to the altar.

"No, I don't want her to see me. She mightn't like it," said Mrs. Knowle.

"Why not?—when your husband is a partner in John Bowerbank's firm, and they have always been such friends? I'm sure I fully expected you would have been asked to the wedding."

"So I was, but I declined to go. I couldn't somehow. I was certain it would be very bad for her, poor thing!" added Mrs. Knowle to herself.

But her little mystery, whatever it was, escaped Mrs. Smiles's penetration, for just then that lady's whole attention was engrossed by the primary object of this sight, gazed at by all assembled in church with the fervid eagerness of women over weddings—the bride.

John Bowerbank's wife—or to be made such in fifteen minutes—was a little lady, fragile and white, whom you could hardly distinguish clearly under her mass of snowy silk, her clouds of lace, and her tremulous wreath of orange-blossoms.

"She is shaking a good deal, poor lamb!" said Mrs. Knowle, half in soliloquy. "And how tightly she holds her father's arm!"

"Mr. Kendal has been a good father, people say; though he won't stand thwarting, he always will have his own way. Perhaps she's sorry to leave him, being the only child."

"Hum!" again soliloquized Mrs. Knowle. "Hush! the service is beginning."

It was soon begun—soon ended—the solemn words which made Emily Kendal John Bowerbank's wife. She rose up from her knees and he rose up too—that grave, gray-haired, commonplace, and yet not ill-looking bridegroom—thirty years at least her senior. No longer nervous now, he gave her his arm, and led her away to the vestry, through the open door of which the two ladies observed him stop, formally and in a business-like way—he was a thorough man of business—to lift her veil, and give her the first conjugal kiss.

"Well! it's all over; but I never thought I should see this day," said Mrs. Knowle, her broad, honest breast relieving itself of much pent-up feeling with a great sigh. "Poor dear girl! poor little Emily!"

"Why will you call her 'poor?'" persisted Mrs. Smiles. "I'm sure I should be delighted to see any one of my girls make so good a marriage; and to such a thoroughly respectable husband—'John Bowerbank & Co., Merchants, Liverpool.' Why, their name is as good as the bank; as you ought to know, who have been in the firm so many years. And as for the gentleman himself, though I never saw him before to-day, he seems really quite the gentleman; and I, for one, would far rather give a daughter to an elderly man—even a widower, of good means and unimpeachable character, than to any harem-scarem young fellow, who would soon make ducks and drakes of her money—and Miss Kendal has a great deal of money, I understand?"

"Yes—more's the pity. Fifty thousand pounds."

"Was it so much?" said Mrs. Smiles, in great awe.

"Yes—for she said to me one day she wished she could change it into fifty thousand pence."

"She must have been out of her senses."

"Perhaps she was, poor dear, for the time. But now she has apparently got into them again, and made a prudent marriage—an admirably prudent marriage. But, oh my dear, when I married Edward Knowle, and he was a clerk and I was a milliner, and we had but two hundred a year between us, we were happy people—happier than these! For we loved one another, and we married for love. And there was not a single 'cause or impediment' in the sight of God or man why we should not marry. Which—God forgive her—is more than I can say of John Bowerbank's wife."

Mrs. Smiles looked so shocked, so frightened, that too-candid Mrs. Knowle could almost have cut her tongue out for the foolish speech she had made. She knew that Mrs. Smiles was a terrible gossip; but she also knew that a certain dim sense of duty and pride, which exists in many great talkers, made her, however unscrupulous over a secret which she had ferreted out or guessed at, if honestly trusted, by no means untrustworthy. With a sudden decision—for the position was critical enough—the good Liverpool lady turned to her London friend—who was not a bad woman in her way—and said earnestly,

"I'm sorry I ever let a word drop, Mrs. Smiles, for it was a very painful business—though it is all over now. I'll tell it you, and depend upon your never telling it again, though it was nothing discreditable, my dear, I do assure you. Indeed, as regards character, not a word could ever be breathed against Emily Kendal, or her father either. They bear a perfectly unblemished name. And perhaps what happened was nothing more than happens to almost every girl in her teens—they fall in love and out of love a dozen times before they marry—but I never thought Emily was that sort of girl either."

"And was she in love? or engaged? Do tell me. Who was it? Any body I know?" said Mrs. Smiles, eagerly.

Mrs. Knowle wished herself at the bottom of the sea before she had let her feelings carry her away into making such a cruel mistake, such a fatal admission; but still the only safe way to remedy it was to tell the whole truth, and then trust to her friend's sense of honor. After all, it was not a very terrible truth. As she had well said, the thing happens dozens of times to dozens of girls.

"I'll tell you the whole story, Mrs. Smiles, if you will promise not to speak of it. Not that 'it' was any thing bad; poor dears! they were so young, it was such a natural thing for them to fall in love; but it caused us—my husband and me—a great deal of trouble at the time, for it happened in our house."

"This love affair?"

"Yes, a real love affair—not a bit like poor John Bowerbank's sober courtship, but an old-fashioned love affair; heart-warm—so warm that Edward said it put him in mind of our own young days. And the people were—"

"I can guess, for I was with you two days of the time of Emily Kendal's visit, and I think I can see as far into a millstone as most people. It was young Stenhouse?"

Mrs. Knowle nodded, with a sad look in her kindly eyes. "Just so! Poor fellow, I have scarcely spoken his name—even to my husband—ever since he sailed to India, a year and half ago. We were so sorry to lose him. He was a clerk in our firm, you know—entered the office as a boy of fifteen—and that was how he came so much to our house while she was visiting us. And he was a fine young fellow, quite the gentleman; and she was a lass in her teens, and a bonny lass she was too, then—so of course they fell in love with one another—and, mercy me! how could I help it! He behaved very honorably, poor fellow! came and told me at once, as soon as ever he had proposed to her—that is, if he ever did formally propose. I rather think not, but that they found each other's feelings by the merest accident. For I remember he said to me, in such a burst of passion as I never saw yet in mortal man, 'I've been an ass, and some folk might call me a knave—for she has fifty thousand pounds, and I haven't a halfpenny!' Poor lad!—poor lad!"

"And what did you do?"

"What could I do—shut the stable-door when the steed was stolen? Why, my dear woman, I told you—the poor things loved one another."

An argument which did not seem to weigh very much with Mrs. Smiles. She drew herself up with dignity.

"A most unfortunate and ill-advised attachment. I, as a mother of a family of daughters, must certainly say—"

"What would you say?"

"That I would consider it my duty to prevent it."

"How could I prevent it?" exclaimed Mrs. Knowle, pathetically, as if the troubles her warm heart had undergone at that time were bitter even in remembrance. "Here were two nice young people—one nineteen, the other five-and-twenty, meeting every day—liking one another's company, finding out continually how well they suited and how dearly they enjoyed being together. In truth, the very sight of them walking under the lilac-trees, or sitting outside the drawing-room window with a heap of books between them, talking, and reading, and laughing to themselves in their innocent, childish way, used to do my heart good. Many a time I thought, if God had been pleased to give Edward and me such a daughter, or if our little Edward, that's lying waiting for his mother, in Hale church-yard—well, that's nonsense!" said the good woman, with a sudden pause and choking of the voice: "all I mean is, that in our childless house those young people were very pleasant company; and I used often to think if either of them was my own, oh, wouldn't I do a deal to make them both happy! But it wasn't to be — it wasn't to be. And now she has gone and married John Bowerbank."

"Not," continued the lady, after a pause, "not that I have a word to say against John Bowerbank. He is Mr. Kendal's friend, and my husband's friend; the three are all about the same age, too. He is a very good man; but he isn't John Stenhouse. And oh me! when I call to mind how fond John Stenhouse was of Emily Kendal, and how fond poor Emily was of him—of all the misery they went through together—of the nights I sat by her bedside till she sobbed herself to sleep — and of the days when young Stenhouse went to and fro between our house and the counting-house, with his face as white as death, and his lips fiercely set, and a look of stony despair in his eyes. Oh! my dear, I think I must have been dreaming when I saw the wedding this morning. How could she do it?"

"Did she do it—what did she do?"

"Well, not much, after all, I suppose," said Mrs. Knowle, with a sigh. "Edward and I vexed ourselves very much about it at the time; and yet such things occur every day, and people think nothing about them. We did, though. We couldn't see any reason on earth why Mr. Kendal should have blamed us so severely for 'allowing' such a thing to happen. Allowing? As if we possibly could have prevented it! As if, believing firmly that a real good marriage with a good man is the best thing that can befall any young woman, it would ever have occurred to us to try and prevent it! But Mr. Kendal thought differently. When John Stonehouse wrote to him for his consent, and my Edward inclosed it in the very civilest, friendliest letter, detailing all Mr. Stenhouse's circumstances and our high respect for him, and his being a fit husband for any girl, except in not having money, which, as Miss Kendal had plenty, didn't signify —well, I say, when the old man came down upon us like a thunderbolt, and dismissed John from the house, and insisted on carrying Emily away, only she took to her bed with a nervous fever and couldn't be moved, I own I was surprised. My dear, the poet says 'Fathers have flinty hearts;" but it's my belief they have no hearts at all. How that old fellow could have looked at that poor little girl of his—his daughter, wasted to a skeleton—lying on her bed with her pretty eyes (that were the image of her mother's when Mr. Kendal married her) fixed on the ceiling with such a hopeless look, and her pretty mouth, that never gave her father a sharp word back, but only whispered to me sometimes, 'Please don't let him be unkind to John'—how he could do it, and call himself a Christian, and go to church every Sunday, *I* don't understand! You must recollect," continued Mrs. Knowle, "that John Stenhouse was not a bad fellow, neither lowborn nor ill-educated—that not a living soul had ever breathed a syllable against his character. There was no earthly reason for refusing him except that he was a clerk in a merchant's office and she was a barrister's daughter; he had nothing, and she had fifty thousand pounds. *That* was the bottom of it, I know—the cursed, cursed money, as my husband said. Mr. Kendal wanted her to make what he called a suitable marriage—

that is, where every thing was right and proper—money equal, position equal—all done according to rule — gentleman coming a courting for a month or two — lady smilingly receiving polite attentions — then gentleman going first to ask papa's consent, and, that given, making a formal offer, and being accepted and married immediately in grand style, with six bridesmaids, and twenty carriages with white horses, just as we had to-day. Oh, how could she do it? But perhaps she couldn't help it. I saw from the first she was a weak, gentle creature. Why, she used to go into hysterics and fainting-fits, when I would have faced that old tyrant with a heart as hard as his own. Bless my life! I would have fought through a regiment of soldiers for the sake of my Edward; but she — the frail, trembling lamb — poor thing — poor thing!"

And the large, loud Lancashire woman, with the womanly heart, dropped a tear or two, which she smothered in her laced pocket-handkerchief, and turned out of the quiet street in Mayfair, where the two ladies were talking and walking, into one that led toward Queen Anne Street.

"For," said she, "I must get a peep at her when she goes away. I was very fond of poor Emily Kendal."

"But tell me the rest of her story," pleaded Mrs. Smiles. "Indeed I will never repeat it. And whom should I repeat it to? for I scarcely know any body in her circle, and she is now removing quite out of it. I suppose she will settle permanently in Liverpool?"

"Yes; John Bowerbank has one of the handsomest houses in all Birkenhead. His long widowhood alone hindered his taking his place at the very top of our Liverpool society. Now he will do it—for he is a social man and likes show—quite a different person from poor John Stenhouse, who would have spent evening after evening by his own fireside with his books or his piano-playing—he was the finest musician ever I knew, and built a chamber organ with his very own hands. I have it still, for he left it to me when he went abroad."

"Why did he go abroad?"

"I'll tell you—at least so far as I know, for he was very communicative up to a certain point, and then he ceased, and held his tongue entirely, and I couldn't 'pump' him, you know. Besides, if I came within a mile of the subject, the look of his face frightened me. He was terribly in love with Emily Kendal."

"It's a bad thing to be terribly in love, and not at all conducive to the comfort of society," observed Mrs. Smiles, sententiously; but Mrs. Knowle was too full of her own remembrances to reply.

"Oh, what a day that was, when, after John Stenhouse's letter, down came Mr. Kendal to Liverpool after his daughter. Oh, the daily storms we lived in—morning, noon, and night—the interviews in our dining-room, and in the poor little thing's bedroom, for she took to her bed the very first day. How we argued, and reasoned, and comforted, and advised—I, and my good man—for we felt to those two young people just as if they were our own children; and we wondered, with an amazement that childless people often feel when they see how other people throw away their blessings, what could have possessed the old father to see his only child almost dying before him, and go on killing her—for her own good, he said; but, as every body else said, just for his own pride and vexation at thwarted authority. Money, too—money was at the root of it all. If John Stenhouse had been in the position of John Bowerbank, Mr. Kendal would have gone down on his knees and worshiped him—I know he would. As it was, he just kicked him out of doors."

"That was rather ungentlemanly."

"I don't mean literally; Mr. Kendal is never that. Besides, he had his own credit to keep up; he had always borne the character of being the best of fathers—as perhaps he had been till this happened. We are all of us very perfect creatures so long as we are not tried. Gracious me! when I looked to-day at that stately, handsome old gentleman, who, when he was asked, 'Who giveth this woman to be married to this man,' looked so smiling and benignant, and remember what I have seen him look like! It's a queer world—a very queer world, my dear."

Mrs. Smiles agreed; she generally agreed in every thing with every body at the time.

"Well, the poor young fellow was dismissed. Of course there was no help for it; the girl being under age, the father had the law in his own hands. Nothing short of an elopement, which no honorable man like John Stenhouse would ever have dreamed of, could have saved poor Emily. And then her money—'her detestable money,' as her lover called it more than once. Every bit of honest pride in him was galled and stung to the quick. 'Her father thinks—all the world will think that I wanted her for her money,' he used to say; and sometimes this feeling was so strong in him that I fancied he was half inclined to draw back and give her up. But I told him not to be such a coward, for it was cowardice; fear of the wicked tongues and not of the good ones. Nobody who saw sweet Emily Kendal and honest John Stenhouse would have doubted that they were marrying for love—real love. But, my dear, I'm growing terribly long-winded, and it's nearly two o'clock: and they were to leave at half past, the bridegroom and the bride. Oh dear me! and once we planned her traveling dress that she was to go away in with poor dear John!"

Here Mrs. Knowle became unintelligible, and Mrs. Smiles fidgeted a little; for, despite her interest in the love-tale, she was beginning to want her lunch.

"Well, the rest of the story lies in a nutshell, for I have never got to the bottom of the matter yet, and I never shall now. John and Emily parted in the old father's presence—he insisted upon that—and my presence too, for Emily begged I would stay. And at the last—oh! how she clung round the young man's neck, and promised him faithfully that she would marry him, and no one but him. And he promised her as solemnly—and John Stenhouse is a man who never breaks his word—that if he were alive on the day she came of age, he would claim her again, and marry her 'in spite of man or devil.' He said that—those very words, for he seemed half maddened by the cruelty shown to her—the tender, delicate girl, made to be loved and taken care of. And then he kissed her—oh, how he kissed her! It makes me cry to think of it even now."

"Poor fellow! But, for all that, it would have been a very imprudent marriage," said Mrs. Smiles, coldly.

"Imprudent or not, it never came about, you see, though what happened I have never found out. Most certainly John Stenhouse formed no other attachment. He worked hard in the office, and out of office hours led a most solitary life. He did not even ask about Emily Kendal; though sometimes when, intentionally, I used to mention her, he listened as if he was drinking in every word. And I took care that during the two years he should hear about her all I heard myself. This was not a great deal, for her father kept her separated from me as much as he could, which was human nature, I suppose. But I had news of her sometimes, and always told them to John. The only thing I did not tell him was a rumor which reached me—so ridiculous it seemed then, that my husband and I only laughed at it—of her intended marriage to John Bowerbank."

"I remember it was I who told you, and how indignant you looked. But you see I was right, after all," said Mrs. Smiles, not without a little air of self-satisfaction.

"Well, no matter now. John never named Emily's name, nor do I know if he ever heard the report or not; but certainly just about that time he went up to London. Whether it was to claim Emily, whether he asked her again and she refused him, or whether he heard the report about her and John Bowerbank, and never did come forward and ask her, goodness only knows! All I know is, that within two months of Emily's coming of age, without my ever seeing him—for I was laid down with that bad fever, you know, and Edward was too miserable about me to care much for any body outside—John Stenhouse had quitted Liverpool and sailed for India. And there he is now, for aught I know. He does not forget us, poor fellow; he writes to us at Christmas always, and this year he sent an Indian shawl to reach me on my birthday. But he never names Emily, and he never gave the slightest explanation about any thing."

"Perhaps," suggested Mrs. Smiles, "there was nothing to explain. The young lady had changed her mind, that was all. And no wonder. A marriage with the head of the firm instead of one of the junior clerks is so very much more suitable. But look! is not that the carriage driving up? Mr. Bowerbank's, I presume. Oh dear! if I could but see one of my daughters driving away in her own carriage!"

Mrs. Knowle did not answer. She stood half hidden behind the groups of idle gazers which always gather to stare at a bride. There was a mingled expression in her frank, rosy face—half pity, half tenderness, yet flitting ever and anon across it a shadow of something else—a something not unlike contempt. Coarse-looking, uncultured woman as she was, she possessed that which makes at once woman's utmost softness and utmost strength—a loving heart and a clear conviction—though she was not clever enough to put it into thoughts, still less into words—of the divineness of Love. Love, which, when mutual, gives and exacts nothing less than the entire soul of man and woman, and enforces as an absolute duty the truth of which marriage is but the outward sign, seal, and ratification—"What God hath joined together let not man put asunder."

"I wonder what made her marry him!" murmured the

good matron of thirty years' standing. "My patience! if I had given up Edward Knowle, what would he have thought of me! What will John Stenhouse think of her?"

"Nothing at all, probably. He may be married by this time himself."

"I don't believe it—I'll never believe it. Men may be bad enough, but they're not so bad as women. They'll not often sell themselves, soul and body, out of mere cowardice, or break a solemn plighted promise from sheer fear."

"But her father—she was bound to obey her father."

"No she wasn't," replied Mrs. Knowle, sternly and strongly. "My dear, you're not bound to obey any man living, not even your own husband, who is a mighty deal closer to you than your father, when he tells you to do a wrong thing. If Edward Knowle said to me, 'Emma, I'm hungry, I want you to chop yourself up into mincemeat for me'—well, perhaps I might do it, if he really wanted it, and it harmed no one but myself. But if he said, 'Emma, I'm hungry, and I want you to go and steal that leg of mutton,' I should say, 'No, sir. God's law is a higher law than obedience to you. Steal your legs of mutton for yourself.' But stop—they've opened the hall door—she's coming."

She came—the little pale bride. Not even the excitement of the bridal gayeties, the breakfast, the Champagne, and the speeches, could make her any thing but pale. She leant on the arm of her father, who was an extremely handsome, gentlemanly, well-dressed, and low-voiced personage. He put her into the carriage with the utmost paternal care, with a kiss and a benediction, both of which she received passively. She seemed altogether a passive, frail, gentle creature, such a one as a brave, strong man would take and shelter in his arms, and love all the dearer for her very helplessness. And John Bowerbank, though elderly, almost old, did not look like a weak man, or an untender man. Far stronger, far tenderer—the two qualities usually go together—than the bride's handsome and elegant father.

"Poor thing!" muttered Mrs. Knowle to herself. "Well, in one sense, it's an escape. He's an honest man, John Bowerbank. Perhaps she may be happy—at least, less unhappy than she looks now. God bless her!"

And with that cordial blessing, unheard, and a few kindly tears, unseen by her for whom they were shed, for in truth the bride did not seem much to hear and see any thing, the carriage drove away. Thus terminated the principal scene, and thus vanished the principal actors in that grand show wedding, which had been quite satisfactory and successful in all its elements, with the exception of one trifling omission, not unfrequently occurring in similar ceremonies—Love.

CHAPTER II.

BEFORE telling the simple sad story—it does not pretend to be any thing but a sad story—of John Bowerbank's wife, I should like to say a word for John Bowerbank.

The most obvious description of him, and almost universal criticism upon him, was the common phrase, "He was a thorough man of business;" a character which, out of business circles, it is a little the fashion to decry, or, at least, to mention with a condescending apology. Hard to say why, since any acute reasoner may perceive that it takes some of the very finest qualities of real manhood to make a "thorough man of business." A man exact, persevering, shrewd, enterprising, with a strong perception of his own rights, and an equally fair judgment, and honest admission of the rights of his neighbor: who from conscience, common sense, and prudence takes care ever to do to others as he would be done by; who has firmness enough to strike the clear balance between justice and generosity; who is honest before he is benevolent, and righteous before he is compassionate; who will defraud no man, nor, if he can help it, suffer any man to defraud him; who is careful in order to be liberal, and accurate that he may compel accuracy in those about him; who, though annoyed by the waste or misappropriation of a pound, would not grudge thousands, spent in a lawful, wise, and creditable way—a man of whom his enemies may say sarcastically that he is a "near" man, a "sharp" man, a man who "can push his way in the world;" yet half the world's work—and good work too—is done by him, and the like of him—done far more successfully, far more nobly, than by your great geniuses, who aim at every thing and effect little or nothing—your grand incompletenesses, who only sadden one by the hopelessness of their failures. Better than to be a poet, whose ignoble life lags haltingly behind his noble poetry; a statesman, who tries to mend the world, and forgets that the first thing to be mended is himself; or a philanthropist, who loves all mankind, but neglects his own family—better far than all these, in the long run, is the thorough man of business, the secret of whose career is the one simple maxim, "Any thing worth doing at all is worth doing well."

Whatever else people might say of John Bowerbank—and they had said much, both bad and good, during his life of nearly sixty years—they always said of him this—that he had never shuffled out of an undertaking nor broken a promise; never begged, borrowed, nor stolen—cheating is stealing—one shilling from any man; and though his aims might not be lofty, and his daily life far removed from the heroic, still he was a good, honest man, and (as I repeat, with exceeding respect for the epithet) a thorough man of business.

But there was nothing the least interesting about him. His figure was short and stumpy, and his gray hair bristled funnily round his smooth bald head. He could not, by any force of imagination, be turned into a romantic personage. That his life had had its romance was not improbable; few lives are without. It might have been —who knows?—connected with a certain grave (which Mrs. Knowle once found, when visiting her own little grave in Hale church-yard, and ever after looked kindlier on the man for the sake of it) which bore the inscription "Jane, wife of Mr. John Bowerbank" (he was not Esquire then), "who died in childbirth, was here interred with her infant son" nearly forty years ago.

But so completely forgotten had been this episode in his life, that most people thought John Bowerbank an old bachelor; and when he grew in years and honors, so much so that it was rumored he had declined being made Sir John Bowerbank solely because knighthood was a small thing, and baronetcy, to a man without heirs, a blank sort of dignity, nobody suspected he would marry; nor, when he did marry, was he suspected of marrying in any but a business-like way—to secure a pleasant mistress for his splendid house, a cheerful companion for his declining years. And, let the truth be owned, he did marry only for this. He was not one bit in love. The solitary passion of his life had blazed up and burnt itself out, or rather been extinguished by the hand of fate, and it was too late to light up any other.

He did not marry Emily Kendal for love, nor—which, perhaps, was the secret of her finally consenting to marry him—had he made any foolish pretense of doing so. He respected her character, he liked her well, in a tender, fatherly sort of way; but "Jane, wife of Mr. John Bowerbank," now sleeping in her peaceful grave, need not have had the slightest jealousy over—nay, would hardly have recognized the middle-aged gentleman who was the "happy bridegroom" that sunshiny morning in St. George's, Hanover Square.

Perhaps this was a good thing for Emily. In her husband's unexacting and undemonstrative regard, more paternal than lover-like, she found the rest which was the only thing for which she craved; and in his steady, sedate, persistent character, which aimed at nothing higher than it accomplished, and sought from her no more than she was able to give, she found a little of the comfort which she once thought was hopeless to her in this world. She, who had begun life with a girl's dreams of perfection, and proved them all false; who, in her weakness—weaker than most women's—had leaned on one stay after another, and found them all pierce her like broken reeds, experienced in her calm, cold marriage with this kind, good, practical man, a certain peace, which, after all the tempests of her youth, was not without its soothing charm. Also, to one of her weak, hesitating nature, the mere sense of her fate being irrevocably settled—of leaning on somebody, and having somebody on whom she was bound to lean—of passing out of the flowery fields and dark precipices of her troubled life into the smooth, hard, iron tramway of duty, conveyed a feeling of relief.

For the first three months of her marriage every body said how well Mrs. John Bowerbank was looking—better than any body ever expected to see Emily Kendal look in this world, for most people had set her down as the doomed inheritor of her mother's disease—consumption, decline, atrophy—whatever name be given to the outward tokens of an inward grief, which kills the spring of youth, and makes life a weariness and the grave the only rest.

It can not be said that marriage caused any great change in John Bowerbank—he was too old for that. But he lost some of his crotchety, old-bachelor ways; moved with a certain air of content and pride about his handsome house, and was carefully mindful of his delicate and sweet-looking young wife, whom he took to state dinner-parties, and introduced among the blooming, florid, and a little too conspicuously dressed Liverpool ladies, where she looked not unlike a lily of the valley in the midst of a bed of tulips and ranunculuses.

So they lived their life, these two. Not a domestic life by any means; Mr. Bowerbank had never been used to that, nor Mrs. Bowerbank neither. She had dreamed of it once—of the honor and happiness of being a poor man's wife; of mending his shirts and stockings; of looking after his dinners and making the best of every thing; counting no economies mean that were to lighten the toil of the bread-winner; no labors hard that were to add to his comfort, toward whom love made even the humblest service the most natural thing in the world.

But this was not Emily's lot. She was a rich woman, married to a rich man; nothing was expected of her but elegant idleness. Once this might have been to her weariness intolerable; but she had long been passive and languid, glad to do nothing, and to be just whatever she fancied, since nobody ever insisted upon her being any thing—a life that some would have called happy, and, especially in its outside aspect, have envied exceedingly.

"She's an old man's darling," said one of the young Liverpool ladies, commenting on Mrs. Bowerbank to her neighbor and occasional, though not very intimate visitor, Mrs. Knowle. "It's better anyhow than being 'a young man's slave.'"

"I'm not sure of that," half-grimly, half-comically replied the other. "I hope, my dear, you'll be pretty much of a slave to your husband (as I am this day to Edward Knowle), or you'd best not marry at all."

But such love-servitude was not Emily's lot. She never trotted after John Bowerbank with his big boots of a morning, or brushed his coat, or found him his gloves; she never ran to open the door of evenings, or settled his cushions for his after-dinner sleep. They had servants to do all that, so why should she? In truth, it never occurred to her to do it.

She dressed herself carefully and sat at the head of her husband's table; she drove in his carriage about the country—solitary, peaceful, meditative drives; or she paid a few courtesy calls after the entertainments to which—arrayed in the most perfect of costumes—he seemed pleased to take her. He never was cross with her; never asked her if she was happy; tried doubtless in his own way to make her so, for he was a kindly-natured man; but he was not observant, nor sensitive, nor over-sympathetic. Besides, he was old, and all his youth, if he ever had any, had been buried long ago in Hale church-yard.

Mrs. Knowle told—not at the time, but afterward—how, one Christmas day, which was one of the rare holidays at the Exchange—and Mr. Bowerbank was a man who never took a holiday illegally—she saw him crossing the long frosted grass of this said church-yard, alone, though he had not been married many months, to stand by that grave, of which the mossy headstone still remained, but the mound had long grown level with the turf. If his eyes could have peered below, he would have found nothing of wife or child but a little handful of bones. Another wife now sat at his splendid, not humble hearth; possibly another child might—

Yes, this was what they said of him, the ill-natured portion of his friends: how, since the offer of the baronetcy, a certain dawning pride of race, the truly English wish to found a family, had come into the head of grave John Bowerbank; that accordingly he had, in his grave and practical way, conceived the idea, however late in life, of marrying, and had accordingly looked round on all his eligible young lady acquaintances, until, in his practical eye, he found one who, for her own sweet sedateness, he thought would be a suitable mate for an elderly man; and accordingly, without much inquiry as to her feelings, and having, indeed, arranged the whole matter, in the most business-like fashion, with his old acquaintance her father, he married Emily Kendal.

But when, after a year—the baronetcy being again offered and accepted—there appeared no heir to these honors, undoubtedly Sir John was very much disappointed. Of course, he did not show it; he was too good a man for that; but the placid mien became colder and colder; and though they were not unhappy—it takes a certain amount of hope even to create disappointment—still day by day the husband and wife went more their own ways;

saw less and less of one another, as is quite easy in the daily life of wealthy people, who have, or think they have, so many duties owed to their position and to society. And though Emily still smiled—her soft, languid, wistful smile—and nobody ever said an unkind word to her, and she, dear soul! had never said an unkind word to any body in her life, still her cheek grew paler and paler, her eyes larger and larger, with a sort of far-away look, as if gazing forward into a not distant heaven for something on earth never found—something lost or incomplete — something without which, though a man should give the whole substance of his house for, it would be utterly in vain.

Marriage must be heaven or hell. Not at first, perhaps, for time softens and mends all things; but after time has had its fair license, and failed; and then comes the dead blank, the hopeless endurance, even if sharper pangs do not intervene; the feeling that the last chance in life has been taken, the last die thrown—and lost.

Probably John Bowerbank did not feel thus—his feelings were never remarkably keen; and he had his business, his days occupied on 'Change, and his evenings devoted, several times a week, to the long, splendid, intensely dull, and entirely respectable Liverpool dinner-parties. But his wife, left all day at home, with no duties to fill up the idle, aimless, weary hours, with no children of her own, and too listless and inactive to adopt the substitute of other childless matrons — Mrs. Knowle, for instance — and take every body else's children who needed it under her motherly wing — to such as poor Emily, a marriage like hers most resembles being slowly frozen alive in the lake of gilded torment, which forms the horror of one of the circles of Dante's Hell.

But nobody noticed it, nobody knew it. Her father, engaged in the same dining-out existence in London that her husband, in a lesser and more harmless degree, enjoyed in Liverpool, never visited her — seldom wrote to her. When he did, his letters breathed the most enviable self-satisfaction that he had done the very best for her; that she was perfectly happy; and it was he, her affectionate father, who had secured, after his own pattern—which, of course, was infallible—her conjugal felicity. And all the world—his world especially—went on as usual, and the people who had most discussed the marriage, pro and con, till the heat of wordy war stretched over a wide area between its two points of Liverpool and London; even these subsided, as all people so soon subside after every marriage, into leaving the two concerned to bear their own cross or enjoy their own content. For, after all, it is their own business, and nobody's else—which it was from the very first, if their affectionate friends could only have believed so.

CHAPTER III.

THE two partners and their wives sat at what was intentionally made a small family dinner of four only, for the discussion of some accidental business of importance which concerned the firm of John Bowerbank and Co. This, however, was deferred until the ladies should retire, though the two Liverpool merchants could not quite forbear, even through game and sweets, to let their conversation flow into its accustomed channel—ships and shipping, cargoes and consignments, cotton "looking up," and indigo "pretty firm;" that mysterious phraseology which sounds so odd outside the commercial circle.

Such and such fragments of their lords' talk fell upon the two ladies' ears. Mrs. Knowle pricked up hers, for she was a shrewd body, and from her very marriage-day had flung herself heart and soul into her Edward's business, until now she was almost capable of going on 'Change herself. But Lady Bowerbank listened idly, or listened not at all, with an equally weary and abstracted air. She went through with more than fine-lady indifference the needful duties of her post as hostess. And continually, in the pauses of conversation, and often during the very midst of it, her eyes wandered from the table where she sat to the expanse of rippling, sunshiny sea or river, for it was bounded by long low walls and hillocks of sand — away, away to the dim, sunset-colored west.

They were dining, not in their magnificent dining-room at Birkenhead, but in one of those sea-side houses which line the Waterloo shore, whither for a change—the utmost change his stay-at-home nature ever dreamed of—Sir John had come for the summer, chiefly on account of somebody or other of his acquaintance having dwelt a little strongly on the extremely pale cheeks of Lady Bowerbank; for he was a kind husband; he never grudged her any pleasure or any good that was plainly suggested to him, though he was not acute at divining her need of it.

Lady Bowerbank had made no objection to the plan; all places were much alike to her; yet she rather liked this place, where the salt breeze was not too strong. It amused her to wander about, and watch the rabbits playing among the sand-hills, or to pick up baskets full of the exquisite tiny shells, for which this shore is famous. Not that she was conchologically inclined, or knew any thing in the world about them, save that they were very pretty. Also, that long ago, in the days which seemed to belong to another life than this, somebody had once brought her a handful of them, which she had kept in her work-box —indeed, kept still for that matter. It was no harm; she had a way of keeping things, even trifles, so long, that from mere force of habit she kept them on still, often for years and years.

The great peculiarity of her character was, that, though weak to resist, she was exceedingly persistent to retain. Such anomalies are not rare, but they are the most difficult to deal with, and the saddest in all one's experience of life.

She made no effort to entertain Mrs. Knowle—indeed, that good lady always entertained herself—but sat idly looking out of the open window, watching the silent ships creep up and down along the Mersey, or the long mysterious trail made by the smoke of some yet unseen steamer, the faint "puff-puff" of whose engines was heard for miles off across the quiet river—far away, even round the curve of the Hoylake shore.

So sat she—gentle Emily Bowerbank—in her lilac pale silk, her rich jewellery, and beautiful lace hanging over her thin white hands: a pretty sight, even though she was so pale; and a great contrast to large, rosy Mrs. Knowle, resplendent in claret-colored satin, and with a brooch on her bosom almost as big as her own heart. Neither conversed, but paid the customary tribute of silence to their respective lords, till both were startled by a sentence, which indeed made Mrs. Knowle color up as if she had been a young girl in her teens, and then sit mute with her eyes fixed on her plate.

"By-the-by, Knowle," said Sir John, leaning back, and folding his hands with the contented aspect of a man who, always temperate, yet keenly enjoys the after-dinner hour of wine and dessert, "I have always forgotten to ask you, what has become of that young man Stenhouse, who left us—was it two or four years ago?—very much against my wish, you remember. You got him, I think, into a house at Bombay?"

"Yes, Sir John," replied Mr. Knowle, a little abruptly. "Pass the wine, Emma, my dear."

"Is he there still? and how is he getting on?"

"Well enough, I believe. He sometimes writes to us, though not often. Sir John, this claret is really capital."

"So I think. But," added he, with the persistency of an unsensitive man, who will not be driven from his point, "to return to Stenhouse. I wish, when you write, you would tell him Mr. Jones is leaving us. In plain truth, there is not a man I would like as senior clerk so much as Stenhouse—John, wasn't his name? John Stenhouse?"

"Yes. Capital fellow, he was," muttered Mr. Knowle. "Accurate as clock-work, and conscientious and persistent as—"

"I'll trouble you for the nut-crackers, Edward," said his helpmate, with a warning frown.

"Indeed," continued Sir John, with a way he had of sticking to his point through all interruptions, "I fully agree with you, Knowle. And what I was about to say was this, that if you still keep up acquaintance with the young man, could you not suggest to him to return home and re-enter our house? we would make it worth his while."

"I don't fancy he'd come, Sir John. He—he dislikes England. But I'll think the matter over, and speak to you about it to-morrow."

"Very well." And Sir John helped himself to another glass of claret, and began talking of something else.

Then, and not till then, the ladies rose; the guest looking hot and red, the hostess pale as death. Emily stood aside to let Mrs. Knowle pass through the door, which was politely held open by Sir John, with a whispered

"Send us in coffee soon, my dear;" but when that good lady reached the drawing-room, she found herself alone, and for half an hour after there was no sign of Lady Bowerbank.

Mrs. Knowle grew exceedingly uncomfortable, not to say alarmed. Never since the marriage had she and Emily renewed their former intimacy, or been on other than the formal terms of visiting acquaintances and partners' wives. Emily did not seem to wish it, though she was scrupulously kind and even affectionate. But then she neither encouraged nor cultivated any body. Life was to her an altogether passive thing. And Mrs. Knowle had had the good sense, and good feeling, never to encroach on this reserve; never, since circumstances were so changed, to make the slightest allusion to their former intimacy, nor to intrude upon the present their painful relations of the past. Thus, little by little, seeing that the silence she desired was unbroken, Lady Bowerbank had gone back from her first shrinking, nervous coldness into comparative cordiality. Still, it was never warm enough to warrant Mrs. Knowle in doing what now was her natural impulse, to seek Emily all over the house, bid her open her heart, and then soothe and comfort her if she could. So she sat, very anxiously, alone in the drawing-room, not liking even to make inquiry of a servant until the mistress reappeared.

A sad sight Emily was. If pale before, she was now ghastly; her eyes red, with black circles round them, as if she had been crying. And as she sat down, and took her coffee from the butler, trying to make some slight observation to her visitor, her hands shook so much that she could hardly hold the cup.

When the servants were gone there ensued a dead pause, at last broken only by Mrs. Knowle's perplexed remark about its being a very fine evening for walking.

"Would you like to walk on the shore? say if you would," cried Emily, eagerly. "I'm not strong enough myself, but my maid would accompany you; and the gentlemen will not be out of the dining-room for hours."

"I don't want to go out and leave you alone, my dear," said Mrs. Knowle, her very heart melting within her as she looked at the trembling hands, the pallid face, where two bright spots of carmine had now risen, one on either cheek, making the large eyes larger and more 'far-away' than ever. She remembered, with a sudden spasm of memory, that pretty, round, merry, girlish face of Emily Kendal, when it first came into her house, and made a brightness in the dark rooms, and flitted like a sunbeam along the garden walks, especially on the Saturday and Sunday when John Stenhouse left his hard counting-house life and his dreary lodgings, and came to bask in Paradise there.

"My dear, I'll not leave you alone," said Mrs. Knowle. "It isn't good for you."

That soft motherly tone, the spell of womanly tenderness, which no woman, married or single, happy or unhappy, is ever proof against, or ever ought to be, unloosed the iron chain which bound the heart of poor Lady Bowerbank. She fell sobbing on Mrs. Knowle's shoulder.

"I must speak to you—only let me speak to you—I shall die if I do not speak to somebody."

That was true. Judge her not harshly, you brave

strong women, who can bear so much. Of course, her duty was silence—total silence, to shut her secret up in her heart, and never breathe to living soul what she had not dared to breathe to her own husband. But this duty, like a few more duties in her short, sad life, Emily had not strength to fulfill. She saw them all, clearly defined enough; perhaps, if she had had any body beside her to help her to do them, they might, weak as her nature was, somehow or other have been done. But her only strength, her love, had been taken from her, and now her life was a mere fragment—a melancholy incompleteness, in which all aims and aspirations remained only such, and never developed into active perfection. Whether the course was right or wrong, dignified or undignified, it was quite true what she said, that she *must* give her confidence to some one—must speak out, or she would die.

"Well, speak then, my poor child. Be assured I will never tell any body—I never did, you know." (For just at the moment she had forgotten Mrs. Smiles, her only breach of confidence.)

"Yes, you were very good to me once, and I—I haven't forgotten it," sobbed Emily. "It was a terrible, terrible time; I wonder I lived through it. But I think it has shortened my life. I shall never be an old woman —I feel that."

"Nonsense, my dear. What would Sir John say to such talk, I wonder?"

Emily neither smiled nor sighed. "Sir John and I are very good friends—he is exceedingly kind to me. Do not suppose I have a shadow of complaint to make against my husband."

It was noticeable that she always called him "my husband—Mr. Bowerbank," and afterward "Sir John." As plain "John," the fond familiar Christian name of other times, she never by any possible chance spoke either of him or to him.

"My dear, if you had any complaint to make, I'm not the woman to listen to it. Wives shouldn't grumble against their husbands. 'For better for worse' runs the Church service. If Edward had his little tantrums—which all men have, bless 'em!—why, I'd bear them as long as I could, or a bit longer; if he grew bad, I'd try to mend him; if he couldn't be mended, but turned out such a villain that I actually despised him—why, I'd run away from him! Ay, though he was my husband, I'm afraid I should run away from him. But I'd do it quietly, my dear, quietly. And I'd never abuse him to other folk. I'd just hold my tongue."

"And I will hold mine—have I not done it hitherto?" gasped rather than spoke poor Emily. "I have a peaceful home—far peacefuller than Queen Anne Street ever was;" and she shuddered involuntarily. "I ought to be thankful for it, and I hope I am. He knows nothing—Sir John, I mean—and he never need know—he would not care. I owe him much kindness—I shall never wrong him—that's quite impossible. But"—here her feeble fingers clutched with the tightness of despair on Mrs. Knowle's wrist, and she looked up at her imploringly—"you must do one thing for me. Promise me you will."

"I never make promises without telling Edward Knowle."

"You may tell him—for it is he who must do it. He can manage it, and he will; say, I entreat, he will."

"What is it, my love?" And, though she spoke soothingly, more than one anxious doubt crossed Mrs. Knowle's mind: "Pray speak out."

"You heard what my husband said. Now your husband must manage, by an excuse he likes—even a lie if necessary—it will be a lawful lie—but he *must* manage it—that some one—you know who—does not come back to Liverpool."

"I understand. You are quite right."

"He must not come, I tell you," and Emily's voice grew shrill with something almost approaching fear. "For I am a very weak woman; I know that I have proved myself so more than once. I am safe, and I want to remain safe. I don't love him, not now, not after he has forsaken me; but oh! for God's sake keep him far away from me. Put the sea between us—hundreds, thousands of miles. Let me be quite sure that I shall never again see his face, or hear the sound of his voice, or his footsteps—you remember I used to know his step along the garden walk quite well. I must not see him—never, nevermore!"

"No, my dear; if I can help it you never shall," said Mrs. Knowle, very firmly, as she held the shrinking, sobbing creature in her arms, crying herself a little, and feeling very angry at somebody or something, she was not quite certain what. But she was certain of one thing, that there had been some great mystery, some heavy wrong-doing somewhere; and though she was not exactly an inquisitive woman, she did like to get to the bottom of things, and still more did she dislike taking the responsibility of acting in the dark.

"Will you tell me one thing, Lady Bowerbank?" asked she, when they both had grown a little calmer; "I don't ask out of idle curiosity, but just that I and my husband, who were, and are still, his warm friends, may be placed in a right position toward him. My dear, just say, in two words, why you did not marry John Stenhouse."

"Because he never asked me—that is, not the second time, as he promised. He promised, you know, solemnly—faithfully, that the day I came of age he would claim me, and we should be married."

"With or without your father's consent?"

"Yes. He said it would be right, and he would do it. If he were alive, he told me, on my birthday, he should write or come to me. But he never wrote, and never came."

"What a strange thing!" said Mrs. Knowle, much perplexed. "And yet I know—I am almost sure—"

She stopped, for in caressing the poor hand she had felt Lady Bowerbank's wedding-ring—the fatal ring. With a sense of dread, lest one word might lay the foundation of harm that now could never be undone, no more than the marriage could be broken, she stopped, hesitated, and finally kept her own counsel.

"Oh, what a day it was—my birthday," pursued Emily, pouring out her long-pent-up grief. "We were giving a ball; I did not wish it, but papa insisted; however, I cared little about it, I was so happy. For when I woke in the morning I knew I should see him before night—I thought he would come rather than write, since he had not seen me for two whole years. I waited in, hour after hour, all that day; and I danced myself sick at night, lest papa might notice I was unhappy. And then I lived on, hoping and hoping all next day, and all the day after—every day for a week. And for many weeks, post after post I watched, and day after day I never crossed the door-sill for an hour without coming in expecting to find his letter or his card. But he never wrote—he never came. And then I heard he had gone to India, and—and that was all."

Emily dropped her head, and the passing light and energy which had come into her features while speaking vanished out of them; she sank back into the pale, passive, quiet woman, John Bowerbank's wife.

"Do you blame him?" asked Mrs. Knowle, softly, with her head turned away. ("For," she owned afterward to her husband, "I was frightened out of my life lest the poor girl should discover any thing in my manner that might set her asking questions.")

"No, I don't blame him. He had been so wronged, so insulted, no wonder his pride took up arms and he let me go: I was but a poor creature to fight for. Or perhaps he had found somebody else he liked better. Your Liverpool girls are so pretty, you know, and he always admired pretty people," added Emily, with a feeble smile. "I never was pretty myself; and perhaps he might be afraid of people saying he married a plain girl for her money."

"No," cried Mrs. Knowle, indignantly, "I'll never believe that. He wasn't such a coward."

"Well, well, whatever it was, does not matter now.

He did not want me—did not care for me—and other people did, and my father was urging me perpetually to marry. I could not help myself—indeed I could not," added she, clasping her hands together in a hopeless resignation. "I was worn out—literally worn out and torn to pieces—and so I married Mr. Bowerbank."

There was a long silence, through which the large drawing-room clock kept ticking and ticking, with a remorseless diligence, unvarying and unwearying as Time itself; and through the open window, from across the now darkening river, came dim voices of sailors in ships slowly dropping down the Mersey, outward bound.

At length Mrs. Knowle roused herself and said,

"My dear, I am very glad you have trusted me to-night; you shall never repent it. I quite agree with you that Mr. Stenhouse must not be asked to come back to Liverpool; Edward will manage it so as to satisfy Sir John. And after to-night, you and I will never name him again."

"No, no. That is," and she hesitated—Emily's piteous hesitation.

But her friend had none. "Decidedly not, Lady Bowerbank. When a woman is once married, she has no right even to think of any man but her own husband. You know, Sir John is a very good, kind gentleman, and very fond of you. And you have many a blessing—and, for all you can tell, it may please God to send you one day a better blessing still."

Emily shook her head.

"I know what you mean, but I don't hope that. I don't even wish it. I could not do my duty to a child.

Better live on as I am living—just pleasing Sir John a little if I can—doing no harm to any body, and by-and-by my whole story will be over, and I myself, as some Scotch song says,

> "'I myself in the auld kirk-yard,
> With the green grass growing over me.'

It's curious," she added, "but sometimes in this mass of bricks and mortar, and these wastes of sea and sand, I feel an actual pleasure in the words 'green grass growing over me.'"

"You are talking nonsense, my dear," said Mrs. Knowle, sharply, though her tears were running down in showers; "you'll live to be an old woman—as old, and as stout, and as comfortable as me."

"Do you think so? Well, I hope I may be half as good and as kind," answered, with a grateful look, poor Lady Bowerbank.

And then the lamps came in, and with them Sir John Bowerbank and Mr. Knowle, both in exceedingly cheerful spirits, having apparently settled quite to their satisfaction the knotty business point to arrange which they had dined together. Their respective wives bestirred themselves, as wives should, to welcome the advent of lords and masters, and after a lively half-hour the little quartette broke up.

But when Mrs. Knowle, as her custom was, immediately poured out to Mr. Knowle every thing that had passed in his absence, "Edward," who was a man of few words, looked exceedingly grave.

"There has been foul play somewhere; I'm sure of that, wife."

"Why—what do you know?"

"John Stenhouse did ask her to marry him; he went up to London on purpose, and was refused. He didn't tell me much, but he let fall as much as that, or something like it."

"And you never told me?" said Mrs. Knowle, a little aggrieved.

"You were very ill, my dear; and when you got better he was gone to India. And somehow I wasn't thinking so much of him as of you. Remember, you were nigh slipping away from me then, old woman."

She gave him a kiss—the placid, tender kiss of forty years' accumulated content, and complained no more.

"Men don't think so much of these things as we do. Poor Emily! well for her she's got a good man for her husband. But, for all that, as you say, my love, I'm certain there has been foul play somewhere."

CHAPTER IV.

De mortuis nil nisi bonum.

I would gladly put this as the motto to the present chapter, and adopt the moral of it, which is a noble and Christian moral, and can not be too tenderly and sedulously acted upon — in the main. But truth forbids silence sometimes—that truth,

> "The evil that men do lives after them;
> The good is often interred with their bones;"

which is as true now as when Shakspeare wrote it. No one, taking a wide and comprehensive view of life, can fail to see what fatal harm is sometimes caused, passively, by the passive dead; how often the living will injure themselves—and more than themselves—for the sake of what they call "respect to the memory of the departed;" some one who, maybe, was once as foolish, obstinate, selfish, cruel as any of us, and in death has perpetuated the ill-doings of his life. From this feeling, corrupted from a virtue into a mere superstition, many a wrong, too late discovered, which ought, years and years before, to have been dragged to the open day, and crushed and trampled under the avenging heel of righteous wrath and noble scorn, is hushed up, suffered to be passed over unrequited, because — alas! the wrong-doers are now far away in the silent land, where, at least, they can injure no more.

Nothing but good of the dead! If good can not be spoken, then keep silence.

Yes, ordinarily. God forbid that when He lays His eternal seal upon the quivering mouth of sinner as well as saint, ours likewise should not respect His awful mandate and be dumb. But there are cases in which silence regarding the dead involves wrong to the living, and that which might have been a solemn warning to many others left behind falls short of its natural lesson—the lesson I would fain have some worldly people lay to heart from this story—the true story, alas! of John Bowerbank's wife. Though it happened long ago, and though place, people, and extraneous circumstances have been, I trust, effectually disguised, still the story itself is no invention, but a fact told to me; and I tell it, after all the actors therein are safely dead and gone, as a lesson to those whom it may concern; especially those who are supposed to need none, and yet fate often reads to them quietly the sharpest lesson of all—the parents of grown-up children.

Lady Bowerbank was sitting quite alone, and dressed in deep mourning, in the dining-room of the house at Queen Anne Street. She had been summoned to London, for the first time since her marriage, by a very sad event—the sudden death of her father. He was not an old man exactly, and had been hitherto remarkably hale and active, living his life—the life of a barrister about town—with apparent enjoyment; making, and spending as fast as he made, a very good income, absorbed chiefly in selfish pleasures, but pleasures of a perfectly reputable and unobjectionable kind. However, in the midst of these Death found and called him. Some hidden heart-disease suddenly developed itself, and he was struck down while making a speech in court. His daughter and son-in-law were telegraphed for, but even before the message reached them he was no more. They carried him back from Westminster Hall to his own door — a corpse.

Of course, deep was the sympathy with his family; and though since her marriage he had so withdrawn himself from her that the slender filial relation which ever existed, or was likely to exist, between a loving girl and a man so essentially selfish, that except by force of the claim of Nature he had no right whatever to be considered a father, had become all but nominal; still, overpowered by the suddenness of the stroke, his daughter mourned for him—mourned, remembering not so much later years as those early childish days when almost every man takes a certain pleasure in paternity, especially being father to a pretty little girl. She recalled how he used to set her on the table after dinner and make her dance to him, or take her walks in the Park with her best clothes on—her muslin frocks, and blue ribbons, and her golden hair flying about, so that, infant as she was, she was fully aware every body noticed her, and asked "Whose charming little girl that was?" Halcyon days these, during which many an imperfect nature and hard heart ride safely over the smooth waters of life, to be shipwrecked afterward. It is not till the storm comes that we find out the real building and timber of the vessel.

After these days came others, in which, to the best of Emily's recollection, her father had taken very little notice of her; for nobody noticed her now very much. She had ceased to be pretty; her beauty was only the round rosiness of infancy, and it slipped away, and there had not yet come that beaming spiritual loveliness which had so charmed the unartistic eye, but clear head and sound heart of John Stenhouse. So she had been, during her teens, a good deal neglected; and, in fact, her young life had only wakened up on that fatal Liverpool visit, the consequences of which turned the careless father into a remorseless judge—a cruel enemy.

But she forgave him that; she was ready to forgive him any thing, as she sat in his easy-chair, before his private desk, the papers of which Sir John, summoned back home immediately after the funeral, had left her to examine alone; she was haunted by sad thoughts of her father—her own poor father—who had so enjoyed the good things of this life—his cosy dining-room—his after-dinner repose — sleeping now, this first night, underground — the eternal sleep of death. She would have liked to think of him otherwise and otherwhere, but somehow she could not; he had been a man so essentially worldly that even after his death one's fancy unconsciously associated him with this world. She knew she ought to dwell upon him as safe and happy in heaven, and yet her thoughts would fly back and back, like gloomy birds of evil omen, and settle in that cheerless, misty cemetery at Kensal Green—where, Sir John Bowerbank had said, some handsome memorial must immediately be erected to distinguish it from the throng of graves; and he left his wife behind in London for a day, in order that she might leisurely examine her father's papers, and find out whether the deceased—(it was melancholy to hear the clever barrister, the social diner-out, already spoken of as merely "the deceased")—had any particular wish regarding his own monument; for Emily's husband was very kindly, very considerate, and in this last sad conjuncture she had been more drawn to him than for many months before.

She had bidden him good-by an hour ago, he starting by the night-mail for Liverpool, and had settled herself alone in the large, desolate dining-room, making a sort of encampment by the fire, that she might feel less dreary. Then she began looking over—drawer by drawer, and paper after paper—the large desk which had been the awe of her childhood and the perplexity of her youth. She could hardly believe that it was really herself then peering into with unhallowed eyes, and turning over with unforbidden hands, those secrets of which we all have some, and which we think are safe from every body, till death comes and teaches differently.

What Mr. Kendal could have been thinking of when he left all these matters—many of which he certainly would not have liked even his daughter to be acquainted with—to such a chance as now befell them, is impossible to say. Probably the truth, unseen and disbelieved, though it stares at us in church-yard and street, and whispers to us in every book or newspaper, that "in the midst of life we are in death," had been wholly unrecognized by this man of the world, or else he might have had a superstitious dread of setting his house in order, and contemplating, in any way, his own dissolution. Certain it was he left no will, and his most private papers were found in the utmost confusion, every thing being exactly as he had quitted his home on the morning of his death, to return thither alive no more.

With a solemn tenderness befitting such an office, his daughter turned over scrap after scrap, opened and looked at letter after letter, just reading as much as seemed necessary, and then burning it, or laying it aside to be burnt. A good many papers she destroyed at once; she did not like even her husband to see them — these relics of a purely selfish life—not absolutely a wicked life, but one self-absorbed and self-enjoying—nothing but self-worship from the beginning to the end.

Lady Bowerbank was growing weary; the hall clock and just struck eleven, resounding through the gloomy old house with a thrill that almost made her start off her chair—she was very feeble and nervous still, though her health had been of late months a little improving. Sick at heart, forlorn and lonely, she put aside heap after heap of letters in unfamiliar handwritings, to be examined by-and-by, when she suddenly came upon one that was — not unfamiliar.

No wonder at its being there; her father and Mr. Stenhouse had had a sharp correspondence; probably this was one of the letters. None of them had ever been shown to her; she had only found out accidentally that such had been sent and received. Eagerly she took up this one, then hesitated—Emily's perpetual hesitation—as to whether it would be a breach of confidence or of duty to read it; when, looking at the envelope, she saw it was not addressed, as the rest of Mr. Stenhouse's letters had been, to Mr. Knowle's house in Liverpool, but to Queen

Anne Street, London. And the post-mark bore a date long subsequent to that unhappy time; a date which, as Emily Bowerbank gazed on, cold shivers of fear ran through her, for it was a week *after* her twenty-first birthday.

"He did write, then. I must read it! I must and will!" she said to herself; and for once that firm "I will"—the want of which had been the great lack of her life—as it is one of the greatest and most fatal deficiencies in any human life or character—came to her aid, and she carried out her purpose. Was it for good or for ill? Alas! the teller of this simple tale—and maybe many a reader—can not possibly decide; except that, as a general rule, to have met open-eyed the most blinding truth is better, ay, and easier in the end, than to live under the blighting shadow of a permanent lie.

The letter addressed to Mr. Kendal by John Stenhouse ran thus:

"Sir,—Though we did not part amicably two years ago, I beg now to appeal to you as to a gentleman and a man of honor, and the father of the lady whom I then, and ever since, steadily determined to make my wife.

"At your desire, I abstained from all communication with her until she became of age, which was a week ago. On that day, and again for six days following, I called at your house, to see her and you, and to beg permission to renew our engagement—or rather to complete it; for it has, as regards myself, never been broken; but I was not admitted. I can not learn any thing about her. I have written to her; I have watched—as far as a gentleman could presume to watch a lady—in the hope of seeing her, and all in vain. I now take the straightforward course of writing direct to you, sir. You may not like me, but you can know nothing against me. Also, you are a father. I entreat you for *her* sake—she did love me once—not to stand in the way of our happiness. That she is true to me I have not the slightest doubt. Tell me where she is, and when I may see her.

"Yours faithfully, JOHN STENHOUSE."

Inclosed with this was a small note, scarcely more than a scrap, apparently written in haste, and blotted as it was folded:

"SIR,—I accept your explicit and complete explanation, and wish your daughter every happiness that circumstances may afford her. Neither she nor you will ever be again intruded upon by your obedient servant,

"JOHN STENHOUSE."

Emily Bowerbank read, and sat petrified. The whole world seemed fading away from her in a sort of dark gray mist. The roaring of waters was in her ears, and a dull knocking pain at her heart. Then all ceased, and she passed into temporary unconsciousness.

When she came to herself she was lying forward with her head on the desk, the letter still grasped in her hand. She remembered at once what had happened, but she did not faint again, not even though she was one of those feeble women whom a very slight thing causes to fall into fainting-fits.

A slight thing—as probably the father who had done it believed it to be, or argued himself into believing—and yet it was the destruction of two lives!

Emily gathered up her feeble thoughts and shattered senses together, and tried to understand the fact thus suddenly revealed to her.

So, John Stenhouse had returned at the appointed time, and once again asked her to marry him. He had loved her, steadily, faithfully, through these two blank years. He had come up to London prepared to meet the sharp ordeal that was inevitably before him—the wounding of his pride—the lacerating of his feelings—all the humbling irritations that, under the best of circumstances, must be borne by a poor proud man who marries a rich man's daughter. Yet he had come, willing and eager to marry her, setting aside every thing except his love for her—a love steady as a rock, true as steel.

For an instant, as soon as this became clear to Emily's half-bewildered brain, there flashed upon her a sudden light—the first and most natural impulse of actual joy. She clasped her hands together; and if ever the poor pale face looked like an angel's, it looked so then.

"He *was* true! He did not forsake me! Oh, thank God!"

And then she remembered all that followed, and how it had all ended in her being what she was now—John Bowerbank's wife.

The dead man had told a lie—or perhaps not a direct lie, but a misstatement—putting forward what he believed and hoped as what really existed. He had evidently informed John Stenhouse that his daughter no longer considered herself engaged to him, and was on the point of marriage with John Bowerbank. Such fabrications are often given as facts by even good people, who hope them until they really believe them. The falsehoods of the wicked can be met—the misstatements of the respectable and worthy can not.

"And a lie that is half a truth is ever the blackest of lies."

So Emily's lover must have believed it, as was scarcely unnatural. But—the father?

When one man has a grudge against another, it may be a small thing to deny him his house and suppress his letters; and such may be, by some people, counted by no means an unwarrantable proceeding on the part of any father who wishes to prevent his daughter's making an imprudent marriage. A little uncandid, perhaps; a little like treating her as a child; but then many young women are little better than children; and parents have, or are supposed to have, all the wisdom, the justice, the prudence on their side, and may take the law into their own hands, and use any means which they think advisable for the ultimate good of their offspring. How can they—the children—just entering on life, and with little or no experience of its countless pitfalls, know what is best for their own happiness? Blind obedience is safest and best.

So would argue many excellent people—so doubtless would have argued the dead lawyer, could he have come back from his newly-filled grave, or from the place wherever it was, that his soul had fled to, and stood before his daughter in the dead of night, as she sat with that fatal letter still clutched in her hands, staring at vacancy.

She was usually a good deal given to weeping—too much so, indeed—she was such a thorough woman in all her weaknesses, poor little Emily! But now she did not weep at all; neither did she rave, nor think any unholy, wicked thoughts, nor curse her father's memory. He was dead, and she must not allow herself to dwell upon what he had done against her, or judge whether his act were right or wrong. She only felt that it had killed her.

Yes, he had killed her, this respectable and respected father—had killed his own daughter—his natural flesh and blood—as completely as if he had slain her with his hand. It might be worth counting—as perhaps the good God may send His angels to count some time, when the secrets of all lives shall be revealed—how many fathers, perhaps some mothers — but women being less selfish than men, these are rarer—with the very best intentions, have done the same.

He had killed her—killed the spring of youth and life within her, not merely by lawful open opposition—though that would have been cruel enough—but by a mean, underhand, cowardly blow, a side-thrust which there was no parrying. By him, worldly man as he was, probably the thing was not realized in its full enormity. How could he, or such as he, understand the loss of love—the one blessing which makes life sacred and beautiful? Or perhaps he thought, like other worldly people, that worldly blessings are all in all, and that he was actually doing his daughter a kindness in keeping her in the sphere she was born to; saving her from sacrificing herself to a man of no wealth and no position, decidedly her inferior in the marriage barter, who, while she gave him every thing, had nothing on earth to offer her except love, which was a commodity of no weight at all with Mr. Kendal.

Be that as it may, he had killed her. Of course, there is this to be said, why had she the weakness to let herself be killed? Why did she take her lover's loss so passively, and so unresistingly allow herself to be married to another? Why, in short, suffer herself to be made a mere victim to circumstances when she should have risen above them, as a strong, brave human being, whether woman or man, ought to do; fight her own battle, and assert her right to live out her own life in her own way, whether she married John Stenhouse or not?

Alas, the question is answered by hundreds of victims —men and women, but especially women—to whose weak helplessness might has become right, and cowardice appeared like dutiful submission. Pass on, pale ghosts, sad shadows of lives that might have been made so happy and so fair: God will remember you, poor suffering ones! But how as to those who have caused you to suffer?

I think, if there ought to be a Gehenna upon earth—for mortal justice must not presume to create Gehennas afterward—it should be opened for the punishment of tyrants—domestic tyrants.

Emily Bowerbank sat till daydawn without attempting so much as to stir. Bewildering, delirious thoughts swept through her poor brain—she who was not much given to think, but only to feel. Whether she fully realized her own position—all she was and all she had lost;

whether, in those long still hours, she went over and over again, in maddened fancy, the contrast between her calm, cold, respectable marriage with honest John Bowerbank—(thank heaven, she felt *he* was not to blame; he never could have known any thing)—and marriage with every pulse of her heart happy and at rest; every aspiration of her soul satisfied; her nature developed, and her mind strengthened; fitted for weal or woe, labor or ease, peace or perplexity, as she would have been had she become the wife of John Stenhouse—all this was never revealed.

She said nothing and did nothing; what was there to do or say? She blamed no one, not even herself; it was too late now. Every thing was too late. She felt in a vague, childish sort of way, like one of the "foolish virgins," whom she had always been so sorry for as a child; her lamp, too, had gone out, and could never be relighted. The door of life was shut, not to be opened more.

Till day dawned—the dreary, drizzly London day, she sat over her father's desk, not attempting, however, to search farther, or to arrange any thing more. Then, with a sudden fear of the servants coming in and finding her there, she hurriedly swept all the letters into a drawer, all but *the* letter, which she took away with her—it concerned nobody but herself—and crept noiselessly away to bed.

Next day, according to her husband's desire, Lady Bowerbank started for Liverpool. It was well she did, for immediately on her reaching home she had a somewhat severe illness, a kind of low gastric fever, which was rather prevalent at the time. No one wondered at it, and every body sympathized with her. "Dear Lady Bowerbank!" they said, in talking her over, "she was such a delicate, tender creature; and what a great shock it must have been for her, the death of her poor dear father!"

CHAPTER V.

PEOPLE do break their hearts sometimes. Not very often, for a large proportion have really no hearts to break; and a few who have them have also that stern power of endurance, which, if they only have strength to live through the first shock, will enable them still to live on —live nobly, heroically, until they come to experience the mysterious internal force of reparation which Heaven has mercifully imparted to every sound body and healthily constituted mind; which turns evil into good, and transmutes dull misery into that active battling with sorrow which in time produces a deeper peace than even happiness.

But here and there are others, like poor Emily Bowerbank, gifted with strong persistency of loving, and almost no other strength—no other persistence in any thing; sweet, gentle, sensitive souls; climbing plants, who, if they find a prop to cling to, bloom bounteously all their days; but, finding no prop, or being rudely torn from it, slip silently to the earth, where they soon wither away, and have no use nor beauty in their lives ever after. This may not be noticeable outside; the result may be attributed to many accidental external causes—worldly misfortune, constitutional feebleness, and so on, but the real cause is—their hearts are broken. Why it should be so—why, above all, Providence should allow it—

should permit the gentle weak ones to succumb to the bad strong ones, and the virtuous to be sacrificed to the vicious—the unselfish and much-enduring to those who have neither tenderness nor generosity—is a mystery that never will be unraveled. We can only leave it with Him, who, dying, prayed to His Father, as Emily Bowerbank tried to pray to the Father in heaven, whenever she thought of her own father, "Forgive them, they know not what they do."

Nevertheless her heart was broken, and she knew it. She recovered from her fever, and by degrees resumed almost her former place in her husband's household, though not in general society; she was quite incapable of that, and, besides, during her tedious convalescence, Sir John had got into a habit of going to his dinner-parties alone. She was, to all appearance, quite well; still she never again took a firm hold on life, never was heard to talk of the future, or to make any plans beyond the month, or the week, and then gradually—so gradually that no one perceived it—not even beyond the day.

She was not in a consumption, for the doctors found no disease in the lungs; it was more what the country people call "a waste"—that is, a gradual sinking of all the powers of the body, and sometimes even of the mind; until mental griefs cease to wound, and of bodily suffering, except weariness and feebleness, there is absolutely none. Not a painful death to die, especially when surrounded by all the luxuries that wealth or kindly care could bestow—every thing, in short, except the one thing—the one amulet of life, which had been taken away from her.

People do not recognize half clearly enough the truth that God would not have created such a thing as mutual love, ending in marriage, had He not meant it to be the one thing needful—not absolutely to the salvation of a human soul, though it is that, or the contrary, oftener than we suspect, but to its perfect development, and, above all, to its happiness. Those who interfere with what is called "a love affair" are doing what they never can undo; destroying what is impossible to rebuild; taking away from two human beings that which no substitute, be it family affection, wealth, worldly honor, or success, can avail to restore. All are valueless when love is not there.

The sod lay green over Mr. Kendal's bones; his life was over; but he had blighted two other lives—lives which might have blossomed into beauty, and carried their perfectness down into coming generations, when his poor selfish existence was forgotten in the dust. He had done it, and it never could be undone.

What had become of John Stenhouse? was a question that Mrs. Knowle often asked herself. Only to herself, however. Constantly as she visited Lady Bowerbank, and more especially since the sad illness which followed the sudden death of Mr. Kendal, his name had, since that first night, never once been breathed between them. It was impossible it could be, between any two honorable women. Nevertheless, the elder matron thought of him a deal more than she would have liked to own, and made many inquiries about him through her husband, but they all resulted in nothing beyond the fact that he was living and working somewhere in India. Mr. Knowle had contrived to prevent all offers being made to him of returning to England.

Still, occasionally he was heard of, to Mrs. Knowle's great satisfaction, though seeing that Emily made no inquiries, her information was carefully kept to herself. But she took a romantic interest, most unworthy of such a very practical and sensible old matron, in the young man and his fortunes; for she never ceased to believe, and asserted repeatedly to her husband, that so true a lover and so honest a man as John Stenhouse could never have forsaken a woman in this mean way; and, though the real truth of the matter might never be discovered, she was as certain as she was of her existence that there had been something wrong somewhere.

"And it may come right yet, who knows? I hope I'm not wicked—and it's ill waiting barefoot for dead men's shoes, but Sir John is over sixty, and he will have had a very fair enjoyment of life if he lives to eighty; and poor Emily will not be much over forty-three even then. Folks do sometimes take the wrong person—become widows and widowers—and then meet their old loves and get married, and end their days happily together after all."

Mr. Knowle shook his gray head.

"It won't be the case here, wife, so you need not think it."

He gave no more explanation, for he was not a talkative man, but his wife noticed that he often rode round two miles out of his way to business in order to inquire how Lady Bowerbank was that morning. And Mrs. Knowle, from paying a formal visit once in three months, got slowly into the habit of driving to Summer Lodge at least twice a week, and spending the morning with Emily. And by degrees she returned to the old tender fashion, and called her not "Lady Bowerbank," but "Emily."

One morning the two ladies were sitting together, one working—for Mrs. Knowle's fingers were never empty of work—and the other reading, or attempting to read, the newspaper. Newspapers were terribly interesting now in all houses, for it was just about the time of the Indian revolt, and, as this generation will long remember, far and near, there was scarcely a family who had not to mourn their dead. Lady Bowerbank, without giving any reasons for it—and indeed none were required, for the sympathy was too universal—had taken a deep interest in the tidings brought mail after mail, and, horrible as they often were, they were not forbidden her, for they seemed to rouse her out of herself to feel for afflictions compared to which her own were nothing. She also began to exert herself and her small strength in a way that surprised both her husband and the doctors: gathering and making contributions in aid of the sufferers, and trying, in a feeble way, to organize schemes for their relief, and find out cases of exceeding need, which, by means of the large Indian connections of the house of Bowerbank and Co., was not difficult to accomplish.

"I should like to do a little good before I go," she said one day, when Mrs. Knowle was urging her not to overexert herself. "I have done so little good in my life, you know."

And so they let her do it; and she spent money, and time, and thought upon these melancholy charities, her husband grudging nothing; he never did. He was a very good man. Many a letter he wrote, investigating difficult cases, and many a time he drove out to lunch in the middle of the day—he that used never to take even a half-holiday from business—in order to tell his wife some piece of news, or ask how she was, or bring her some little delicacy from market or hothouse, if she chanced to be especially fanciful or feeble that day; for she was very fanciful, as sickly people often are; but she strove against it in a pathetic way; and Mrs. Knowle noticed how invariably she tried to look grateful and pleased at Sir John's little attentions, and to smile steadily as long as he remained in the room.

"I have really got a piece of news for you to-day, my dear," said he, sitting down beside her, "though it is not for you so much as for Mrs. Knowle—at least half for one and half for the other. You shall share the pleasure between you. Guess."

The two ladies tried, in all politeness, but failed signally, both of them.

"Well, then, first, Lady Bowerbank, it concerns you. That widow with three children—Mrs. Hamilton, you know, whose husband was shot at Bareilly, and who wrote you such a pretty letter of thanks—she is coming home by next mail."

"With all her children, I hope! Poor thing!"

"You need not say 'poor thing,' for it is not only with her children—she brings a husband too."

"Then he was not shot, after all?"

"Yes he was," said Sir John. "But you women are curious creatures. This is her second husband. She has married the gentleman who saved her life and that of her three children, and brought her hundreds of miles across country and through indescribable perils. As she has not a halfpenny, and he is pretty well off, perhaps, poor woman! she might have done worse. You will think so, Mrs. Knowle, for you know the person—our old clerk, John Stenhouse."

"John Stenhouse! Married!" exclaimed Mrs. Knowle; as with an agitation she could hardly conceal, she glanced toward the sofa where Lady Bowerbank lay. But this tidings, which had powerfully affected the good lady herself, seemed to have passed quite harmlessly over Emily. She scarcely turned or showed any sign of emotion beyond a feeble fluttering of the fingers, which were soon stilled and folded upon one another over her heart—an involuntary attitude of hers, something like Chantrey's figure of Resignation.

"Why on earth should not the young man be married?" said Sir John, smiling. "My dear lady, you look as vexed as if you had wanted to have him for your second! I must certainly tell Knowle of this. What do you say, Lady Bowerbank?"

Lady Bowerbank said quietly, "I think people should always marry whoever they choose, and that nobody should blame or criticise them for it. Nobody but themselves can know the whole circumstances."

"Quite right. You are a sensible woman, Emily," said the old man, looking tenderly at his young wife, who yet seemed so much nearer the other world than he. "Well, I must go back now, for I am full of business. You'll wait here to dinner, Mrs. Knowle?"

Mrs. Knowle muttered some excuse concerning "Edward." She looked exceedingly nervous and uncomfortable still.

"Well, do as you like. Only stay as long as you can—stay and grumble at your friend Stenhouse and his marriage. By-the-by, I think I shall write to meet them at Southampton; it would only be civil, and I liked Stenhouse. What shall I give him—your good wishes?"

"If you please."

"And mine," said Emily, half raising herself from the sofa. "I knew him once—we met at Mrs. Knowle's. He will remember me—Emily Kendal."

"Very well, my dear."

After Sir John was gone, Mrs. Knowle took her friend's hand in hers and held it, but she did not attempt to speak; she literally did not know what to say. Lady Bowerbank's manner, so gentle, so composed, had completely puzzled, nay, frightened her. She could not believe it natural. But it was natural; there was no affectation of strength about it, no high heroic self-suppression. Emily lay, pale indeed, but not paler than usual, her eyes open, and fixed with a soft, steady gaze on the white spring clouds that sailed in mountainous masses across the dark blue sky; great heights and depths of heaven, into which the soul, when it is loosely held to earth, seems to pierce with an intense and yet calm desire, that soothes all pain, and makes every thing level and at rest.

"I am glad of this—very glad," she said, after a long pause, and without any explanation. "He ought to be married, and he will be sure to make a good, kind husband to whomever he chooses for his wife; and no doubt he has chosen wisely and well."

"I hope he has," said Mrs. Knowle, rather tartly. She was but human, and she did not like the destruction of her little romance.

"I am sure of it. The man who could love one woman so faithfully as he once loved me—"

Mrs. Knowle turned round eagerly.

Emily colored, even through the paleness of mortal disease. "Yes, it was so. He was never untrue to me. I can't tell you any particulars, and I never found it out myself till a little while ago. But he did come back, to the very day, and claimed me. Only—I was never told."

"And whose doing was that?"

"My father's."

Mrs. Knowle almost started from her chair. "What an atrocious—"

"Hush! it is too late now. And, besides, it might have come to the same thing in the end. Feel here!" and she took Mrs. Knowle's hand and put it to her heart, which was beating violently and irregularly. "*He* does not know it—my good husband I mean. Was he not good to me this morning? Nobody knows it, I think. But I know it," and she smiled. "I am quite certain—safely certain—that I am dying."

"Don't say that. You must not—you ought not." And Mrs. Knowle tried a little to reason her out of that conviction, which seemed to be the source of all her strength, and the soothing of all her sorrows.

"No—no. This world has been a little too hard

for me," Emily said; "but in the other I may begin again, and be strong. Do you think he has forgiven me?"

"Who, my poor child?"

"John Stenhouse. You see, I might have obeyed my father, and not married him; but then I ought not to have married at all. Nobody ought, loving another person all the time. But I was so weak—and— Never mind. It does not matter much now."

"John has married, you see," said Mrs. Knowle, partly with a lurking sense of indignation at him, and partly from a vague feeling that even now it was her duty to impress that fact salutarily upon Sir John Bowerbank's wife. Both the wrath and the caution passed harmlessly over the gentle spirit, that was already loosing its cables from earthly shores, and feeling soft, pure airs blowing toward it from the land unseen.

"Yes, he has married; I can quite understand how it came about: just the sort of marriage he would be sure to make—of pity, and tenderness, and duty. And it may turn out a very happy one. He will love her very much when — when I am quite gone away. I hope she is a good woman."

"I hope so," said Mrs. Knowle, rather huskily.

"Would you mind trying to find out? I don't mean that I am ever likely to have any acquaintance with them, but I should like to know about him and her. And something about her three children too. He will have to work hard to maintain so large a family."

"Very hard."

It was strange how the two women seemed to have

changed places. Emily talked, Mrs. Knowle was all but silent.

"You are sure you don't mind making these inquiries? Or I would ask my husband. Yes, perhaps, after all, it will be better to ask my husband. He might befriend them very much, and I am sure he would like to do it."

"In the way he once wanted — by getting John Stenhouse into the firm again? Do you mean that? and do you wish it, Emily?"

"No, not wish it exactly. But"—and she opened her eyes wide, clear, and pure — pure alike with the innocence of sorrow and the peace of coming death, and fixed them steadily on Mrs. Knowle's face — "I should not be afraid of his coming to Liverpool—not now."

Mrs. Knowle fairly laid her head on the sofa pillow and sobbed. Then she rose up, saying in a cheerful voice,

"Well, my dear, I have staid talking quite long enough for one day, so good-by. I'll keep a look-out after the Stenhouses. Meantime lie down and get a sleep if you can, and take care to be quite bright by the time Sir John comes in to dinner."

"Oh yes, I always try to do that. I like to please him. He is very good to me," said Emily Bowerbank.

CHAPTER VI.

Lady Bowerbank was, as she said, dying; that is, the seeds of death were firmly sown in her constitution, but they were very slow of developing themselves. Perhaps the exceeding peace in which, externally, her daily life was passed, partly caused this; but chiefly it was because, if she had seen an end to happiness, so she had to all its bitterest elements, its turmoil, trial, restlessness, and pain. She was not strong enough to suffer, and now she had ceased to suffer any more. She even seemed for a while to rally, and to take an interest in things about her—the tender, farewell interest of one soon departing. She was especially sedulous in all duties to her husband—at least those which she was able to perform. But she had long sunk into a thorough invalid wife, most kindly watched and tended, though more by his orders than by his personal care, while he went his own ways, and fell back gradually into much of his old "bachelor" life, as it had been spent in the long interregnum between his first marriage and his union with poor Emily Kendal.

"Sir John is quite comfortable: he will not miss me very much," Mrs. Knowle once heard her say, more meditatively than complainingly. But that lady, who had so keen a sense of wifely duty, even without love, never took any notice of the remark.

And when, according to promise, she had learnt all attainable facts about the Stenhouses—how that they lived in London, on Mr. Stenhouse's not too large salary in a merchant's office, and he was reported to be a most kind husband to the widow, and a careful father to the three fatherless children—after this, the prudent matron said as little as possible to Lady Bowerbank on the subject of her old lover.

Only once, when, after as long an interval as it was possible for civility to admit of, Mr. Stenhouse answered the congratulations he had received on his marriage in a letter to Mrs. Knowle, containing the brief message—"his own and his wife's compliments, and thanks to Sir John and Lady Bowerbank"—Emily's eyes filled with tears.

"He might have been a little kinder," she said. "But he does not know, and he can not forgive. He never will forgive me—till I die."

And meantime the two, once lovers, lived on, and did their duty to the husband and the wife unto whom Fate had united them. Whether bitter thoughts ever came—whether in the dead of night either woke up and remembered the past, their young, bright, innocent mutual love, and the cruelty that snatched it from them and turned it into a curse; whether their hearts ever burned within them against man, or, alas! against Providence, because in this short, short mortal life they were not made happy—they whose happiness would have injured no one, and who needed nothing in the world to make them happy except a little love—these were mysteries which must remain forever undisclosed.

But month by month there was disclosed the plain sad fact that Sir John Bowerbank's second marriage was not likely to be of much longer duration than his first one, which most people had altogether forgotten; and much was the sympathy excited both for him and for the sweet, fragile creature who was fading away, peacefully and contentedly, it was evident, but still fading, no one quite knew how or why. All the Liverpool doctors, and more than one London physician, were brought to his wife by Sir John, in undemonstrative but evident anxiety; but they could not cure her—they could not even find out what was the matter with her. Hereditary weakness, want of stamina, deficiency of vital force—they called her disease, or no disease, by all these fine names; but no human being guessed the root of it except Mrs. Knowle.

She, honest woman, as she sat knitting beside her "Edward," who was getting an old man now—stout, and a little infirm with rheumatism, and sometimes a little cross too with the weight of business, but still at heart the same hearty, kindly "goodman" as ever—would often say with a sigh, "Ah, poor Emily! if those two had only been left to fight the battle out together as we did, my dear, how much better it would have been!"

At which Mr. Knowle, who never sentimentalized in his life, just assented, smiled at his "old woman," and perhaps a little weary of the subject, generally went to sleep.

How the Stenhouses struggled on, for it must have been a struggle at best, with their small income and the three children, Mrs. Knowle could not easily learn; John Stenhouse seemed determined to drop entirely out of the range of his old Liverpool friends. To any letters—and Mrs. Knowle wrote him several—he always returned polite, but long-delayed and unsatisfactory answers, telling her nothing that she wished to know, and inquiring of nothing which, she hardly knew why, she would have liked him to inquire about.

"And there is that poor thing dying, and he does not even know it!" lamented she sometimes. To which her husband only answered with the common-sense question,

"And what would be the good of it if he did know?"

Nor on her side was Emily aware—and Mrs. Knowle took care to keep it from her, lest it might disturb her peaceful dying—that his struggle was the equally hard struggle of living: grinding poverty; a delicate, nervous, broken-spirited wife; three hungry children to be fed, from duty, without the natural fatherly love to sweeten it; and, above all, the daily blank in the life of a strong, faithful, single-hearted man, who, having once taken it into his head, or heart, to love one woman, never can learn to unlove her to the end of his days. Such men there are, but they are very, very rare, and John Stenhouse happened to be one of them.

So he locked his secret up in his breast, and, whether or not his marriage was a happy one, went on working steadily and patiently for his wife and for the children, not his own, whom Providence had sent to him. He slipped away from all his old associates, till even Mr. and Mrs. Knowle were half inclined to do as he apparently wished, and let him go.

But the one person who, with an almost fateful pertinacity, held to him, was Sir John Bowerbank. Whether he, too, was the sort of person who, once taking a liking, great or small, never relinquishes it, or whether some other secret inner sympathy attracted him to young Stenhouse, as being not unlike what he himself had been as a young man, certain it was that the head of the firm never lost sight of his former clerk; and when, on Mr. Knowle's suggesting the advisability of a junior partner, the question arose who should be adopted into such a valuable and responsible situation, the first person Sir John proposed to whom the offer should be made was Mr. Stenhouse.

Edward Knowle was greatly amazed—nay, perplexed. He rubbed up his hair with a troubled aspect.

"Stop a bit; I think—I think I should like to speak to my wife about this."

Sir John looked undisguised surprise. "As you please. But it never would occur to me to consult my wife on business matters."

"Indeed!" said the other, catching eagerly at the opportunity, "I wish you would. I really think you had better—in this matter."

"Why?"

"You see," awkwardly explained Mr. Knowle, "a partner, which also implies a partner's wife, is a serious thing to the women-kind, bringing about much intimacy, and all that. I fancy—of course it's only a fancy of mine—that the ladies would both like to be consulted about it. Shall my wife go and speak to Lady Bowerbank?"

"If she chooses; but it is really great nonsense bringing domestic affairs into a mere question of business. It will cause delay, while every post is a matter of consequence. I can not see the use of it at all. In fact, with your consent—" and his manner implied with or without it, for Sir John Bowerbank was a very obstinate man in his way, as was well known to his partner—"with your consent, I shall write and make the offer to the young man to-night."

He did so, and it was declined—declined immediately and point-blank, without any reasons being assigned for the refusal.

Sir John was considerably annoyed. To the answer, which had come, not by letter, but by telegram, so eager apparently was the young man to renounce the proffered kindness, he wrote again, suggesting easier terms—terms so favorable that no man in his senses seemed likely to refuse them, and yet by return of post refused they were.

"The man must be mad," said Sir John to his partner.

"Perhaps," was the brief reply.

"Why, he has three children and a delicate wife, and scarcely enough salary to keep them in bread and cheese; for you know, at Lady Bowerbank's desire, I found out all about them. She was interested in the wife, and might write and advise her to persuade her husband out of his folly. I must speak to Lady Bowerbank."

Meantime Lady Bowerbank had been spoken to. In fear and trembling the matter had been broken to her by good Mrs. Knowle; but there was no need for uneasiness; Emily evinced not the slightest sign of agitation. She merely said that she thought such a partnership would be the best thing possible, both for the firm and for Mr. Stenhouse, and that she hoped it would come about speedily. And then she lay looking into the sunset over the sea, with a strange, soft expression in her eyes.

"You are sure—quite sure, my dear Emily, that you have no objection?"

"No; why should I?" And she added again still more earnestly, "Oh no—not now."

"And by that," commented Mrs. Knowle, as she repeated the conversation to her husband, "I am certain Emily feels that she is dying."

They talked the whole matter over for a while, conjugally and confidentially, in their own room, for they had been asked to dine and sleep that night at Summer Lodge, as indeed they very often were now, and then went back to the drawing-room.

There, white indeed as a dying face, but eager with all the strength of life, lay poor Emily, her husband sitting beside her sofa in his quiet, attentive, elderly way, and trying, as well as he could, to make little bits of talk, concerning the news of the day in Liverpool, to amuse her during the hour and a half that he and his guests dined, and she rested alone, for she had now ceased entirely to join the circle at meals.

"Come here, Mrs. Knowle, and say if you do not agree with me—you women understand one another so well. I have been telling my wife about that young man's exceeding folly—your friend Stenhouse, I mean—in refusing to enter our firm. It must be a mere crotchet—some offense taken, or the like, for which we can't afford to lose such a useful partner, or to let a fine young fellow cut his own throat in that way. I want Lady Bowerbank to write to his wife, and reason with her. She has a right; for Lady Bowerbank has done all sorts of kind things to Mrs. Stenhouse."

"Kindness implies no right," said Emily, hastily and tremulously. "I don't know her. I can not write to her. What could I say?"

"Just a little common sense—that such a chance as this does not happen to a man twice in a lifetime; that Stenhouse should take advantage of it. He is very poor. I hear he can but just put bread into the mouths of those three children. If he were to join us he would make his fortune."

"Make his fortune," repeated Emily, wistfully. "Ah! if that had been—once. But it is too late now."

"Too late, my dear! Nonsense. The young man can not be over thirty yet."

"Thirty-one and a half."

Sir John Bowerbank looked exceedingly surprised for the moment. "I forgot—you said you knew him."

"Yes, I did know him, as Mrs. Knowle is aware. I met him at her house. I was once going to be married to him. He was very fond of me."

Quite quietly, without the slightest sign of emotion, Emily said these words, as if it had been a fact communicated concerning a third person; so utterly divided from the world and the passions of it seemed that frail creature, who already stood close on the portals of the world to come.

"Shall I go away?" whispered Mrs. Knowle, and yet she dreaded to do it, for there was something so unearthly in Emily's expression just then.

"Oh no, do not leave me. You can tell my husband

any thing he wishes to know. Dear husband! you are not angry with me? You know I was a poor weak thing always, and now all will soon be over. It is far the best —far the best."

"I do not understand," said, with a distressed air, Sir John Bowerbank.

No, he did not; it was not in him to understand. And when, in few words, for her breath was short and her strength small, she told him all the story—not that she had married him without loving him, for this he knew from the first; but that she had loved another, from whom she had been so cruelly separated; that from that day her poor young life had withered up at its very roots; still, still the worthy man seemed as if he could not understand. He was sixty years old, and the tale belonged to youth and love; to a time which, if he had ever known, had now entirely passed away even from his remembrance. He just looked perplexed, and a little sorry, and patted, with a soothing gesture, the wasted hands that were held out to him entreatingly.

"Do not excite yourself—pray do not, my dear! It is so very bad for you. Just tell me what you wish, and I will try to do it."

"And you are not angry?"

"About this young man? No, no. Of course, it was a great pity, but the thing happens every day. Don't fret about it, Emily. You are very comfortable as you are—at least I hope so."

"Yes," said Emily; and her tears ceased, and her quivering features settled into composure. No, he could not understand—this good, kindly-meaning, elderly man, no more than the tens of thousands of respectable men and women of this world ever do understand—the full meaning of Love. Love, happy or unhappy, mutual or unreturned, perfect or unfulfilled, but still real, true, heart-warm love, which is a gift direct from Love divine, and which ever to know, or to have known, is a blessing which fills a whole lifetime.

"You perceive now, Sir John," said Lady Bowerbank, laying over his her shrunken hand, where the wedding-ring hung as loosely as the great hoop of diamonds that guarded it, "you perceive why Mr. Stenhouse is so insensible to all your kindness. He thinks himself wronged, and he was wronged—cruelly. He was made to believe one thing and I another, and so we were parted. Please tell my husband how it was, Mrs. Knowle, "I have no strength for speaking much."

"Don't speak at all, for where is the good of it?" said Sir John, who evidently disliked the discussion of the matter. "Things can't be mended now, my dear! He has got a wife and you a husband. So, even if I were to die, it would be of no use. You could not marry him."

"I was not thinking of marrying, but of dying. Husband, I am certain I am dying; and it is hard to die without his having forgiven me, for he was a good man, and he was terribly wronged. Often—often I thought of asking you, but I had not courage. Now I have. Will you do one thing for me?"

"What, my dear?"

"Let me see John Stenhouse again—for one half hour—just one ten minutes—before I die!"

"Don't talk of dying; you will live many years yet, I trust," said Sir John, earnestly.

Emily shook her head.

"Ah! you know better than that. And I would not ask such a kindness unless I were dying. It is not wrong; surely you do not think so?" added she, imploringly. "I only want to tell him the truth; that it was not I who deceived him; I want to save him—he is a good man, you know—from having his whole life embittered and his future injured by thinking of me as a wicked, faithless woman, who first jilted him, and then let her rich husband insult him by showing him kindness. The truth would set all right—just three words of honest, simple truth. Husband, may I see him? Mrs. Knowle, speak for me, please."

"I really think your wife is right, Sir John," said plain-speaking Mrs. Knowle.

"Very well. Settle it among yourselves, you women-kind!" answered Sir John, as he rose up. "Only take care that Lady Bowerbank does not overexert herself."

"Thank you," breathed rather than spoke the poor girl; in her excessive fragileness, she seemed wasting back into thin girlhood again. "And you will forgive me, because I can not either harm you or grieve you much; I shall be dead so very soon — quietly dead, you know, as your first wife is, whom you never talked to me about. I wish you had, now and then. Were you very fond of her? And I dare say she was very fond of you?"

The old man suddenly sat down again, covering his eyes with his hand.

"Don't mention her, please. Poor little Jane—*my* Janie. *She* loved me."

And as he sat beside the wife of his prosperous later days, who, whether living or dying, only coldly esteemed him, and was grateful to him, perhaps the old man's thoughts went back, with a sudden leap of memory, to the wife of his youth and his poverty, so fond, so simple, so tender, and so true. When he took his hand away there were traces of tears on the withered cheeks, and he rose hastily to depart.

"Well, my dear, we need speak no more on this matter. You can see Mr. Stenhouse whenever you like, and if you can persuade him to enter our firm, so much the better. Impress upon him that capital is of no moment; a young, active, business-like man is the one thing needed, both by Mr. Knowle and myself. Isn't it so, Mrs. Knowle? You'll write the letter, perhaps? And you will take good care of my wife here, and not let her mope, eh?"

"I will, Sir John."

"Good afternoon, then."

And he went away, leaving the women alone.

CHAPTER VII.

WHAT John Stenhouse said to his wife when he got Mrs. Knowle's letter—a very brief, simple letter, dictated by Lady Bowerbank at her bedside, and merely stating that she wished to see her old friend again, as she did not think she was long for this world — what he said or what he felt, this history can not tell. He was not a man likely to have confided much of his own previous history to his wife, nor, when Mrs. Knowle afterward saw the lady, did that acute matron think her a person likely to have evinced much interest concerning her husband's early fortunes or lost love — a nice, pretty-faced, gentle creature, languid, and a little uninteresting, besides being a little lazy, as Indian ladies are apt to be. Doubtless the marriage had grown, as so many marriages do grow, out of mere circumstances, and after it the husband had gone back very much to his own old life — the life of action, or business, or, at best, of general kindly benevolence —a life in which his wife took little part, or, indeed, was capable of taking it.

When John Stenhouse visited Liverpool — for, after showing the letter to Mrs. Stenhouse, in whom it did not excite the least curiosity, he started North at once, every one of his old acquaintance, especially the Knowles, noticed a visible change in him — a certain hardness, reticence, and self-containedness, deeper than even the reserve of his bachelor days — as if the man had withdrawn into himself, went his own ways, and carried out his own life with a grave and sad independence. He spoke of his hôme and of his wife with a careful tenderness, but his eye did not moisten nor his face kindle when naming either, and there was nothing of that total change from frosty coldness to sunshiny warmth which is often seen in the looks and manner of a man who marries ever so late in life, if he marries with all his heart in the union. In this man's heart, good and true as it was, and would always remain, faithful till death, for honor's and conscience sake, to the woman he had taken to himself, still, as any one who knew the difference could plainly see, and as Edward and Emma Knowle saw at a glance, the sacred marriage torch, ever burning yet ever unconsumed, had never really been lighted—never would be.

But Stenhouse had been always a silent and undemonstrative man; and his experience abroad had made him more so, and more sedulous than even in his youth over the keeping up of all outward observances. Even when he sat listening to Mrs. Knowle's account of Lady Bowerbank's failing health and the hopelessness of her recovery, and again to that other story, which it had been arranged she should tell him, and not Emily, of the circumstances of her marriage to Sir John, and the letter found in Mr. Kendal's desk afterward, he exhibited outwardly nothing more than a sad gravity; in fact, he hardly spoke six consecutive words.

"So like a man!" cried Mrs. Knowle, half bitterly, when she was retailing the conversation to her husband.

"I think it was like a man," said honest Edward

Knowle; and his wife, woman as she was, quick, impulsive, and hard to believe in what she did not clearly see, recognized dimly what her husband meant. She respected, and in years to come learned daily to respect more, the manly endurance which, beholding the absolute and inevitable, accepts it, and, whatever the man suffers, makes no sign.

"Thank you," Mr. Stenhouse had said, holding out his hand to Mrs. Knowle, "thank you for all your kindness; to me myself—and—to her! Is she able to see me? If so, had we not better go at once?"

Mrs. Knowle ordered the carriage, and they drove across country—the miles upon miles of flat country which mark the Liverpool shore—a long level of roads, fields, and hedges—hedges, fields, and roads—sometimes green, perhaps, and not ugly, but tame and uninteresting as a loveless life—as the life which had been meted out to these two human creatures, who, left to their own holy instincts, would have met and mingled together, and flowed on harmoniously as one perfect existence. Now?

Mr. Stenhouse and Mrs. Knowle conversed very little during their drive, and then not concerning any thing of the past. Only once, with unnecessary caution, Mrs. Knowle screwed up her courage to its utmost pitch and said,

"Perhaps it would be better if you did not speak to Emily about her father." John Stenhouse's face turned purple-red, and his eyes flamed.

"No, I will remember he is dead—dead." And within a minute or two he said—the bitterest thing he ever was known to say—"Mrs. Knowle, my father died a month before I was born, and my mother seven years afterward. Perhaps it's true what a cynical friend of mine used to declare, 'that when he chose a wife, he would take care she was a miserable orphan.'"

But they were reaching the door, where scarcely any visitors now entered except good Mrs. Knowle. Soon they passed through the splendid empty house, where the mistress had been missing so long that her absence was scarcely noticed. The large, handsome drawing-room was just as bright, even though the sofa in the corner where Emily used to lie was vacated, and had been for some days. She now occupied a small room much quieter and farther removed, which had been hastily fitted up for her comfort. In a few days more she would vanish even from that into her own chamber and bed, never to be carried thence till carried away in that narrow couch of eternal rest where we all shall be laid some day. And that day was not very far off now to the weary soul and worn-out body of Emily Bowerbank. As she said many a time, life had been too hard for her; she was glad to go to sleep.

When the strong, hearty, healthy man, still young in years, and with all his life before him, passed out of the bright, cheerful drawing-room, full of all human sights and sounds—rich furniture, the scent of exotics, and the shrill note of cage-birds singing—to that small inner chamber where the light was subdued, and there was a faint, oppressive perfume to make up for the lack of fresh air; while a sedate old woman, the nurse of Emily's childish days, sat sewing at the window, but turning every minute at the slightest cough or movement of the almost motionless figure on the sofa, John Stenhouse drew back involuntarily. He had not realized till now all that he had lost—all that he was losing. Though he had been told it over and over again, he never really recognized that the woman he once loved so passionately—the pretty bright girl, with her rosy cheeks, her laughing eyes, and her heart full of the fondest, most innocent love, was dying.

He was married now—another woman owned his duty, and possessed a great deal of the tenderness that no honorable man can fail to give to a creature so utterly dependent on him as a wife is—but Emily Kendal had been his first love. All the memories of it, and of her, rushed upon him with an agony irrepressible. He grasped Mrs. Knowle by the arm as she was going into the sick-room.

"Wait a minute—stay!—say I'll come presently."

And he rushed away, right down the staircase, and through the first open door—for it was high summer, and the air was full of sunshine and of roses—into the garden.

It was half an hour before he returned, which gave time for them to meet, as alone was possible these two could meet—as old friends—calm, tender, self-possessed—friends over whom hung the sacred shadow of the eternal parting—at least the parting which we call eternal in this world—though it often makes closer and nearer, for the rest of life, those who otherwise would have been forever divided.

Perhaps Emily felt this; for, as she raised herself a little from her sofa, and held out her hand to Mr. Stenhouse, there was not a trace of agitation or confusion in her manner.

"I am very glad to see you. It was so kind of you to come. Did you leave your wife quite well? and all the children?"

Commonplace, simple words they were—the simplest, most natural, that could possibly be chosen—and yet they were the best and safest. They took off the edge of that sharp agony which was thrilling through every fibre of the strong man's heart. They brought him back to the commonplace daily world, to his daily duties, and his ordinary ways. The wholesome, saving present came between him and the delirious past. And though it was Emily's old smile, her very tone of voice, and a trick of manner she had—how well he recalled it, of half extending her hand, drawing it back, and then putting it forward again, with the uncertainty that was the weak point in her character—still he had no desire to snatch her to his arms, and hold her there, in her old familiar place, like any mortal woman. He felt inclined rather to stand apart and gaze at her, as she lay, consecrated from earthly emotion in her almost superhuman peace, or else to fall on his knees and worship her, as Dante worshiped his Beatrice when he met her in the fields of Paradise. And he found himself powerless to say any other words than one or two, as brief and inexpressive as her own.

"My wife and the children are well. It was very good of you to send for me, after I had been so rude, so ungrateful almost, to your husband."

Emily bent her head, acquiescing; and then, as if with a great effort,

"I had something to say to you—something I thought

you would listen to, from me, now. I entreat you to accept this partnership. It will be a good thing for you, and an equally good thing for Sir John and Mr. Knowle. You would like Sir John very much if you knew him well. He knew nothing about you and me till lately. And he has been such a good, good husband to me."

"Thank God for that! If—if he had been any thing else than good to you—"

And then, shocked by the sound of his own harsh voice jarring on the stillness of the room, and still more so by perceiving the sudden tremor that came over Lady Bowerbank, he stopped, recognizing the sanctity of sickness—of near advancing death.

"Yes," he added, almost in a whisper, "I feel very grateful to Sir John Bowerbank; I am not ashamed of his knowing—indeed, I have been asking Mrs. Knowle to tell him—how very poor we are, and are likely to remain; and that if he really still wishes me to accept his offer, I will do my utmost to prove deserving of it."

"Will you? oh, will you?" clasping her hands in her old, pretty childish way at any thing she was very glad of.

John Stenhouse turned away.

"It is not easy, for I will do it because you wish it—for your sake."

"No; do it for your own," said Emily, solemnly, with all the old childish manner gone. "Do it, that you may take a wise man's advantage of this chance of getting on in the world, and living fully the life that is before you. Think, a life of twenty, thirty years, with work to do, and money to use, and influence to make the most of, for the good of yourself and all that belong to you. That is what I want. I want you to lead your own noble, active, useful life—just as I once planned it—though it was not to be beside me, and though I shall not even see it; for I am going away, John—you know that?"

He could not deny it; he did not even attempt to do so; he just moved his lips, but they would not form a sound.

"Yes, going away—in a few days, or a few weeks more, to where I know I shall be quite happy—happier than I ever could be here. I only wished before I went to let you know the truth. She," glancing to Mrs. Knowle, "she has told you all?"

"Yes," he muttered, but attempted not, nor did Emily offer, any farther explanation. One a husband, the other a wife, with the shadow of the dead father between them—it was impossible. The past was over and done. But the present was peace—all peace.

"And now good-by, and God bless you," said Emily, faintly. "Give my love to your wife. Does she know any thing about me?"

"No; I never told her."

"Ah! well, let that be as you choose. And one thing—I know I have forgotten one thing that I had to say to you—Mrs. Knowle, what is it? Oh, my head! Please, Mrs. Knowle, will you help me?" with the querulous tone and wandering eye which told at once how fast her sand of life was running. "Yes, I remember now; it was to give you this," taking a valuable diamond brooch from under her pillow, "and to ask you, if ever you have a little daughter of your own, to give it to her from me.

And perhaps, if your wife did not object, you wouldn't mind calling her Emily?"

Nobody answered or stirred, not even Mrs. Knowle, who stood at the window in nurse's vacated place; nor John Stenhouse, who sat opposite the sofa where Lady Bowerbank lay—sat, with his hands clasped tightly on his knees, looking at her, as if he wished to carry away the last picture of her, vivid as life and youth, permanent as love and death.

At length he moved, and, taking the brooch from her hand, kissed both, and so bade her farewell.

"If you come soon to settle in Liverpool, perhaps I may see you once more," said she, gently, and with a sort of compassion in her voice, for she saw that he was absolutely dumb with sorrow. But both knew that this was only a fiction to hide the last good-by; and when the door closed between them, both felt that they never would see one another again.

They never did, though Lady Bowerbank lived for several weeks longer, and even after the time when the Stenhouses came to settle in Liverpool. She heard all about them from Mrs. Knowle, who, in her customary active way, was exceedingly helpful to the rather helpless Indian lady; and she seemed to take a faint, flickering interest—the last interest of her fading life—in the house they fixed on, the manner they furnished it, and their general household ways. Nay, she sent many little gifts to them—harmless, domestic gifts, such as not even the proudest man could reject, and which, without making any external show of giving, greatly added to the comfort of Mr. Stenhouse's home. But she never asked to see him again. She seemed to feel that the last meeting had been a peaceful closing of every thing that bound her to life, and every thing that made death painful; apparently she did not wish to revive either, but lay perfectly at rest, waiting patiently for the supreme call.

It came at last, quite suddenly, as often happens in consumption, when both the watchers and the patient are lulled into a hope that it is still far distant. She had no one with her, and no time to say farewell to any body; only the nurse, running to her and bending over her, fancied there came through the choking of the expiring breath the words "John—dear John."

Consequently the woman fetched Sir John, and told him, and Mrs. Knowle, and every body, that Lady Bowerbank's last words had been her husband's name. Nobody contradicted the fact.

* * * * * *

It may be thought a proof of the hardness of John Stenhouse's heart to state that except the one day of Lady Bowerbank's funeral, when, out of respect to her memory, the office of Bowerbank and Co. was closed, and the clerks had liberty to enjoy themselves as they pleased —and she would have been glad of it, dear, kindly heart! —except on this occasion the junior partner of the firm was never an hour absent from his desk. He came early —he went late—he filled the place of both his senior partners—Mr. Knowle, who was laid up with an attack of rheumatism, and Sir John, from whom, of course, little could be expected just now. In every way he did his duty like a man; and not one of those excellent gentlemen on 'Change, with whom he daily transacted business, giving promise that the new blood which had come into the firm would make the house of Bowerbank and Co. higher than ever among Liverpool merchants—not one of them ever suspected that within the week a light had gone out of this young man's life which nothing in the world could ever relume.

Nevertheless, John Stenhouse's life has neither been useless nor sad. Moderately prosperous, and widely honored by all who know him, externally he may be considered a happy and successful man. And his home, if a little dull sometimes, is always quiet and comfortable. In course of time it was brightened by a little daughter —his very own little daughter—and he called her Emily. In compliment—and very right too, every body said—to the head of the firm and his deceased wife, poor Lady Bowerbank.

Emily's instinct—true woman's instinct—was correct. Sir John and Mr. Stenhouse became fast friends. Such strange likings often occur, under circumstances which in meaner natures produce only jealousy and aversion. But these three—the two men left living, and the sweet woman happily dead—were all good people, none of whom had intentionally wronged the other, but had all been sinned against by the one selfish, hard heart, which was now a mere handful of dust. Still, by the merciful ordinance of Providence, evil itself is limited in its power against good, especially when after it comes the solemn, healing hand of inevitable fate, which the foolish and bad resist, but by which the wise and good are calmed and soothed.

When Emily was dead, the two honest men who had

loved and mourned her—one with the wild angry passion of loss, the other with a half-remorseful tenderness—were unconsciously drawn to one another in a way neither could have explained or desired to explain, but both felt it was so. They sought one another's company shyly and doubtfully at first; afterward with a yearning sort of curiosity; finally out of warm regard. The great difference of age between them, which might have been that of father and son, and the fact that the one had never had a father nor the other a son, also combined to prevent all feeling of rivalry, and to form a bond of mutual attraction and mutual usefulness. And she who was gone, though her name was never once named between them till Mr. Stenhouse asked Sir John's permission to give it to his baby daughter, constituted a tie stronger than any thing external.

Mr. Knowle was a little surprised, and so was Mrs. Knowle, to see the great cordiality and even intimacy which in the course of a year sprang up between the senior and junior partners. But the Knowles were both such kindly people that, though they did not understand it—indeed, would have expected things to be altogether different, they were exceedingly glad it was so—exceedingly tender, too, in a half sad sort of way, over the baby Emily, whom good Mrs. Knowle took to with a warmth surpassing even her universal and ardent affection for all babies.

And so the three households of the firm of John Bowerbank and Co. still subsist—two rich and childless, one much poorer, but not without many blessings. There is, at all events, wherewithal to put food into the little mouths, and clothes on the little bodies, and instruction into the little minds; and John Stenhouse is a good father, who, in a literal sense, "makes no step-bairns," but is equally just and tender with his own and his wife's daughters. As a parent of young children he has been almost faultless; what he may be when the little maidens grow up and take to marrying, Heaven knows! But the sharp experience of his own life may be all the better for theirs.

People do say that one of them is not likely to be poor all her life, but will be chosen by Sir John Bowerbank as his heiress, at least so far as regards the late Lady Bowerbank's fortune; his own, Sir John openly declares, he means to divide among charitable institutions. Poor little Emily! now running about under the shady alleys of Birkenhead Park in her cotton frock, and with occasional holes in her shoes, she knows not what may be her destiny! Nor does her father—good man—who watches her and guards her, and is both father and mother to her, for Mrs. Stenhouse, though sweet as ever, has sunk into confirmed laziness and elegant invalidism. Her girls are good children, but the apple of the father's eye is his own little daughter; and no doubt even now he thinks with a certain vague dread of the young man who may be coming some day to snatch her from him.

Still, under all circumstances, even the alarming catastrophe of Emily's marriage, I think John Stenhouse will prove himself a just, an unselfish, and a loving father. And if—human nature being weak at best—he is ever tempted to be otherwise, he will think, as he does think, in many a wakeful midnight, with his wife fast asleep beside him, of that quiet grave, within sound of the waves on Waterloo shore, where lies buried the love of his youth—the one woman who would have made him really happy and been happy herself—who, instead of dying thus, might have lived to be the light of his home and the mother of his children—poor Emily Kendal.

E

PARSON GARLAND'S DAUGHTER.

PARSON GARLAND'S DAUGHTER.

CHAPTER I.

The Reverend William Garland was, in the primitive sense of the word (*vide* Chaucer and others), and as it is still used in remote English parishes, of which his own formed one of the remotest and smallest, emphatically a "parson." Whether legally he could be termed rector, vicar, perpetual curate, or incumbent, I do not know; in his own place he was rarely called any thing but "the parson," just as the only other educated person within the boundary of the parish was called "the squire." They divided the land between them—and the people's hearts, though in both cases the division was notably unequal. But with this said squire—Richard Crux, of Cruxham Hall—the present story has little to do, more than to mention his name, and the fact of his residence within the parish (at the shooting season, for two months in every twelve), in order to show what a lonely parish it must have been, and what a shut-up, solitary existence this was for any man of education and refinement to lead. Yet the Reverend William Garland had led it for more than twenty years, and now, though over seventy, he still continued to discharge, single-handed, without even a week's absence, the duties of pastor to that small and simple flock.

A very simple flock they were, in truth, many of them never having been in their lives farther than the nearest market-town, ten miles off. They subsisted chiefly by farm labor and fishing; for, being only half a mile from the coast—the southern coast of England—they now and then roused themselves sufficiently to secure a little of the deep-sea riches that lay close at hand, and drive a mild and innocent piscatory trade, chiefly in lobsters.

But, on the whole, the aspect of the place and its few inhabitants was as if they and it had grown up out of the earth somehow, and remained there, stationary as cabbages, with no need to toil for their existence, and no power or will to change it—at least this was the impression it would probably have made upon a stranger, who, in crossing the miles upon miles of waving downs, ending in those sheer precipices of chalk rock which form the often-sung "white cliffs of Albion," came upon the tiny village of Immeridge.

It was almost a compliment to call it a village, for it consisted of a mere handful of cottages, one being elevated into the dignity of the post-office and general shop, a single house, and the parsonage. The church, as old as the Norman Conquest, was very small, and its churchyard contained so few graves that every one of them was a separate chronicle; and by going over them, you might guess, fairly enough, at the village history for centuries. All its family records of joy and sorrow, birth, marriage, and death, lay covered over in peace by the green turf here.

Here, too, lay the secret of what struck every accidental worshiper in the church, and every stray visitant to the village and parsonage, as such a remarkable thing—that a man like the Reverend William Garland should ever have been found at Immeridge, or, being so located, could possibly have remained there, as he had done, for twenty long years.

Just between the parsonage garden-gate and the chancel-window was a head-stone, notable only for its plainness and for the brevity of the inscription upon it. There was only a name, "Mary Garland," and three dates of the three epochs which record all lives—"born," "married," "died." Between the first and second was an interval of forty years; between the second and third one year only. Underneath—the letters being so equally old and moss-covered that the oddity did not at first strike a passer-by—was a second inscription, "Also of the Reverend William Garland, her husband, who died ——, aged —— years;" blanks being left for the figures, to be filled up—when? by some hand unknown.

In that grave, which the present generation at Immeridge almost forgot existed, and which only an occasional old man or woman gave a sigh to, in watching the parson's gown sweep past it, Sunday after Sunday, on his way from his own gate to the vestry door—in that little grave lay the mystery, such as it was, of Mr. Garland's life from manhood to old age.

He had fallen in love with her—the "her" who to other people was now a poor handful of dust, but which to him was still a living and real woman and wife—fallen in love, not very early, for he was a shy man and a hard student, but soon after he got his fellowship. They were quite alone in the world—orphans, with no near kin, he being the last of an old county family, having gone up to Cambridge as a sizar, and thence worked his way to considerable honor; and she, of no family at all, having worked her way also, and earned her bread hardly as a resident governess. It was an attachment which, as neither had any thing to marry upon except love, might fairly be characterized as "imprudent;" but there was no one to tell them so, and the mere love made them happy. So, as they were both young enough to wait, and as some one of the livings in the gift of college was certain to fall to Mr. Garland's lot in time, they did wait, silently and patiently, for fifteen years.

No doubt it was a sad alternative. Of a truth, this sitting watching for dead men's shoes is one of the hardest trials to human endurance and human goodness; but somehow they bore it, these two, and were not actually unhappy—that is, they were less unhappy than if they had parted, on the prudential motives which, had they not luckily been two lonely creatures, would have been worried into them by affectionate friends and relatives. As it was, they were at least allowed to blight their lives in their own way.

At length the living of Immeridge fell, in customary rotation, to the eldest fellow, and though it was a very poor one, and the next one due was considerably richer, still William Garland decided not to let it pass him by. He, and Mary Keith too, were willing to risk any poverty that was not actual want sooner than longer separation. So they married; and as blessings, like sorrows, rarely come alone, a few days after her wedding, she was left a legacy which doubled their income, and made the brave facing of narrow means a needless courage, to be smiled over, contentedly and half proudly, in the years to come—the bright, easy, sunshiny years which never came.

For within thirteen months Mrs. Garland was taken out of her husband's arms, and laid to sleep until the resurrection morning, under that green grass, between the church chancel and the parsonage gate. She died—more than peacefully—thankfully, telling him she had been "so very happy;" and she left him a bit of herself—not the little daughter he had longed for, but a baby son, who for days was scarcely taken notice of, and whom nobody expected to live. The boy did live nevertheless; and the first interest his father showed in him, or in any earthly thing, was in christening him, as near to his mother's name as possible, Marius Keith Garland; and from that hour William Garland roused himself, almost by miracle, from the stunning stroke of his sorrow; and grave college fellow as he had been only a few months before—and even his brief married life was only beginning to shake him out of his long-habitual old-bachelor ways—he made himself at once both father and mother to the puny infant—his only child.

For at fifty, a man who has had the blessing—ay, even if a fatal blessing, of loving one woman all his life—who has married, and lived happy with her only for a year, is a little less likely than most men to marry again. Mr. Garland never did so. Whether, through a certain want of energy, which perhaps had been the weak point in his character, and influenced his fortunes in sadder ways than he himself suspected, or whether the wound, which scarcely showed outside, had in truth withered up the springs of life and manly ambition forever, certain it was that he never tried to better himself by leaving the little village which had witnessed his crowning joy and utmost anguish, which was his son's birthplace and his wife's grave. He settled down in this out-of-the-world nook, discharged faithfully and fully all his duties there, but sought no others. He refused all attractions from without—though these were not wanting to a man of his cultivated tastes, for he was a first-rate mathematician, and, for the two often go together, a scientific musician likewise. He never revisited his old college haunts, and after a few years seemed to have not a thought or interest beyond the boundary of his parish and its duties, such as they were.

Not that he was in any way soured; a man of his sweet nature could not be, especially by a sorrow which had come direct from Providence, and had no wrong or bitterness in it. But it had fallen upon him too late in life for him to recover from it; and though his heart was not crushed or broken, for with a woman's gentleness he also seemed to possess a woman's miraculous strength in affliction, still his masculine ambition was killed within him. He could not rise and go back into the world, and make himself a new path in it; he preferred to take his child to his bosom, and hide himself in the quiet home which for one little year *she* had made so happy; narrowing his wishes down to his duties, and hers, which he had also to fulfill, and so spending, as it were, in the shadow of her perpetual invisible presence, the remainder of his uneventful days.

A life which some may think small, limited, unworthy of a man, and a man of education and intellect. Possibly: I neither defend it nor apologize for it; I merely record it as it was, and had been for twenty years; for now young Keith Garland (since his school-days he had dropped the "Marius" as being odd and heathenish, and because the boys turned it into "Polly") was actually grown up from the forlorn, puling baby into a fine young man, whom his father, justly considering the difference of half a century between parent and child, was too wise to educate entirely himself, but had sent first to a public school and then to college—the same quiet old college at Cambridge where Mr. Garland had spent so large a portion of his life.

Of course that cost a good deal—quite one half of his income; but he did not grudge it. He never grudged any thing to his boy, nor restricted him in aught but what was wrong. And though Marius did wrong things sometimes, the parson's only son was not a bad boy—not more selfish than only children are prone to be; very unlike his father, and still more unlike his mother, having neither the delicate refinement of mind and body of the former, nor the noble moral nature, generous, frank, and brave, which had made Mary Keith beloved till her dying day by a man far cleverer and handsomer than herself; still, young Garland was a fine fellow, full of animal life and activity, with a sufficient quantum of brains and affections to serve as ballast for both—a good ship, well built and sound, capable of many a voyage, if only it should please Heaven to put a steady captain on board, and a quick-eyed steersman at the helm.

But why farther describe the lad? He was like most lads of his age—neither better nor worse than his neighbors—fairly well liked both in the little world of Immeridge and the larger one of his college. And to his father—well, to the solitary parson, this one untried vessel was his argosy of price, on which all his life's stores, youth's memories, manhood's pride, and old age's hope, were solemnly embarked, as men sometimes (and women, alas! only too often) do embark their whole treasures in a single ship, and sit and watch it from the shore, sailing, sailing far away—whither, God knows!—the only certainty, often the only reliance, in such an awful watch being the firm faith that He *does* know.

Mr. Garland had just sent his son back to college after the first long vacation spent at home, partly in reading—or what Keith called such, and partly in wandering up and down country in the lovely September days, with his gun on his shoulder, though it was seldom that he brought home a bird. Indeed, the youth had, his father thought, an unlimited faculty for doing nothing; and after many weeks of that valuable employment, it was a certain satisfaction, in spite of the pang of parting in the fatherly heart, which circumstances had made likewise almost motherly in its tenderness and its anxiety, to feel that the lad was safe back at his work again; for Keith always worked hard, and conscientiously too, so far as the conscience of twenty years goes, when he was really within the walls of his college.

In the still October sunshine, which streamed in one

unbroken flood over the smooth downs, and dazzled whitely where they broke abruptly into high chalk cliffs, walked the parson, gazing idly on these long familiar green slopes, and on the glittering sea with its specks of ships, each seeming stationary, yet in reality gliding, gliding away, every minute farther and farther, like human lives, into the under world. Mr. Garland had bidden his son good-by only an hour or two before, and his mind absently followed the lad from these known places to others equally well known, which belonged to his earlier world, lingering dreamily over those same old college walls which had been his own home for so many years. He had never revisited them, never wished to revisit them; but his fancy hung over the thought of them—those gray cloisters and courts, those green leafy avenues, with the fondness that most University men have for their Alma Mater, the place mixed up with all their youthful hopes, and dreams, and friendships, to which they cling tenderly to the last day of their lives.

Mr. Garland liked to picture his boy there, with all his future before him—a future full of high hopes, college honors, worldly successes, and, by-and-by, domestic joys; for the good man was eager, as we all are, to plan for our successors a brighter destiny than our own, fraught with all our blessings and none of our woes; profiting by our experience and omitting our mistakes; carrying out victoriously all that we desired, yet failed to do; and enjoying fully every bliss that to us Heaven's inscrutable wisdom denied. There must have been a curious simplicity, as well as youthfulness of feeling, still latent in the old man of seventy, for, as he walked along, he amused himself with planning his son's future almost as a woman would have done; for his secluded life had kept in him that freshness and unworldliness which women generally retain much longer than men, and which often makes a woman who was elderly in her teens, in old age as young in heart as a maiden of twenty. It was almost childlike; nay, he smiled at it himself—the way the good clergyman speculated about his boy, as he slowly meandered on, his soft white hair floating over his coat collar, and his hands clasped behind him over his lengthy, and, it must be owned, rather shabby coat-tails.

Marius—the father alone still called him Marius—was to take holy orders—that is, if he had no strong objections thereto; but he should never be forced into any thing. He might win his degree and as much of college honors as he could, but he was not to struggle for a fellowship; there was no need, since he would inherit his mother's little fortune; and a fellowship hindered marriage, which the twenty-years solitary widower still believed to be the purest aim and highest blessing of any man's existence.

"Yes, Marius must marry," said he to himself, with a half sigh. "And his lot shall not be like mine. He shall marry early—as soon as ever he is in full orders, and can get a good curacy—perhaps even a living: I can still bring some influence to bear."

And with a pleased look he called to mind a very friendly letter from his bishop lately received, and another from a mathematical dean in a neighboring diocese, urging the publication of a book on some abstruse topic whereon Mr. Garland had wasted gallons of "midnight oil," and quires of valuable paper, during the last two solitary winters at Immeridge Parsonage.

"Perhaps I could make it into a book after all, and so get my name known a little, which might be useful to my son."

Not to himself; that phase of ambition never crossed the parson's imagination. Nor had he ever been able to make use of any body for himself. But his son? Many a scheme of most childlike Machiavelianism did he concoct, as he climbed slowly up, and as slowly descended, these eminences of green turf, round which the cliff-swallows and an occasional sea-gull were merrily circling. These schemes were solely for his boy's benefit—acquaintances to make, influential people to be cultivated, and so on, and so on, even to the last and most vital question of all—where in the wide world was Keith to find for himself a wife?

At Cambridge, certainly not; for, at the date of this history, wider even than now was the gulf between Dons and undergraduates, rendering the entrance of the latter into any thing like family life very difficult, nearly impossible. And at Immeridge Keith's lot was worse. Not a household in the parish contained any youthful women-kind above the rank of laborers' daughters, except Cruxham Hall, by-the-by; but the Misses Crux were quite elderly, and, save at church, the young man had never beheld them, otherwise the father might have built a charming little romance, since, knowing he came of as good blood as the Cruxes, it never occurred to him that a marriage between the hall and the parsonage would be in the least a *mésalliance*. If, indeed, he had a weak point, this true, honest Christian man, it was that, having been, as the phrase is, "a gentleman born," and having lived all his life among gentlemen, he was a little sensitive on the point of gentlemanhood—that is, he liked his intimate associates to be of good birth, good breeding, and possessed of those nameless refinements which to be perfect must be known by the absence of any demonstration thereof, even as the test of pure water is its being as colorless and tasteless as it is clear.

"Yes," meditated the good man, "Miss Crux is not bad—pretty, and quite a gentlewoman; she would have done had she been ten years younger. But now, where in the wide world is Marius to look out for a wife?"

And then he laughed at his own folly in so seriously arguing the matter, when the boy was only a boy, not one-and-twenty yet.

"The idea of marrying can never have entered his head. What an old idiot I am to let it enter into mine!"

But, in spite of himself, he could not quite dismiss the Alnaschar-like vision, born perhaps out of the unwonted gravity and tenderness, more manly than boylike, with which Keith had bidden him good-by that morning; the vision of his only son bringing to the parsonage a wife, who of course would be the parson's daughter.

"My daughter! yes, she would be that. Only to think! I should actually have a daughter."

And with a sudden gleam of remembrance there flashed back upon the old man's fancy that old dream, dreamed before Keith was born or thought of—that vision of beauty which to most men takes a shape feminine—the father's delight—the little daughter.

What if, by-and-by, this dream should be realized? Not exactly as he had first desired it—the little girl all his own, growing up from babyhood to womanhood as his ideal daughter, but as his daughter-in-law—next best —who might be a very perfect woman too—pretty, of course, though he did not absolutely exact it; her mother, that is, her mother-in-law, had not been pretty, yet was not Mary Garland the essence of all grace and all ladyhood? Of course Keith's wife would be a lady, well educated, possibly clever—Mr. Garland disliked stupid women. But still he would give up the brilliancy if she had good common sense and household wisdom—the true, delicate, feminine wisdom which alone makes harmony in a household, and welds together its jarring qualities into a smooth surface of family peace. A sweet temper, above all, she must have—this paragon of daughters-in-law; a nature calm and even, placid and bright, like that which for thirteen little months had spread such a sunshine through the parsonage rooms, that to this day the sunshine had never quite gone out of them. The woman that was to come—the parson's "daughter," would bring it half back again, and shine upon the evening of his days like the dim but lovely reflection of days departed.

The tears came into Mr. Garland's eyes as he thought of all Keith's wife would be to him, and all he would try to be to her, till he loved her already as if she had been a real existence—as she was, of course, somewhere in the world. He wondered where, and what she was like, and what happy chance would bring her and his boy together?

"'Truly I am a very foolish, fond old man,'" said he

to himself, quoting "Lear," and then, after his dreamy, meditative fashion, wandering away from the subject in hand to speculate on the play in general, and especially on the character of Lear, whom he always thought had been considerably overpitied and overrated.

"I should like to write a criticism on him—the weak, ambitious, vain, exacting old fellow; what better daughters could he expect to have? He who could so exile Cordelia and curse Regan scarcely deserved a better fate. I fancy our children are very much to us as we are to them. I hope never to feel the 'serpent's tooth;' but oh, I hope still more that I shall never play old Lear to my boy Marius. She was a sensible woman, that poor Cordelia—

"'Sure I shall never marry like my sisters,
To love my father all.'

And when Keith marries, I must make up my mind to some sacrifices; I can not expect him to 'love his father all!' Heigh-ho! Can that be actually Valley Farm gate?"

He found he had walked six or seven miles across country to the nearest farm-house out of his own parish, where twice or thrice a year he was in the habit of calling. It belonged to a worthy old couple, Mr. and Mrs. Love, who had inhabited it for half a century, and made it into the pretty place that it certainly was. Keith had always been fond of going there, and was a sort of spoiled pet to the childless pair, and his father was grateful to any body who was kind to Keith. So, as the sun was now sloping westward, he thought he would just climb the one little hill above—somehow this year Mr. Garland had felt the hills higher, and the valleys deeper than they used to be—and invite himself to tea and a rest in Mrs. Love's parlor. He always liked a chat with the old lady, and Marius had not mentioned having seen her lately; possibly because the college man had not found that simple old couple so interesting as formerly, and had been less often to the farm, which neglect the father determined to make up with a little extra civility.

"Is Mrs. Love at home?" he asked of a girl who stood feeding poultry by the stable-door—a servant evidently, though for a minute the parson had doubted it, being struck by the grace of her attitude and the prettiness of her face. But her arms were red and dirty, and so was her gown; and the moment she opened her mouth it was quite clear she was only a farm-servant.

"The missus bean't at home, please, sir," answered she, dropping a courtesy, and blushing red as a peony; "but the measter be about somewheres; would 'ee like to see 'un, Mr. Garland?"

"You know me, it seems, my girl," said the parson, stopping to give a second look into the face which really would have been pretty had it only been clean. "Do you belong to Immeridge?"

"No, sir; I do come from C——," naming a town several miles off.

"And you live as servant here?"

"Yes, sir."

"Well, you have a kind, good mistress, I know that, and you look like a good girl, who would be dutiful and attentive to old folk. I hope you will long remain here, and be a comfort to them. Tell your master I am taking a rest in the parlor; he must not hurry himself."

So the good parson sauntered in at the always open door, a little pleased, in spite of its dirt, by the pretty face; he so seldom saw a new face at all, and this one attracted him for the moment, just like a new roadside flower. He soon forgot it, however, for, being weary, he had scarcely sat down in Mr. Love's easy arm-chair before he fell sound asleep.

When he awoke it was to see the servant-girl standing beside him, examining him curiously. Her master had not come in, for which absence she made some confused explanation in an accent so broad—so much broader than even Mr. Garland was used to, that he gave up the attempt to understand it, especially as he was very hungry, and there lay ready prepared beside him a capital tea, which was evidently meant for his benefit.

"You are a sensible lass, and a kindly," said he, as he fell to with earnest appetite, noticing also that she had "cleaned herself up" to wait upon him, and was really very comely.

But his glance was only momentary; though, as he ate his meal, he spoke to her from time to time with that gentle but slightly reserved manner which, people said sometimes, was the only fault the parson had in his parish; he was a little too dignified and distant with his inferiors. Not that he meant any unkindness, but simply that he did not quite understand them.

Having finished his tea, he left all courteous messages for the master and mistress, and thanked the girl for her civilities.

"And what is your name?" asked he, absently, as he drew on his gloves.

"Charlotte."

"Good-by, then, Charlotte, and thank you. My compliments to your master and mistress, and say I shall call again some day before long."

He put a shilling into her hand and went his way.

CHAPTER II.

Mr. Garland was sitting in his study, where, to save fires, and trouble to his one old servant—almost as old as himself—he very often sat all day—these long, quiet winter days, which he usually spent quite alone, or, rather, with one invisible companionship, perhaps nearer to him in winter than in the summer season, for she—his wife Mary—had died in early spring, and his last memories of her were connected with the winter afternoons and evenings, when she used to lie on that sofa, pale but peaceful, with the fire-glow shining on her light hair; for, even though useless, she liked to stay beside him, and he fancied he could write his sermons better when she was there. So she often lay for hours almost silent—Mrs. Garland was never a great talker—watching him as he wrote, and thinking. He often wondered in after years what she could have been thinking about, and whether she had any dim prevision of his lonely years to come, which made her look so strangely sweet and grave.

It was all over now, long, long ago, but the memory of it and of her was vivid yet. Even to this day, on a Saturday afternoon, the parson would lift up his eyes from his sermon, half expecting to see her lying there, looking at him with those eyes of love which had warmed his inmost heart his whole life through—a love which death only would quench in closing them forever.

Mr. Garland sighed, but it was a sigh of remembrance rather than of sorrow. Time had long since taken the sting out of his grief; besides, he was not quite forlorn—no man ever can be who has once been thoroughly happy. He pushed his sermon aside for a time, and took up and reread his son Keith's Christmas letter, on this, the first Christmas that they had ever been apart.

Keith had written to say he was working very hard—so hard that he thought it advisable to remain at college during the brief vacation. And in this letter he made, for the first time, a hesitating request for a little more money. Altogether, though affectionate enough, even pathetically so, in its regrets for his unavoidable absence, it was not so satisfactory an epistle as Keith was wont to write, and had written weekly from school and college ever since his first separation from home. Still, he was working hard, as he always had worked, both at school and college. A certain light-mindedness of youth had sometimes worried his elderly father a little, but the parson's heart had never yet had cause to ache on account of his boy.

"I think," he said to himself, as he once more drew toward him the manuscript sheets of his sermon—a Christmas sermon on the prodigal son—only half finished, and, alas! never to be finished—"I think, after all, his mother would have been rather proud of him."

And as Mr. Garland sat leaning his head on his hand—both the hand and the profile, though brown with exposure to weather, being almost woman-like in their delicacy of outline—his mild eye wandered to the empty sofa, so little used all these years that it was still covered with the washed-out, faded chintz which Mrs. Garland had made new for it when they were first married. His fancy slipped back to those early days, and all the blank days which followed — not mournfully, for the life between, also of God's appointing, had been safely lived through, and the reunion could not be so very far off now.

"Still I should like first to leave my boy happy — as happy as I was myself. Poor lad! what a dull Christmas he must be having, except for work; it is good to feel that he works so hard. But I should not like him to settle into a dull, dry, college life—a mere bookworm, and not a man at all. No, no. Just a few years of good steady work — as a young fellow ought to work — and then a living—a home—and a wife. My dear lad!"

The parson settled himself once more to his writing; but he had scarcely done so and was pausing a moment, pen in hand, with the end of the incomplete sentence running in his head, when there came a knock to his study door.

"Come in," said Mr. Garland, a little surprised; for it was a rule that only matters of vital moment were allowed to disturb him on Saturdays. "Any body ill in the village, Jane?"

"No, sir, not that I know of," replied — not his servant, but a visitor very rarely seen at Immeridge — Mrs. Love, of Valley Farm. The old lady stood hesitating in the doorway, her cloak powdered and her boots clogged with snow.

"Sorry to disturb you, sir; hope you'll excuse it," said she, dropping a nervous courtesy.

"Certainly, my good friend," said the parson, placing her comfortably by the study fireside with that chivalric gentleness of demeanor which he always showed to all women. "But how could you think of coming all the way from Valley Farm in this inclement weather?"

"I never thought about the weather," returned Mrs. Love, and the fixed smile which she had persistently kept up slowly faded; "I had a—a sort of a message to you, sir, and I thought—my good man thought—I had best come over and deliver it myself."

"How very kind of you," answered the parson, cordially; "and how—we'll tell Jane to get you some tea at once."

The old woman stopped him with his hand on the bell.

"Oh no!—please, sir—oh don't; I couldn't swallow any tea—I—I—"

She burst into tears.

Mr. Garland sat down beside her and took her hand, as he was wont to do with any of his parishioners in affliction. Some people said of him that in ordinary life he held too much aloof from them; that, with his excessively refined tastes, feelings, and sympathies, the gulf between himself and the humble, rough, illiterate folk around him was such that, though he had dwelt so long among them, nothing but a great sorrow could altogether bridge it over. But when sorrow did really come to any one of them, no man could be more tender, more gentle, more truly sympathetic than the parson.

"I am sure there is something on your mind, my friend. You shall tell me what it is presently."

"I don't know how to say it, sir. It's about—about—oh, I wish you knew without my telling!—Your son—"

The father turned pale.

"Nothing wrong with my son? I heard from him a week ago. Has he written to you lately?"

"No; I dare say he didn't like to write. In truth, Mr. Garland, your son hasn't been behaving quite well to my good man and me."

For that was the form in which she and Mr. Love had decided she should open the subject, and so break it gradually—the cruel secret which as yet she only knew, but which she dreaded every hour some chance waft of gossip might bring to Keith's father's ears.

Mr. Garland's color returned — nay; he turned hotly red.

"My son not behaving well to you! There must be some mistake, Mrs. Love; he is not in the habit— But if you will tell me what his offense is, perhaps I can explain it."

Mrs. Love shook her head.

"It isn't that, sir; we would have borne a deal without taking any offense, we were so fond of him. Oh me! I'm as grieved as if it had been a son of my own who had gone astray."

"Gone astray!" repeated Mr. Garland, sharply; "stop! you forget it is my son you are referring to."

"It's him, sure enough; though, if all the world had told me, I wouldn't have believed it of him any more than you would, sir. But the girl herself confessed, and whatever she is now, she wasn't a bad girl once; and she never told me a lie, never deceived me in the smallest way before. And she has been my servant for a year, and I've known her ever since she was a baby—poor little thing!"

"Mrs. Love," said the parson, recovering himself a little from his bewilderment, and speaking with distant dignity, "may I ask you to explain yourself a little clearer? What can I or my son possibly have to do with your difficulties as regards your domestic servants?"

"No, sir," drying her tears, and speaking rather warmly; "but when a young gentleman condescends to keep company with a domestic servant—when he makes believe to visit the master and mistress, and under pretense of that, meets the girl at all hours and in all sorts of places; and after he's gone, the other servants joke her; and at last—never mind how, sir—it's all found out. And she doesn't deny it, but brazens it to my face, and says he's her sweetheart, and that she knows he will marry her at once—and—oh, sir—oh, Mr. Garland!"

For the old man had sat down, sick and faint, like a woman.

"Never mind me, Mrs. Love; go on with your story. Who is the girl?"

"Lotty—that is, Charlotte Dean—Thomas Dean the plowman's daughter."

"And—the young man? You do not mean—you can not possibly mean to imply that the young man is my son?"

"Ah! but he is, though; not a doubt about it," said Mrs. Love, shaking her head. "And I thought, sir—my good man and me both thought—that it would be better to come and tell you at once, before you heard it otherways."

"It? What is *it?* But I beg your pardon. I guess the whole story. Oh, my unfortunate boy!"

Mr. Garland put his hand to his face—his honest face, which burnt crimson, though he was an old man. To many men—alas! many fathers—the news of such an error—such a crime, would have been nothing, causing only a smile or a jeer, or perhaps a flash of passing irritation at the extreme folly of the thing; but it was quite different—it always had been quite different with William Garland, Mary Keith's lover and husband. The groan that burst from him went to Mrs. Love's heart. "And I thought to myself," she owned afterward, "perhaps those folk are best off who never have any children."

She was terribly sorry for him, yet knew not in what form to administer consolation to a gentleman so far above herself in education and manners, and who, she could not help seeing, took the fact which she had communicated—one of a class of facts only too common here, as alas! in many other rural districts—so much more to heart than even she had expected he would.

"Don't give way, sir," she said at last—"don't, or I shall wish that I had never told you."

"It was right to tell me. Let me hear the whole story—at least, what you suppose it to be."

Mr. Garland sat upright, clasped his hands upon his knee, and prepared to listen, as he had listened many a time to many a similar story of misery and sin, but it had never come home to him till now. Still he sat, with his grave, fixed eyes, and sad, shut mouth, and tried to force himself to listen to it, calmly, fairly, and justly, as if it had been any other story of his parish, or about any other ordinary sinner—not his own son.

Mrs. Love repeated, with many emendations and extensions, the tale she had previously told. She said the —love affair shall it be called? but the word belongs to a different sort of courtship, and a higher form of love—had been carried on so clandestinely, that, though it must have lasted three months at least, she had not a suspicion of it. The discovery had happened through the merest chance, and after it the girl had disappeared.

"Disappeared?" repeated Mr. Garland, eagerly.

"Yes, sir, that's my trouble—that's my fear—which I came to tell you before all the neighborhood gets talking of it. She slipped away in the middle of the night, taking nothing with her but the clothes she stood in, saying not a word to any body, leaving no scrap of writing—for that matter, I don't believe she can write beyond signing her name. What she has gone and done nobody knows—whether she has made away with herself, or run off to her sweetheart at Cambridge—"

Mr. Garland trembled, he hardly knew at which of these two alternatives, for one would be an escape out of the other.

"God forgive me!" he cried, starting up, and thrusting the idea from him—the horrible idea that would come—how by her death the girl would be got rid of. His first horror at his son's misdoing having passed over, he was painfully conscious of a desire to hush up and hide the sin at any cost. To save Keith—only Keith—

was the not unnatural parental instinct; all parents may comprehend and pardon it.

But by-and-by the good man woke up to something beyond the mere instinct of parenthood—that impulse for the preservation of offspring which comes next to self-preservation—in mothers, God bless them! often first. He became conscious of that large duty—abstract, impersonal, involving simple right and wrong—which, if even the fondest parents lose sight of, their tenderness degenerates into mere selfishness, and their devotion to their own children becomes an actual moral offense in the sight of Him who holds the supreme balance of justice as the Great Father of all men.

"This girl, whom you say my son has led away, though I will not and can not believe it, Mrs. Love, except on stronger evidence than seems to have convinced you—what sort of girl is she?"

"You have seen her yourself, Mr. Garland. She told me she got your tea for you the last time you were at Valley Farm—a rosy, black-haired lass, pretty enough, but slatternly, which was not wonderful, considering the folk she came from. Her father drank himself to death, and then her step-mother turned her out of doors. I took her for charity, and lest, being so pretty, she should come to any harm. Oh dear me! if I'd only kept my eyes open! But who would have thought it of Master Keith?"

"We'll not think it," said the clergyman, in a low tone, but hard and unnatural. "I refuse to think the worst of my own son, as I would of any other man's, until I am certain of it. Just describe the young woman to me till I recollect her."

He did so, in time — the dirty-aproned, red-handed, rough-haired farm-servant, whose handsome face he had remarked; who had waited upon him with such especial civility — why, he knew now — and to whom, in departing, he had given—and she had taken with the ordinary servant-girl's humble "Thank you, sir" — a shilling.

And this—this was his son's ideal woman—the object of the boy's first love! Lawful, or unlawful, remained to be proved—still his first love.

To a man who had never had but one love in all his life, and she Mary Keith — Mary Garland — no wonder such a discovery came with an almost stunning sense of repulsion.

"Did she say" — the parson's lips faltered over the question, and he did not own even to himself why he asked it, or what he desired its answer to be — "Did she say, positively, that she knew my son would marry her?"

"She certainly did. But you know they always say that, these poor creatures, and perhaps they really think it, or the men tell them so. Men are a wicked lot, Mr. Garland—wickeder, at first, than we women. But then, when we once get bad, we go down, down, lower and lower, till we stop at nothing but the bottomless pit. Oh me! if that should be the end of poor Lotty!"

"You did like her, then?" said Mr. Garland, turning round sharply. "Speak out just as you would to any body else—not me."

"Yes, I liked her in a sort of way. She was very ignorant, but she was not so rough as some o' them; and she had an affectionate heart. She was an honest girl, spite of her bad bringing up, when I took her. I'm sure of that. And such a child—only sixteen. He shouldn't have brought her to shame!"

"Shame!" said Mr. Garland, almost fiercely; "don't say that. Say nothing you can not prove. Remember you are speaking of my son—my only son—his mother's son. Mrs. Love," with a look of agony that, momentary as it was, whenever the good woman afterward recalled it, brought tears into her eyes—"Mrs. Love, you remember his mother?"

"Yes, sir, I do, and that's what makes me and my good man so sorry."

"There is no need to be sorry till you are quite sure of this. Some explanation may be found. I will go at once to my son. He said he should spend the whole of the Christmas hard at work at Cambridge."

And he remembered Keith's last letter—all his letters for weeks and months back, which, if this story were true, must have been one long concealment. Not deception exactly—the father was too just to accuse him of that—but concealment. He that for twenty years had been open as daylight, frank as childhood, to the tender parent, who, by his unlimited trust and unlimited love, had never given him cause to be any thing different!

The blow fell hard. Many parents only get what they earn. By harshness, want of confidence, and total want of sympathy, they themselves, with their own blind hands, open the gulf which divides them from their children. But in this case there had been nothing of the kind. Never a cloud had come between father and son until this cloud—the heaviest, short of death, which could possibly have arisen. And how was it to be removed? For, whether the case was one of mere disgraceful folly or of actual sin, of the thing itself there could be little doubt. His boy—his honest, gentlemanly, honorable boy—had made love to a common farm-servant; a girl who could necessarily have only the lowest allurements of womanhood — the personal beauty that pleases, and the ignorance that amuses. She might have suited the taste of some foolish, coarse fellow, in whom all the elements of manhood and gentlemanhood were wanting; but Keith—

Mr. Garland knew well — none better — that a man's whole character and destiny is often decided by the sort of woman with whom he first falls in love. This poor boy!—if he had "fallen in love" with Charlotte Dean, it must have been with the meanest half of his nature, in the most degrading form of the passion. Nay, it could not properly be called love at all, but that other ugly word which the Bible uses, though we have grown too refined to do so — not, God forgive us! to practice it, to extenuate it, to slur it over or gloss it under with every sort of mild poetical periphrasis, or else to philosophize upon it as a kind of sad necessity, when, instead, we ought to face it as what it is; call it by its right name; pull it down from its high places; tear the sham, sentimental covering off it, and then trample it under foot as that vile thing, of which, however the heathen world may have regarded it, Christ's Revelation speaks undoubtedly and unshrinkingly thus:

"But the abominable, and murderers, and whoremongers, and all liars, shall have their part in the lake which burneth with fire and brimstone, which is the second death."

And whatever the farther allegory may imply, one thing is certain, that the first death comes to such sinners even in this world.

"My poor, poor boy! And he only twenty yet! My miserable boy!"

It may throw some light upon this man's character—the man whom Mary Garland had loved so long, and been so happy with, and to whom, in dying, she had trusted her child, with the one prayer that he might grow up-like his father—it lets light, I say, upon the character of Mr. Garland, that the first outcry of his parental grief was that of David for Absalom, "My son, my son!" Only that—only for his son. He did not think of himself at all; there was no sense of personal wrong, no dread of personal disgrace at the scandal which such a story must inevitably bring on the clergyman whose only child was guilty of such misdoing, and at the weakening thereby of his influence in the parish. A proud, or vain, or self-conscious man would at once have thought of these things; but, though Mr. Garland did afterward think of them—it would not have been human nature that he should not—he thought of them only secondarily. His strongest grief was altogether on his son's account; first, for the sin; next, for the misery.

"I must start for Cambridge at once, Mrs. Love. Whatever has happened—whether the girl has gone to him, or whether that other dreadful thing you feared has happened, which God forbid! my boy will be all the better and safer for having his father beside him."

"He will, sir, indeed!" said Mrs. Love, earnestly. "Poor dear lad! he has got something like a father. And now, Mr. Garland, I must go home, or my good man will be thinking I'm lost in the snow."

"My kind old friend, how I have been forgetting you!"

Mrs. Love told afterward, with a tender garrulity, how Mr. Garland had insisted on her having tea in the study before she left; how he poured it out for her himself, and waited upon her with an ancient courtesy, not overlooking her smallest needs; "though I could see all the time," she added, "that the dear gentleman hardly knew what he was doing." At last she departed, and the parson was left alone, face to face with his heavy care.

Nothing so heavy had befallen him since his wife's death. Then, it seemed as if Fate, weary of persecuting him, had spent her last shaft and let him rest. Not a single anxiety, not even a week's sickness to himself or his boy, had since darkened the parsonage doors till now. But this grief. It was so strange and sudden, so utterly unforeseen, that, at first, when he had closed the gate upon Mrs. Love and returned to his study, which looked exactly as it looked an hour before, he could hardly persuade himself that all was not a nightmare dream.

He sat for a little with his head upon his hands, trying to realize it, and gradually all came clear. He perceived that, whether or not true in its worst and blackest form —in a measure the tale must be true—at least sufficiently so to lay upon Keith's future life, and upon all after relations between father and son, a cloud, a doubt — the first deception on one side, the first distrust on the other; like the fatal

"Little rift within the lute,
That by-and-by will make the music mute."

"It is the beginning of sorrows," said the old man to himself; and he clasped his hands, half in submission, half in despair, and looked into the embers of the forgotten fire with a hard, dry-eyed anguish, pitiful to see. The young suffer and have still hope, for themselves and for others; but the old, who have nothing to look forward to, and in whom the sharp experience of life had deadened the excitement of the struggle with pain, as well as the expectation of its happy ending, the grief of the old has always a sort of passiveness, sadder than any sorrows of earlier years.

"What should I do?" sighed the parson to himself; "for something must be done, and I have nobody to help me. No one could have helped me—except one."

But she slept where this affliction and every other could touch her not, and her husband was thankful for it.

"I wish I slept beside you, my poor Mary!"

For the first time for many years the widower uttered her name, spoke it out quite loud, until he himself started at the sound. But, uttering it, he felt as if his solitude were made no longer empty—as if in the dreary blank of the room she came and put her airy arms about his neck, in the long familiar way, sharing his burden as she had so often shared it, and in some mysterious fashion giving him the comfort that love only can give—a wife's love—in life, and, for all we know, afterward.

Mr. Garland roused himself, drew his chair to the study table, put by his sermon, and began to make his plans for the impending journey. This was rather a serious matter, for he never traveled, and knew nothing about railways, the nearest of which did not approach Immeridge by ten or a dozen miles—Keith, who was a practical young fellow, always settled his comings and goings without troubling his father. In Mr. Garland's utter ignorance, it was necessary to take counsel of Jane before forming any plans whatever. And now there came upon him the nervous apprehension as to how much Jane knew — how much any body knew — whether, when he ascended the pulpit to-morrow, every body would not know it?

A shiver of fear ran through him — actual fear; that moral cowardice which men have so much more than women, especially men of the parson's excessively delicate and refined nature. That dread of public opinion—that shrinking from public reproach, to escape which some will bear any amount of inward torture, attacked him in his weakest, tenderest point. His bravery gave way; he thought, if he could only start at once — that very Saturday night or Sunday morning—and so escape all?

Escape what? The sin? Supposing it existed. Alas! sin no man can ever escape from. The shame? That too, if inevitable, would have to be endured. Ay, in its sharpest form; for while, rightly and justly, no son is held responsible for, nor in any honest judgment, can be dishonored by, the wickedness of his parents, there is also a certain measure of justice in the world's opinion that a parent is not quite blameless for the misdeeds of his son. Exceptions there are, solemn and sad; but in most instances the comment of society at large is not made altogether unfairly, as in the case of Eli (bitterly did this poor father—father and priest also—recur to the words), "His sons made themselves vile, and he restrained them not."

No, there was no escape. The thing must be met and faced. Whether it turned out great or small—a mere annoyance or a life-long disgrace, there was no use in running away from it. Besides, if he left home, he would have had to shut up the church. Was the house of God to be closed because the minister was a coward, and dared not meet his people? *She* would not have advised such an act, she who had always before her eyes the fear of God, and that only—never the fear of man.

"No, I will not do it!" said the parson to himself. "Besides, for my boy's sake, I ought to keep an honest front till I have proved there is cause to be ashamed."

So he bestirred himself, rang for Jane, and told her, to her exceeding surprise, that she must pack up his portmanteau, and find some conveyance to take him across country, for that he was going to see Master Keith on Monday morning.

"Bless 'ee, sir, I'm so glad! And when shall you be back again?"

When indeed—or how!

He hoped, he said—with a sad hypocrisy of cheeriness—to return by next Sunday, unless his son particularly wished to detain him longer.

"You may be sure o' that, sir. Master Keith often said there wasn't any thing would make him so happy as a visit from his father."

"Did he say that?" with an eager clutch at the merest

straws of comfort out of that great treasure of love which seemed drifting hopelessly away from him. And he thought reproachfully—the self-reproach to which tender hearts like his are so prone — that perhaps he too had erred; that if he had not shut himself up so closely in his study, thereby leaving Keith too much alone — if he had tried more to win his boy's confidence and sympathy—had been to him, not less of a father, but more of a friend, this might not have happened.

"I will try and act differently now," he said, vainly repeating, and forming many a resolution for the future, when only the present cloud should have passed by.

It felt lighter next morning, which was a bright, clear frosty Sunday, and Mr. Garland had been all his life painfully sensitive to atmospheric influence. And when, as he entered the church, all things appeared the same as usual—no one pointed the finger or looked hard at him either in his coming or going—he began to hope that the story had not reached Immeridge; that perhaps, as Mrs. Love was not a gossiping woman, and had acted so wisely and kindly hitherto, all might be hushed up, and in time quite forgotten.

He put it as far from his mind as he could, and tried to serve his Maker and to instruct his people throughout that strange Sunday; but when night closed the whole matter came back upon him with relentless pain. In his complete uncertainty, he kept picturing to himself, over and over again, the two bitter alternatives — of the girl, Charlotte Dean, visiting Keith Garland to his disgrace—perhaps shaming him openly before his college; or else

—as Mrs. Love suggested—the victim might have punished the seducer in a still more terrible way—a way which Keith could never forget all his life long. And with horrible vividness Mr. Garland's fancy recalled a scene he once beheld in his youth, of a drowned girl dragged with boat-hooks from the bottom of a pond. He seemed to see it all over again, only the ghastly, swollen face was the face of the girl Dean, with the rosy cheeks and the curly black hair—pretty enough—but with the prettiness of mere physical beauty. How could Keith have ever cared for it.

Still, there the fact was, undeniable; and a worse tragedy might follow—her death, or the scarcely less blighting misery of her living.

"Nevertheless, I will not judge until I know the whole truth. Keith will surely tell it to me when I see him to-morrow."

And with a desperate clinging to that to-morrow, which must at least end his suspense, and bring a solution to some of his difficulties, Mr. Garland packed up his portmanteau—very helplessly—but he did not like to ask Jane to do it, as it was Sunday, and he never gave her any extra work on Sundays.

Besides, he kept out of the old woman's sight as much as possible, for she would ask questions about Master Keith, and send him messages, and talk about the great delight he would have in seeing his father, till the poor father felt as if driven wild.

When Jane was gone to bed, and the house all empty and still, the parson went to his little store of money, and took out thence as much as was required for his journey;

then, with a second thought, he went back and took it all; "for," he said to himself, "who knows?"

Also he put away his books and papers, locked his writing-table—for the first time these many years—and made other little arrangements concerning his affairs, which seemed to him advisable considering his years, and the painful nature of his journey—"for," he again repeated, "who knows?"

Finally, he laid his head on his solitary pillow, and thought, with a kind of sad curiosity, how strange it would feel the next night to be sleeping, for the first time for twenty years and more, under his old college roof, far away from that little mound over which he could hear the elm-trees soughing outside, and without remembering which he seldom closed his eyes at night or opened them in the morning.

"May God help me to do right, however hard it be!" was his last prayer before he slept. "O God, my Father in heaven, teach me to be a good father to my Mary's son."

CHAPTER III.

It was about four o'clock on a winter afternoon when Mr. Garland stood at the gate of his old college, for the first time since he had left it twenty years ago, to take possession of the living of Immeridge, and to be married to Mary Keith. How well he remembered that October morning, soft and sweet as May, when his long-delayed happiness, come at last, had colored his life with all the hues of spring, though he was nearly fifty years old. Now, all things outside looked, as they were with himself, at the day's end and the year's. The only bit of color in the murky winter sky was the rift of sunset behind the pinnacles of his familiar chapel—the most beautiful chapel, he often used to think, that mortal hands have ever built. Its airy architecture came out against the fading light as perfectly as ever, and the old man stood and looked at it for a minute or two with exceeding tenderness. The twenty years between—the happiness and the woe, slipped away for the time being—nay, he went back far longer, and was again a young man at college, with the world all before him, or a busy student, an early made Don, thinking his college the queen of all colleges, and his University the very centre of the world.

He could have believed he had only quitted it yesterday, the place was so little changed. Its smooth square lawn was green as ever; and across the white mist which was slowly rising up over it—as in so many winter afternoons of old—there shone the same cheerful glimmer from the buttery door, and from the tall windows where the few men who remained "up" at Christmas were dining in hall—Keith among them of course.

The parson thought he would wait till hall was over, and then go unobserved to his son's rooms. A sudden meeting might vex or confuse the lad, or any chance companion who was with him might notice something unusual in this unexpected parent-visit. Better that father and son should meet alone, and quietly, when Mr. Garland too might be better able to command himself; for, now that the moment was come, he felt an involuntary nervousness creeping over him as to how his son would comport himself; an uneasiness whether he might find, not the boy Keith at all, but a strange man—all the hardness and wickedness of exhibiting youthful manhood.

Poor Keith! Gradually, during the long meditative day, all the father's anger toward him had melted away. And now, weary with his long journey, feeling within himself, as if it had fallen upon him with a sad suddenness, the inevitable weakness of age, conscious also of a certain forlornness in thus coming back, a stranger, to the familiar places, the parson's heart yearned over his boy, his only child, the tenderest, nay, the only tender tie he had left in the world. When, in the darkening twilight, he watched two or three black figures issuing out, and moving round the gravel-walk of the quadrangle, eye and ear became involuntarily intent, in case he might detect the light footstep and lively laugh that he knew so well.

Nevertheless he shrank still more under the shadow of the gateway, whence, himself unobserved, he could watch each young man that passed.

No, none of them was Keith, who must have gone straight to his rooms. Not being quite certain where these were, and growing every moment more weary in body and in mind, he went back to the gate-keeper, smiling at himself for his own silly surprise that this was not the quaint, white-bearded old fellow that used to be called "Moses," who of course was dead and buried years ago.

"Can you show me Mr. Garland's room?"

"Up that staircase, next to the buttery, first door on left hand," was the answer, given rather carelessly—more carelessly than Fellows were used to be addressed in the parson's time. He felt this a little, and then recollected that he was no longer at home in his own college; that he revisited it merely as a stranger, who could only be judged by his exterior, which was probably out of date, and shabby, even for a country parson. So he said, with a little dignity of manner,

"Thank you. I know the rooms now quite well; I was a Fellow here myself for fifteen years."

"Oh, indeed, sir;" the porter's tone changed, and he respectfully touched his hat. "But I'm afraid, sir, you'll not find Mr. Garland. His rooms are locked up; though I think his bed-maker has the key, as he said he might come back before term."

"Come back! Has he gone away?"

"Yes, sir; he left two days ago."

The poor father leaned against the gateway to keep

himself from falling. All strength seemed to have slipped out of him. Then he said, feebly trying to keep up a coloring of indifference,

"Two days ago, did you say? That was Saturday."

"Yes, sir, Saturday—a sudden journey; for he told me the day before he meant to stay up and read all Christmas. But young men don't always know their own minds, and there's sometimes a little more than meets the eye—eh, sir!" added the jolly porter, with a twinkle in his own.

But Mr. Garland noticed it not. He asked, first eagerly, then with assumed carelessness,

"And where—perhaps he mentioned where he was going?"

"Not he. He wanted it kept dark, I fancy, for he told me not to send on his letters unless he was not back in a week or two, and then to forward them to his governor."

"To—what did you say?"

"His father. But, bless my soul," as a sudden idea dawned in the good fellow's mind, not unfamiliar with young men's difficulties, "maybe you're his father, sir."

"Yes," said the old man, briefly. And then he asked permission to sit down for a minute in the porter's room. "I have had a long journey here, and my son and I have—" he paused for a second in search of some fragment of truth which would save him from betraying himself or Keith—"have somehow missed one another."

"So I perceive; very annoying to you, sir. Will you come nearer to the fire? You're very cold, I see."

The rest and warmth came only just in time. As Mr. Garland sat down, he felt a sickness like death stealing over him, during which his only care was to preserve some sort of decent appearance externally, so as to save Keith's credit, and hide every thing as long as it could possibly be hid.

The civil gate-keeper left him, and then he cowered over the fire, trying to steady his shaking limbs and rally his feeble strength, and think of what was to be done next.

The present conjuncture was one he had never foreseen. That Keith should actually have left college—gone away no one knew where—leaving no clew except what slender information might be got at by inquiries humiliating to the father and likely to bring disgrace upon the son—it was very hard to bear! A sudden flight it must have been; and at least Keith's intention of reading all Christmas had not been a deception. But why had he ordered his letters to be forwarded to Immeridge? Either he had nothing to conceal, or he wished to blind his father's eyes with the daily expectation of his coming, and so prevent pursuit or inquiry. Or, a third possibility, perhaps he was now reckless of both. Perhaps he had taken the girl, Charlotte Dean, away with him; and, as she so confidently asserted he would, had married her.

Married her—a common servant! Old as he was, Mr. Garland's blood—his honest, honorable, gentle blood—of which secretly he was not a little proud, seemed to boil in his veins at the thought. Hot indignation, bitter shame, outraged affection, filled him by turns against the son who could so disgrace himself and his lineage. He started to his feet with the energy of youth, uncertain where to go or what to do, except that he felt he must go and do something. But it was in vain. The moment he tried to stand his head swam round, and he dropped back into his chair.

There he sat a long time, half stupid, it seemed, hearing through a sort of doze the college porter talking and "chaffing" with some young fellows outside. Within, he watched the blazing, crackling, cheerful-looking fire, and felt himself a poor, forlorn, feeble old man, who had not strength to do any thing, even if there was any thing to be done.

There was nothing. Either by accident or design, Keith had left behind him not a single clew to his whereabouts. So long as a hope remained that the young man had not compromised—nay, ruined himself for life, his credit ought to be saved, and that could only be done by the most cautious silence.

Never throughout all his simple, virtuous days, had Mr. Garland acted the hypocrite before, but now he did it. He called the porter, entered into conversation with him about college matters, and got from him by various inquiries as much information concerning Keith as could safely be obtained. This was little enough; the young man had apparently been living steadily and creditably, and reading hard all term. No outward vicious signs had betrayed him to the small college world; so far, his credit was secure.

The father took care still to maintain it. With a pathetic diplomacy, he managed to convey to the porter the idea that his disappointment was very trifling, and his son's absence of no particular moment. He took counsel of the man as to what inn he should put up at for a night or two, just to revisit his old Cambridge haunts and old friends.

"Why not turn into your son's rooms at once, sir? It's very often done at vacation-time, and you, of course, could get permission directly. Shall I see about it? and we'll have the rooms open and every thing comfortable for you in an hour or two."

Mr. Garland thought a minute and then consented, for it was the simplest plan, and he felt so weary, helpless, and forlorn. If he had only somewhere to lay his head for the night, he might wake in the morning strengthened, and able to judge and to act. Just now he was capable of neither. He had so long lived out of the world that every thing—even the ordinary noises of the street, confused and troubled him. He longed to be at Immeridge again, laying his head down on his own peaceful pillow, within only a stone's throw of that still peacefuller pillow where it would one day lie. The craving that we all have at times, and stronger as we grow older, to

"Lie down like a timid child,
And sleep away the life of care
Which we have borne and still must bear,"

came over him heavily. He turned out into the foggy night, and, while Keith's rooms were being got ready for him, walked round and round the familiar paths, past the chapel, and the high ivy-covered wall, and along by the willows at the water-side to the bridge over the Cam. There he paused, and mechanically stood leaning in the old spot where he used to lean for hours in his early-morning or late-at-night "constitutional" nearly half a century ago.

Was it actually half a century? Yet there was no perceptible change. Up and down the river the lights of the different colleges flickered in their old places, and the stars overhead — Ursa Major, Ursa Minor, Orion's Belt, and the silvery duplex wave of the Milky Way—shone just as in those days when he used to dabble in astronomy. The only change was in himself. And yet, somehow, his life had been so single, so true — such a faithful life, in short—faithful to God and man—that he did not feel greatly altered even now, except perhaps that —as on this winter night—the human lights were growing dimmer, and the heavenly ones larger and clearer, as he neared his journey's end.

Under this starry stillness the parson's mind became calmer, and his thoughts less bewildered as to the position in which he was, and the next step it was advisable to take.

Evidently to attempt to track Keith was useless. A cleverer, more worldly man would have found the pursuit difficult; to Mr. Garland it seemed impossible. Nothing short of applying to the police, and hunting down his own son by means of a detective officer, could have availed any thing—perhaps not even that. Keith might be already married, though that was improbable.

The parson—for a parson and a married man—knew surprisingly little of the marriage laws; still he was aware that both surrogates and registrars refuse a license, and clergymen decline to officiate when, as in this case, both parties are under age, and the marriage is without the consent of parents. Mr. Garland tried to recall all the small practical legal facts concerning his own simple, happy, holy marriage to the long-plighted, pure woman of his choice, and the contrast between it and such a marriage as this he feared smote the father's heart with an inexpressible pang. It could not be! His son—his own son—and hers could not so degrade himself. And as for that other possibility—seduction without marriage—it was a crime of which he tried to believe Keith utterly incapable.

Well, he could do nothing; he could only sit still and wait. Before term began Keith must reappear at college, unless he was quite reckless as to his own future. If he were—if he had done any thing bad enough to bring upon him public disgrace—better his father should be here to stand by him. Who else should do it? Even if the lad had sinned, he was still only a lad; and whose duty was it but his father's to throw over him the shield of calm parental wisdom, equal-handed justice, and patient love?

Mr. Garland had been fatherless—or, rather, worse than fatherless—himself; he had known what it was to stand alone and unprotected against the world. As he paced the solitary bridge—which in the days of his youth he had paced so often—with lighter, younger feet, but a heart heavy with its own burden of now forgotten cares, he recalled some words which then had often seemed to him worse than meaningless, a cruel mockery, "Like a father pitieth his children, so the Lord pitieth them that fear Him." But time had taught him its merciful lesson; he understood them now. As he looked up to the steadfast stars, which seemed singing in their courses through the changeless heaven, and remembered how he too had been led, as it were, by an invisible hand, through his long course of seventy years, and how his boy had it all yet to run, there came into him a feeling of compassion so intense, so divine, that he seemed to comprehend, in a sense clearer than he had ever yet preached it, the all-perfect Fatherhood of God.

With such thoughts—most thankful for them and for the peace they brought—Mr. Garland went back and installed himself in his son's rooms, which, of course, he had never yet seen, though he had often heard Keith's description of them. But he found them smaller and poorer than he expected. No extra luxuries, such as young men at college can so easily waste their substance in, brightened the shabby furniture, which seemed coeval with the parson's own college days. No indications of light or coarse tastes decked the walls; no portraits of ballet-girls or prize-fighters; not even a University boat-race. All was quite plain and humble; the lad had evidently been, so far, an honest lad, true to himself and to his father, spending scarcely one unnecessary penny out of the allowance, which he knew, for his father had told him, was not too easily spared.

"Poor fellow! poor fellow!" sighed the parson, as he settled himself in his son's arm-chair, gathered up the books—and very shabby second-hand books they were—that he found strewn about just as Keith had left them, then made his own tea out of the broken-lidded tea-pot, pulled off his boots, and put his tired feet into Keith's well-worn slippers. As he did it, thus taking possession of the rooms, and enjoying their owner's unconscious hospitality, some faint sense of comfort stole into him—a hope that things were not so very dark after all, or, at darkest, might brighten soon.

He refreshed himself with his favorite meal, and then, lulled by the warmth and silence of the solitary fire, gradually the weakness of age crept over him. He fell fast asleep, and dreamt he was a young man once more, working hard for his first examination. And then, somehow or other, he was married, and sitting in his study at Immeridge, with his wife Mary sitting beside him on the rocking-chair which she had bought but never used, rocking her infant in her arms. She looked so young, so sweet! and the baby was such a pretty baby—just what Keith used to be—and there was such a heavenly light shining round the two, that, though she did not speak to him, nor he to her, and though, while dreaming, he had some dim consciousness that it was only a dream—that she was not alive at all—still Mr. Garland felt quite happy. And even when he woke he was happy still.

He spent fourteen days, one creeping after the other before he was aware, at Cambridge, living in his son's rooms, waiting for Keith's return. At first he was terribly restless; could not bear to stir across the threshold; started at every footstep on the stair without; and kept his "oak sported" continually, lest any body should intrude upon him. Gradually this state of mind ceased. His nature was essentially of the passive kind; besides, he was old, and age takes every thing quietly. After the first shock, he seemed almost to have reconciled himself to whatever might happen. His present pain he kept entirely to himself, merely writing to Immeridge that he meant to remain at Cambridge till term, and stating the same to the few acquaintances whom he made here—old Fellows who, hearing of him from the porter, called upon him, and invited him almost daily to dine in hall. Nobody asked him any unpleasant questions, or any questions at all. Indeed, he felt keenly what people living long in country solitudes are apt to forget, how soon a man may slip entirely out of the petty world where he thought himself such an important item, and how little the said world will trouble itself about him when it has ceased to get any thing out of him.

So, after a brief fit of moralizing, Mr. Garland fell back, in a strange ghostly fashion, into his old college ways, spending his mornings in University library, and usually dining in hall at the old familiar table with some Fellow or other. But he rarely went into Combination-room: he usually returned to his solitary fire, and settled himself there, sometimes reading, sometimes sleeping, or sitting half asleep, half awake, scarcely able to distinguish the present from the past. He made no outward show of grief, never spoke to any body of his affairs, or of the suspense he was enduring; he endured all quite passively and unresistingly, as was the habit of his life; but if Keith had seen his father's face he would have found it ten years older since Christmas-day.

The last day of vacation came, and then Mr. Garland could neither eat nor sleep; never stirred outside the door, but sat counting every beat of the clock, and trembling at every step upon the stair. When he had almost given up hope, when it was quite late in the evening, Keith appeared.

Some one must have told the young man that his father was there, for he came in without showing any surprise. Agitated he was to the last degree, but he did not start nor shrink back. Over him, too, had come a change; he was not a boy any more.

He opened the door and walked steadily into the room. His father rose and met him as steadily; for at sight of him the old man's nervousness vanished, and anger, or rather the righteous paternal displeasure which yet had no personal vindictiveness, began to revive. He felt that the critical moment had come; that between father and son there could be no more disguise, no delay, no momentary hypocrisy of friendliness; all must come out at once. Possibly Keith felt this too, for he approached no nearer, and made no attempt to take his father's unoffered hand. Still, he was the first to speak—some muttered words about "this unexpected visit."

"I know it is unexpected and undesired. I found you absent, and took the liberty of remaining in your rooms till you came back."

"The liberty—oh, father!"

"Stop," said Mr. Garland, checking his son's advance toward him. "You must answer me a few questions first. Where have you been?"

"To Ely."

"No farther?"

"No. I had not money enough for traveling."

"Then you have been at Ely all this time?"

Keith assented.

"And—answer me the truth, the honest truth, my son, for you never told me a lie yet"—and the father's tone was almost entreating—"were you alone?"

"I was not."

The parson recoiled, and his next words were hard and sharp.

"Tell me—don't be a coward, for that is worst of all—tell me at once, Are you married?"

The youth hung his head, blushing crimson; but he said without hesitation, "Yes, father."

The father never spoke, nor even looked at him again. He passed him by, walking uprightly, steadily, and sternly to the door. Then he took his coat, hat, and stick.

"Father, where are you going?"

"Do not follow me—you have no right," was the hoarse answer.

"No right!"

"No." And Mr. Garland turned and looked his son full in the face, his own gleaming with passion, the natural passion of an honest man and an outraged parent. "No, not the smallest right. I have no son now."

So saying, and not trusting himself to say another word, the old man went out into the cold dark night, closing the door behind him.

CHAPTER IV.

An hour later, having succeeded in calming down the burst of passion which had shaken all the little strength of his helpless seventy years, Mr. Garland determined to go back to his son's rooms. He would not suffer himself to be carried away by blind anger; he would at least find out the true state of things—the whole truth, before he condemned Keith, before he even attempted to judge him; for justice, that quality rare enough in all men, and, alas! often rarest in men that are fathers, even though in them it is most needed and most divine—strict, impartial justice had been all his life Parson Garland's idol.

His first indignation having subsided, though he deeply despised his son—ay, despised him; for the delicate, high-minded gentleman felt his very soul revolt from such a marriage, and such a wife as Keith had chosen—still the youth was his son, his very flesh and blood. Nothing could break that tie. And though it had not existed—though they had been only guardian and ward—oh, that they had!—at the hands of this just man any other man's son would have found equal justice.

Nor, angry as he was, did his anger blind Mr. Garland to the common-sense fact that when a young man makes a foolish or disgraceful marriage, whoever else he may injure by it, the person whom he most injures is himself.

When he thought of this, through the father's storm of wrath gleamed rifts of the tenderest, the most agonized compassion. Only twenty yet, and his fate sealed for life, as every man's must be who has bound himself to a woman of whom he knows little, while what he does know makes the future appear as hopeless as the future of all hastily-conceived, passion-prompted, unequal marriages always must be, and deserve to be. Unhappy Keith!

Yet, however madly he had acted as regarded himself, however deceitfully—no, not deceitfully, but uncandidly, he had behaved toward his father, still he should have justice. Where in the wide world might he hope to find it, if not at the hands of his own father?

Mr. Garland turned back from his weary walk up and down Trinity Avenue and the lonely courts of Clare Hall—any where that he thought he was least likely to meet people, and just before ten o'clock struck came into his own college. He entered his son's room without having formed any definite plan of action. He did not even trust himself to speculate on what the next hour might bring, or whether it would not find him, as in his passion he had said, but was a little sorry for it now, without a son, without one tie in the wide world to bind his thoughts from that future world where now seemed his only rest.

Gaining Keith's door, he opened it, but gently—so gently that the young man did not hear, or was too absorbed to notice him. He was sitting over the fire, his hands propping his head, and his elbows on his knees, in an attitude of dull despair. When he turned his face round, its haggardness struck to the father's heart.

"Well, Keith?"

"Well, sir. Will you take a chair?"

But the lad did not stir from his own, and his manner was indifferent, almost sullen, as if he no longer cared what became of him.

"I have come back to you," said his father, sitting down opposite to him, though a long way off, "just to speak a few words, such as no one can speak to you except your father: to ask you how all this happened—how you could be so misguided, so insane? Do you not know, my poor boy"—in spite of his will there was a piteous tenderness in Mr. Garland's voice—"that by this act you have ruined your prospects for life?"

"Very likely I have."

"For—am I right?—this girl you have married is the girl Mrs. Love told me about—her servant, Charlotte Dean."

"Yes, it is Charlotte Dean, now Charlotte Garland. You can't mend it or alter it, sir; she is my wife, Charlotte Garland."

The poor fellow seemed to brazen the truth out in its hardest form, that he might hide himself behind it as a sort of shield—a defense against his own conscience and against his father.

That miserable father! only he felt his son to be more miserable even than himself. To one who knew, in all its depth of sanctity, what a real marriage is, the perfection of that pure love, happiness before wedlock, and unutterable joy afterward—the thought of all his son had lost and thrown away, with a frantic folly that the lad might yet give half a lifetime to recall, came upon him with such an agony of pity that, instead of reproaching Keith, he could have stood and wept over him, even as one weeps for the dead. But weeping was of no avail; the deed was done. Keith had distinctly said, though in a tone oh! how different from a young man's first proud utterance of the word—"my wife."

"Tell me," said the father; "don't be afraid, but tell me just as you would tell any other man—any friend of your own age, how this came about? When were you married?"

"Yesterday."

"Not until yesterday?"

"No; we had to wait for the fourteen days' residence and the license, which, after all, I was forced to get with a lie—the first lie I ever told in my life."

"What was that?"

"I made oath I was over age, or, she being only sixteen, they would not have granted it. Do you want to know any more? I'll tell you any thing or every thing. Nothing can alter it now!"

The young man spoke recklessly; but in listening a gleam of hope darted through the parent's mind—involuntarily, or he would never have given expression to it.

"Stop a minute; would not a false oath make the marriage illegal?"

"Father," cried Keith, fiercely, "don't speak of that. Don't put such things into my head, or make me a worse scamp than I am already. No, it is not illegal; I took care of that—unless you go to law and try to prove it so. Do if you dare!"

"I have no intention of the kind," said Mr. Garland, gently—nay, humbly—for his conscience smote him a little. "You have chosen your own lot, and must abide by it."

"So I mean to do."

Frantic as the lad was—seemingly driven half mad with remorse, or dread at what he had done, or grief at having displeased his father—there was a certain spirit and courage in him which the father could not but notice and respect.

"Tell me, Keith, what made you bring yourself to this pass?"

"I could not help it. She followed me here; it was the greatest chance, the greatest mercy that nobody saw her. She begged, entreated—nay, she almost compelled me to marry her."

Mr. Garland paused—considered; a hot blush, like a maiden's, mounted into his withered cheek as he regarded his son, his motherless boy, whom he used to carry about as an innocent baby in his arms.

"There is one thing which Mrs. Love hinted at, but which I refused to believe. I will not believe it upon any word but your own. Keith, was there any cause—just cause—why this girl should 'compel' you to marry her?"

"Yes." The young man hung his head, and could not look at his old father.

He drew back—this good father, this righteous, honorable man, who had held all women sacred, first for his mother's sake, and then for that of the one woman he adored; above all, for God's sake, whom the pure in heart alone shall ever see. He turned with an unmistakable repugnance even from his own son, and the son saw it.

"Don't mistake, father—don't think of her worse than she really is, because what she is I made her. It was my fault. God forgive me!"

"In that case," returned the parson, slowly and deliberately, "she, and no other woman in all this world, ought to be the wife of Keith Garland."

He said no more; never till his dying day did he say any more, making of his son no farther inquiries, and putting the matter altogether beyond argument or discussion. He accepted it as it stood, a life-long grief, an inevitable ill, but one to be faced in its naked truth as a simple question of right and wrong.

To any one of Mr. Garland's clear judgment, unbiased by worldly sophistries, the decision could not for a moment hang doubtful. Not even had it rested with him to allow or forbid the marriage, which, had he met his son before that fatal yesterday, might have been possible. But now the matter was taken quite out of his hands; he was saved at least from the terrible position of being the arbiter of his son's future. Keith was already married; and, even were his wife ten times more objectionable than she was, there could be no question as to the duty owed to her, if merley as Keith's wife, and Mr. Garland's daughter.

His daughter! Oh, the bitterness of that word to the parson's heart! Oh, the hopes and longings, and remembrances that were swept away at once as by a flood! His son was married; had brought him his long-expected daughter; and that daughter was Charlotte Dean!

Well, the dream was all over; it was not to be. Mr. Garland felt his old passiveness creeping over him, stupefying him both to present pain and to the future that was coming. He only hoped he should not live very long. With a sort of dull pleasure, he felt how completely, within the last two weeks, his strength had slipped away; how he had lost entirely that green old age which had so many enjoyments, and had looked forward to many more.

He sat silent, could have sat on thus for hours, when he was roused by his son's bitter cry.

"Oh father! can't you speak to me? can't you help me? Tell me what in the wide world I am to do!"

"My poor, poor boy!"

Mr. Garland came forward and touched Keith's clenched hand, gently patting it after the caressing habit of his childhood. Then the young man altogether broke down, and sobbed, first at his old father's knees, and then upon his neck, like the prodigal son in the parable, which parable the parson henceforward could not read in church without many quavering and broken tones, and he never preached upon it afterward.

Far into the night did they sit together, father and son, regarding steadfastly their mutual misfortune—for that it was a misfortune, Keith, if he did not actually acknowledge, never denied—and trying to see if there was any way out of it.

The young man did not notice then, being too much

self-absorbed, but he remembered afterward, when that honored white head was hidden from him in the dust, how that, in all their conversation, his father seemed to take for granted that it was a mutual misfortune, to be shared and striven with together; that he never once hinted at breaking the parental bond, or cutting adrift the son whom God had given him — not for his own pleasure, but as a solemn charge which not the most foolish or even wicked act, on the son's part, could ever entirely disannul. "For," as the parson was once heard to say, long afterward, when some intrusive friend suggested how much better he had been to Keith than Keith to him, "we did not ask life of our fathers; we gave life to our children."

So now, from duty as well as love, he assumed the father's most painful office, and, old as he was, tried to enter into that brief frenzy of youth which had ended in such a disastrous fatality, for such even the bridegroom evidently now felt it to be. Keith scarcely spoke of his wife at all; but of the difficulties and dangers of his own position, and the blighting of his prospects, he talked freely and very bitterly. Especially he dreaded lest by any miserable chance the college authorities should find out his marriage.

"But it must be found out. You could not possibly intend to keep it concealed?"

"Well, to tell the truth, I had not thought much about the matter," answered Keith, somewhat confused by his father's air of grave surprise — nay, displeasure. "She only entreated me to marry her—she did not expect any more. And I thought if I could but keep all quiet till

I had got through my necessary terms — taken my degree, and been ordained—"

"Stop!" cried Mr. Garland, and his voice shook with the violent effort he made to control himself; "you have forgotten one result, the inevitable result of the step you have taken, or rather of the evil you have done, for the last act was the only possible redemption of the first. You knew what was my heart's desire ever since you were born — that you should enter the church — to succeed in all I failed in—to do all I had not strength to do. Now this can never be."

Keith looked up, startled.

"No, I say never! No son of mine shall ever offer to the Holiest a blemished offering. Never will I see brought to the service of my God a life corrupted at its very source, and which will take years of repentance and atonement to make it a fit example to other lives, as that of a minister of the Gospel ought to be. No, my son, I forgive you; I will help you to begin anew in whatever way seems best, but one thing I exact as an inevitable necessity—you can never be a clergyman!"

Keith was terribly overcome. He had not thought much about his destined profession; he had accepted it simply as his destiny, the one most natural and best pleasing to his father; but, now that the father himself forbade it, and for such a cause—now that it was shut out from him with all its pleasant associations and expectations, he felt the disappointment and humiliation very sore.

"Then, sir," said he, at last, "since I am never to enter the Church, perhaps you would wish me to leave college?"

"Most certainly; and as soon as you can."

That, too, was a great blow, and one evidently unexpected. Keith writhed under it. He dropped his head between his hands in a hopeless despair.

"Oh, what will become of me?"

Still, he did not attempt to argue. He knew he was wholly dependent on his father, for the income which would be his one day could not come to him till his father died; that, in plain truth, here he was, cast upon his own resources, burdened with a wife, and—God forgive the young man, and the sin which turned blessings into curses!—he was thankful it was now only a wife. But his circumstances were desperate enough, especially if he had to quit college, which he felt must be, for he knew by experience that in some things his gentle old father could be hard as adamant and remorseless as fate.

But Mr. Garland was too just a man to assert his mere will without giving his reasons for the same, especially to a grown-up son, whose relations with a father ought to be reverent indeed, yet perfectly independent and free.

"In the first place, Keith"—after this day he never called him Marius—"you could not possibly keep your marriage secret; and if you could, you ought not. To live for months and years under false colors, acting a daily lie, and continually under the dread of its discovery, is a position that would ruin any young man. He ought not to expose himself to the temptation, and if he did one would almost despise him for doing so. No, my son; look things straight in the face—it is best. Do not be what is almost worse than a knave—a coward."

"I am not a coward, father," cried Keith, starting up and pacing vehemently the room — the shabby, but cheery little room—with all its books strewn about it, its heterogeneous oddities and delicious untidinesses, yet such a room as a man remembers all his life with the tenderness belonging to his hard-working, hopeful, happy college days. "I am not a coward, and I am ready to meet all the consequences of my folly—my confounded folly;" and he stamped with his foot like an angry child, and something like childish tears came into his eyes as he looked round the room. "It's bad enough to leave college, to put aside my future, for I was reading hard—indeed I was, father—to have all brought to light, and be set down by the men here as a fool—the merest fool—for marrying her."

"Better be a fool than a villain," said the father, sternly.

"You are right," returned the son, humbly. "I will not be afraid again. And now, sir," continued he, after a little, "just tell me what I am to do. I'll put myself entirely in your hands, myself and her too, poor little thing! Poor little thing!" repeated he again, "she is but sixteen, and she is so fond of me!"

"Where is she staying now?" asked Mr. Garland, not harshly, but turning away his face, for he would fain hide the expression of intense repugnance that he knew must be visible there.

"At Ely still. She could not be moved. She has been very ill. She was only just able to be taken to church yesterday to be married, but then it made her so happy."

"And you left her to-day?"

"Yes. She insisted that I should go; she knew it would injure me if I was missing at the beginning of term; she doesn't think of herself much—you used to say women seldom do—my mother never did."

"Silence!" cried Mr. Garland, in the harshest tone his son had ever heard from him. "Do not dare even to name your mother."

Keith was silent.

"I pity you; I will not forsake you," the parson went on, his hands shaking as he spoke, and his whole face aflame. "I will help you to redeem yourself, if possible. But never dare for one instant to compare your marriage to my marriage, your wife to mine. What can you know—you miserable boy—of such a love as ours? How could you, and the hundreds of foolish lads like you, understand what a man's love is—one pure love for one pure woman—founded on thorough knowledge and long-tested fidelity; tried by many temptations, clung to through years of delay and hopelessness, and then perfected openly, honorably, in sight of God and man, by the closest union with which mortal life can be blessed. Keith Garland, you may live many years—live not unworthily or unhappily, but you will never know, never comprehend a marriage such as mine."

Keith answered nothing. Imperfect as his nature was, half-developed, and perhaps inferior, or he never could have been allured by Charlotte Dean, still, if he did not understand his father, he was awed by him.

"Well," he said at last, "as I have made my bed, so I must lie upon it. It is useless to blame me more—I blame myself only too much. Do not talk to me, but show me how to act. If you insist on my quitting college you take the bread out of my mouth, so tell me how I am to earn it elsewhere—for myself and my wife; for I can't leave her to starve, and I can't let her go back into service again, as she proposed yesterday. Now she is my wife," added he, bitterly, "that would hardly be creditable."

"Certainly not."

"If I were alone," Keith went on, "I could manage well enough. Any young man 'without encumbrances,' as the phrase runs; with strength in his limbs and a little money in his pocket, can always earn his living and make his way in the world."

"How? What would you do?"

"One thing, certainly, which I have often longed to do, only I fancied it would vex you to part with me; but you'll not care for that now. I would emigrate."

"Emigrate!" cried Mr. Garland, much startled; and then he folded his hands, and asked calmly, "Where?"

"To Canada or New Zealand. I would borrow two hundred pounds or so, start off by the next ship, and try my luck. I'd like it too," added the young fellow, with his eyes brightening. "Oh, if I had only the world before me once more, with never a clog behind!"

The word — the cruel word — came out involuntarily, and perhaps he was ashamed of having uttered it, for he blushed deeply, and began to apologize.

"You see, of course, when a fellow is married, he isn't quite so free as he was before. And then she is so very fond of me!"

"There are times," answered the father, gravely, "times in a man's life when he would be thankful that any woman was fond of him—when he would give his whole substance for love and can not get it—he has thrown it away. When shall you go back to see her—I mean, Mrs. Keith Garland?"

Keith started, and then recollected himself, blushing violently.

"I had forgotten. Of course, that is her name, and she ought to be called by it."

"Unquestionably."

"Father," and Keith regarded him with a puzzled yet contrite look, as if recalled to his own unfulfilled duties by the far bitterer parental duties of which Mr. Garland never shirked one. "Oh, father, you are very good to me."

Then, as a sort of escape from the agitating emotions of the hour, the young man turned his attention to practical things—made up the fire, got out bread and cheese, and beer, and a solitary bottle of wine, administering to his father's wants in many little tender ways, as had been his habit ever since he was a tiny fellow—a precocious, petted, only child—but still Keith's was one of those kindly natures which can bear spoiling; if rather featherheaded, he was decidedly warm-hearted, and if light-minded abroad, was very good at home.

Their supper ended, the two seated themselves over the fire, and calmly discussed what was best to be done, avoiding alike all recriminations, angers, and despairs. The son was only too eager to see the sunny half of life, and the father knew enough of its storms not to wish to imbitter it to himself or his boy by one unnecessary pang.

The plan of emigrating to Canada, which country, with a sad shrinking, Mr. Garland substituted for the more distant New Zealand, was carefully gone into by him, and he found, from Keith's full acquaintance with all its chances, difficulties, and advantages, that the lad's bias thereto had been very strong — strong enough to make his future more hopeful than had at first appeared. To none of his son's schemes did the parson make objection, not even to his plan of raising money for himself. His father's assistance the lad never asked, nor did Mr. Garland offer it. He thought it best not. It gladdened him, amid all his pain, to see Keith so thoroughly and honorably independent. Perhaps the frantic plunge he had made, blindfold, into all the anxieties and responsibilities of manhood, might shake him out of his boyish thoughtlessness — act upon him with the stimulus of a cold bath, and brace his energies for the real business of life.

The father earnestly hoped so. Young as Keith looked, with his round, rosy, beardless cheeks, and his curly hair, there was a firmness and earnestness in the lad's expression which Mr. Garland had not perceived before, and which comforted him amid all his heavy care; for he knew, of his own knowledge, how life is never hopeless, and how the good God can make all things, even trials such as this, to work together for good, if we work also with Him, and in His own righteous way.

So, before going to rest, all was settled so far as was

then possible, for there was no time to be lost. The best way to avoid scandal was to escape it.

Keith mentioned hesitatingly that he knew of a ship that was to sail in a fortnight; and, short as the time was, Mr. Garland decided that he had better go.

"We can end all college matters easily enough," added he, "and all the easier that you will have your father here at hand."

"I know that," said Keith, contritely and gratefully. Then, after a pause, "But about her?"

"Do you mean your wife?"

"Yes"—and it was pitiful to see the cloud of repugnance and annoyance that came over the young husband's face—"I can not take her with me; you must see that, father. It would be quite impracticable."

"I never had the slightest intention of suggesting it."

"Then what can be done with her? She has no home—absolutely not a relative living—thank goodness for the same! And she is so young, so pretty! You don't know how pretty she is, father!"

The father half smiled, and then told how he had seen her at Valley Farm. With a certain feeling not unlike compassion, he recalled the fresh young face and rather attractive manner of the creature, now cast aside as a burden and encumbrance, more than half despised.

"Valley Farm—that is an idea," cried Keith, eagerly. "Perhaps Mrs. Love would take her back—not as a servant, but as a boarder—that is, if you did not object to her being so near you. She would not intrude; she will be very humble, poor thing! And at least it would give her a decent, respectable home. Do you consent, father?"

"No!" Mr. Garland replied, not immediately, but after a long pause, during which Keith waited patiently, with an aspect of dreary humiliation. "My son's wife can have but one home—either his or mine. Go to Canada, as you desire, for two years, and either send for her there, or earn enough to return and settle in England. In the mean time I will take your wife back with me to the parsonage."

"Oh father! oh my good, good father!"

For the second time the young man fell on his knees—on his very knees—before the parent, who had given him something better than mere life—the love and patience which helps one to live it; who had been to him at once just and merciful; like the Father in Heaven, as all parents should try to be to all their children.

Mr. Garland did not speak, only leaned over his son and patted his head, while two tears—the rare, pathetic tears of old age—stole down his cheeks. But Keith wept like a little child.

CHAPTER V.

EUSTON SQUARE terminus in the dim dawn of a winter morning—nay, before the dawn; for the gas-lamps were still burning here and there along the platform, where a little knot of people—porters, and passengers, and passengers' friends — were assisting at the departure of the early train for Liverpool. It happened to be one of those oftenest chosen by emigrants, of which the greatest number necessarily leave either from this station or Waterloo. You can easily detect these sad, outward-bound folk from ordinary passengers, even were it not for their heterogeneous heaps of luggage—not common luggage, but masses of property, which plainly speak of leaving home "for good." Ah! is it, can it ever be for good? Huge packages of amorphous character, canvas bags, heavy sea-chests, and smaller boxes marked "Wanted on the voyage," show plainly that few of them are ever likely to return to England. And opposite the line of second and third class carriages—sometimes first-class, but seldomer; first-class is more accustomed to keep its feelings under control—hang groups, mostly of women, some crying, loudly or quietly, as their natures may be; some silent, with bleared and swollen faces, that seem to have wept all tears dry, and settled into sheer exhaustion. They, and the men too, have a look of having been up all night—a long night of forced composure or parting anguish, terrible as death. But the men carry it off far the best, either with a miserable hard stolidity, that has something savage in it, or else with a false jocularity; it is chiefly the women who break down.

"You see, father, there are other folk bidding good-by to old England as well as I," said one young passenger —a second-class passenger he was, although quite a gentleman to look at—" other folk who look as if they had not slept much last night, as I own I didn't."

"Nor I," said Mr. Garland.

The parson was walking slowly up and down, leaning on his son's arm. All was over and done; Keith had quitted college, and, through the father's protecting care, quitted it without any outward exposure. They had been three days in London making final arrangements. Now the very last day—the last hour—of parting had arrived. Even the ticket was taken, and the rugs and other impedimenta packed into the carriage; nothing was left to do or say. No need for aught but the few last words, which in such circumstances never will come, or come as the merest commonplaces.

"We have found our lodgings very comfortable, as I hope your hotel has been," observed Keith; "and it was very kind of you to get them for us. The landlady said she knew you long ago."

"Not me, but your mother, who once befriended the woman. She always did contrive to help every body—your mother, I mean."

"I know that," said Keith, softly.

"Is your wife well to-day? Did you leave her tolerably composed?"

"Yes, she is a good girl—a very good girl. She would not trouble me more than she could help. She sat up all night helping me to pack, and would have come with me to the train, but I told her you might not like it."

Mr. Garland was silent.

"But she will be ready at the lodgings any hour you please to name, or she will meet you at the railway station, whichever you prefer. Shall you start for Immeridge to-day?"

"Possibly; I am not quite certain. Hark! was not that the bell for departure?"

"No, the five-minutes' bell."

The old man clung to his son's arm, leaning heavier and heavier, though he still firmly planted each foot on the ground, and walked with head erect and tearless eyes. Looking at him, Keith felt, for the moment, that he would have given all his hopes in life, every prospect of worldly advantage, every indulgence in that frantic, youthful passion misnamed love, to have staid behind, and cheered and solaced the few remaining years of his dear old father.

He was sorry he had said so much about his wife; and the few words more he had meant to say, begging that when they did meet—for Mr. Garland had not seen her yet—he would be kind to her, and put up with her many shortcomings, faded entirely out of the young fellow's mind. It was one of those sad cases in which a man can not, as the Scripture ordains—and as, under certain exceptional circumstances, a man is bound to do—"leave father and mother, and cleave unto his wife." Here there was in truth no wife to cleave to, no vestige of the real marriage of heart and soul, which alone constitutes "one flesh;" husband and wife, sufficient each to each. Poor Keith—if he ever looked into the future! But he did not—he dared not.

All he felt was—with a pent-up grief choking him at the throat, and a bitter remorse gnawing like a wild beast at his heart—that in a minute or two more he should have parted from his father—his good father, who had done every thing in the world for him, who had been both father and mother to him ever since he was born. That, for all he could tell, he might never again behold those venerable white hairs, that dear familiar face—withered indeed, but pleasant and fresh to look on as that of a young girl—pleasanter and dearer far, as now seemed to Keith, than that pretty red and white face which had so taken his foolish fancy, and for which he had sacrificed and suffered—ay, and caused others to suffer—so much.

"Oh father!" he cried, in exceeding bitterness of soul, "I wish I were not going away from you! Tell me—at this last minute—shall I stay?"

And at that final moment the father paused. Paused to consider, not his own feelings—they could have given an easy solution of the difficulty—but his son's good. He ran over rapidly all the arguments which, during many a solitary walk, and many a weary, wakeful night, he had carefully weighed; all the exigencies of the future—the bitter, perhaps fatal future, which Keith had brought upon himself. The same reasons which held good then, did so now. No momentary outburst of emotion could set them aside. The plain common sense of the matter was, that the youth and his girl-wife—so madly, so unsuitably allied — were better parted. That the safest chance to make a man of the one, and a woman fit, or at least less unfit, to be his wife, of the other, was to part them — for a time. Of their separation little harm could come. Keith was fast bound, and would keep constant to his wife — if only from conscience and self-respect; nay, he was perhaps safer far away from her, where he could only remember her prettiness and her love, than if perpetually jarred upon and irritated by those fatal deficiencies which he already felt — and his father could see that he felt—only too keenly.

No, Keith must go. It was better for him that he went.

Of himself, and his own life to come—that short, short vista, out of which all the brightness now seemed faded —the parson did not think much. He remembered only his own seventy years and his son's twenty, with perhaps half a century more yet to run. No, not a chance must be left untried of redeeming the past and softening the future. Keith must go.

"My boy," he said, "I am glad you said that; I shall not forget it. But I do not wish you to stay. When a man has put his hand to the plow, let him not look back. Go to Canada, and do your best there, like a brave young fellow as you are — as I would wish my son to be. Go! and I will try to keep alive and hearty till you return."

"Of course you will!" answered Keith—fiercely almost —and when he spoke the departure-bell was heard really ringing.

Father and son turned face to face, and then grasped hands, in the tight, silent grip with which men express —or conceal their feelings.

A minute more, and where the busy train had been was an empty space — a few porters hurrying away to other work, or sharply calling "This way out" to the knot of women left weeping on the platform, and one old man who stood, not weeping, but leaning heavily on his stick, and gazing, in a sort of abstraction, upon the long black serpent, with its white-coiling breath, that went puffing and snorting away, first slow — then faster —faster—till it disappeared into the dim distance, carrying with it the delight of his eyes for twenty years.

Yes, Keith was gone—quite gone now. The old man had lost his only child.

There must have been something in the parson's aspect which told his sad story, for one of the porters, roughly beginning to order him from the platform — as they did the poor sobbing women — stopped, and said civilly,

"This is your way, sir. Shall I get you a cab?"

"Thank you."

But, on trying to walk, Mr. Garland felt so feeble that involuntarily he put out his hand for support.

"Sit you down here, sir, and I'll find you a cab in two minutes."

It might have been two or ten, he could not say, for he felt so utterly bewildered and weary, when he was roused by a light touch on his arm, and saw a young woman standing at the end of the bench — a young woman — scarcely even a "young person," as the intermediate phrase is, and not a "young lady" by any means.

"If you please, Mr. Garland, I be here, sir."

The strong west-country accent, the humble manner, like a servant's, and the dress—a mere servant's dress also—were sufficient, even if she had not called him by his name, to inform the parson who she was—his "daughter," Charlotte Garland.

Exhausted as he was, all the blood seemed to rush to his heart, rousing him out of his stupor, and bringing him back at once to the bitter reality of things. He turned—to examine sharply—he tried hard that it should not be unjustly—this girl, who had proved such a fatality to him and his.

She was like—and yet unlike—what he had remembered of her. Her face he could not see—she had a thick veil on; but her ungloved hands, not coarse now—sickness had wasted and whitened them—were shaking violently. Nevertheless, the voice in which she addressed him was composed, and not unsweet, even to the parson's most sensitive ear.

He rose and gave her his seat. "I believe—I can not be mistaken—you are Mrs. Keith Garland?"

"Yes, sir."

"Are you here alone?"

"Quite alone."

She said it half inaudibly, but very quietly, without any of the torrents of tears, the noisy demonstrative grief of the women around, which was what Mr. Garland had somehow expected. And when she lifted up her veil he saw, not the pretty, rosy girl who had worked so much woe, but a thin, sickly-looking creature, who was evidently doing her utmost to use a woman's self-control. There was a fixed repression in the small and close-sat mouth; a mute, restrained, unappealing sorrow in the heavy eyes, which touched him in spite of himself.

She waited for him to speak again, but finding he did not, she said, still in the same humble tone,

"Beg pardon, sir, for coming up to 'ee, but I thought you might miss of I, and that would gie 'un a deal more trouble."

As she spoke Mr. Garland winced terribly. He could not help it. He, so sensitive to small refinements, how should he endure constant association with this girl, however harmless and even affectionate she might be?

"I thought you were safe at your lodgings," said he, abruptly. "What did you come here for?"

A foolish, nay, a cruel question, as he saw next minute, but the girl did not resent it; and though her features twitched and quivered, she did not cry.

"I couldn't help coming, just to see the last of him; he's my husband, sir. But he didn't see I; I took care o' that."

"Where were you, then?"

"Just behind that lamp. I saw you and him a-walking together, up and down, such a long time—oh! such a long time! And then you bid him good-by, and he got into the carriage." She faltered—broke down a little.

"Poor girl!" said Mr. Garland, taking her hand, which he had not yet done; and as he did it, he was conscious of a momentary warmth of heart toward this forlorn creature, scarcely more than a child, thus strangely left to his charge, and to whom the law, if nothing else, had given the external title of his "daughter."

Charlotte did not respond in any equal or filial way. Her limp, pallid hand just touched his and dropped away again. She was evidently terribly afraid of him.

The civil porter came up with the information that a cab was waiting.

"We must go now," said Mr. Garland. "Come!" He paused, considering what to call her—what he ought to call her—this young woman, who, however he felt toward her, was his son's wife, and must be treated as such. Then, with an effort, he said, "Come, Charlotte."

She obeyed with the humble, deferential air which was to him so painful, and yet, perhaps, the contrary would have been worse. He tried to think so—tried to hope the best. As she sat beside him in the cab, he made several attempts at ordinary conversation, showing her the London streets they passed, and so on; but she seemed quite stupid, either with grief or shyness, and only replied in monosyllables; so he took refuge in covertly observing the pretty face. Beyond question it was very pretty, with almost a Greek profile, only less inane than those correct outlines usually are—dark eyes, and a quantity of rich blue-black hair. But there was the servant's bonnet, gown, and shawl, tawdry with violent contrasts of color; the servant's gloveless hands; and, above all, the unmistakable servant's air—half awkward, half shy, in the presence of an acknowledged superior.

He could make no more out of her than this until the two were sitting face to face—he pointed to a chair, or she would have remained standing—in the little lodging-house parlor. With both of them, the first passion of parting had subsided; the wrench was over; and let their hearts bleed inwardly how they might, outwardly they had to go back to the duties of the common work-a-day world.

The first thing that startled them into this was the landlady's bringing up breakfast; it was scarcely nine o'clock, and yet it seemed already the middle of the day.

"We'll wait a bit," said Charlotte, hesitating; perhaps she remembered the day when she gave the parson his tea at Valley Farm. Perhaps he remembered it too; but these things must not be remembered.

"No, we'll not wait, if you please. Will you give me some breakfast?"

He pointed to her seat, assuming his own opposite; and so they sat down together, as father and daughter-in-law, and took the initiative step in their new life.

Their meal ended—and it gave to both a certain sense of ease and comfort, as if the first and worst difficulty had been got over satisfactorily—the parson spoke to her, trying to do it gently and kindly, in the manner he used toward his parish school-children.

"We must now consider our plans, my dear. You know, of course, that you are coming back with me to Immeridge?"

"Yes; he told me so."

"And are you satisfied with the arrangement?"

"Eh, sir?"

"Do speak out," said Mr. Garland, a little sharply. "I should be sorry to take you home with me if you did not approve of it. I do not wish to treat you as a child, or as—as an inferior person."

Charlotte Garland opened her great eyes — childish eyes they were, almost; there was no badness in them, and a certain appealing simplicity—a "Don't hurt me!" sort of look. Evidently she did not half understand what was being said to her. But she looked up into the kind face of Keith's father, and understood it better than his words.

"Yes, sir, I'd like to go with you, and thank you kindly," said she.

"Very well; suppose we go home to-day?"

And then he remembered what a changed home he was returning to—changed in what it had lost, and far worse, for he had grown used to Keith's absence, in the additional burden it had gained—a burden which, to an old man of his solitary and settled ways, would be obnoxious every hour of the day. And yet it was but duty—as this Christian man read his duty—therefore it must be done.

Nevertheless, the more he pondered over it the more perplexing it grew, not merely in its larger aspect, but in the minutiæ of things. He had written to his housekeeper, saying merely "that Mr. Keith was married, and was going to Canada, leaving his wife at the parsonage till his return." This intelligence, in all its naked brevity, would, he knew, soon speed all round the parish, perhaps even to Valley Farm, where the truth would be at once guessed. How it would finally come out at Immeridge, or whether the whole story was not already public, Mr. Garland could not tell, and took no means of learning.

He was a thoroughly honest man, this Parson Garland. His candid soul, clear as daylight itself, had no fear of coming to the light. Those poor shams—so common that they cease to be thought mean, and are called by pretty names—such as "keeping up appearances," "wearing a good face before the world," or even that last and saddest sham of all, euphuistically translated as "*laver son linge sale chez lui*:" all these forms of elegant hypocrisy were to him unknown and impossible. He never did, consciously, what he was ashamed of doing, and therefore never dreaded the world's knowing that he did it. If he himself thought it right to take home to Immeridge Parsonage his son's wife, what business had the world to meddle with the matter?

He did not feel it necessary to advertise to all his neighbors who and what Mrs. Keith Garland had been—to bruit publicly his own private griefs and his son's errors. But his silence was not deceit—he never tried to deceive any body; he was resolved, whatever happened, he never would. That morbid dread of public opinion, which shrinks not so much from the thing itself, whether misfortune, disgrace, or even crime, as from society's knowing it, was not the form in which temptation came to Mr. Garland. It might have done once, for he was naturally very sensitive to love and hatred, praise and blame; but time and his long solitary life had taught him better wisdom. To him—accustomed to live alone, face to face with the All-seeing Eye—the stare, whether kindly or malign, of mere fellow-creatures seemed comparatively a very little thing.

Still he was conscious of many perplexities that would

arise from bringing Charlotte home as his daughter-in-law. The first one—a trivial and yet annoying thing—dawned upon him as she sat opposite to him, huddled up in the arm-chair which he had made her take, for she looked very pale and wan, though she made no complaint.

It was years — twenty years since the parson had noticed women's dress; but he had an artistic eye, and remembering what used to please him once in the only woman he ever admired—and yet she was not pretty—he saw at once that something was amiss in the undoubtedly pretty Charlotte Garland. He could not exactly tell what it was, except that the flimsy cotton gown and gaudy-patterned shawl were very different from the unity of harmonious color, the decorous simplicity of shape, to which he had been accustomed, and by which an ordinary or even a plain woman can make herself lovesome, not to say lovely, if she chooses.

Also there was that unmistakable something, or lack of something, which convinced him that when she came under the sharp eyes of Jane, the old servant—who had been servant to his wife — would discover at once that Mrs. Keith Garland was "not a lady."

This, alas! was in degree inevitable; still, some external amendment might be made, only he did not like to hurt Charlotte's feelings by doing it.

"Excuse me," he said, at last, "but have you any other gown than this? It is scarcely warm enough for traveling."

"So *he* said," she always referred to Keith as "he;" "and that it wasn't fit for me to wear now; and he left me some of his money to buy clothes, and told me he would send me more by-and-by. I wasn't to be a burden upon you, sir."

"Poor fellow!" said the father, softly.

"I was always handy at my fingers, though I had no book-learning, please, sir," pursued Charlotte, timidly. "If I might go out and buy some stuff, I could make a Sunday gown for myself when I get home—I mean—I beg your pardon if I've said any thing wrong," added she, in great confusion.

"No, my dear. Immeridge is your home."

"Thank'ee, sir," with a return to the humble, servant-girl manner so terribly annoying to Mr. Garland. He struggled to conquer himself, however, and suggested that they should take the landlady into council, and before leaving London should spend Keith's money, perhaps a little more—but he did not hint this—in supplying a suitable wardrobe for Keith's wife.

Charlotte caught at the idea, and whether for love's sake or vanity's sake—the not wonderful vanity of sixteen—she took, during three whole days, a world of labor and no little enjoyment over her new clothes. She also accommodated herself to them so well, that when she was dressed in them, a fellow-traveler who resigned his place to her in the railway carriage, spoke of her as "that young lady."

Fortunately she talked little during the journey; indeed, the parson had been relieved to find, during their three days' association together, that familiarity with him did not make her grow more voluble, but rather more silent; also, that when he talked to her, which he forced himself to do as much as possible, she sometimes seemed to notice the difference in their speech, and try, blunderingly, but eagerly, to correct her own. Seeing this, he once or twice corrected her himself in some glaring error of grammar or pronunciation, which reproof she took meekly enough, and did not make the mistake again.

Still the *ci-devant* Charlotte Dean could by no possibility be exalted into a heroine of romance. She was just a common servant-girl, or seemed so, to the parson, who, in criticising her, had to contend not only with personal pain, but with all the prejudices of his class, and the sensitiveness of a nature peculiarly alive to all that was graceful and delicate, or the contrary. His only hope was, that in these three days he saw nothing wrong about Charlotte, nothing actually coarse, or wicked, or unwomanly; and then she was so very young. She must have been a mere child — too childish to have learned any thing very bad — when she came under the strict guardianship of Mrs. Love, of whom, however, she seldom spoke, or in any way reverted to her former life.

Nor did Mr. Garland. He covered it over, and left it with the Judge of all.

Nevertheless, as, with this young woman sitting by his side, he traveled through the fair southern counties, along the very same route which he had once taken—(it seemed sometimes only a day, and sometimes a lifetime ago)—with another, and oh! what a different woman, whom he was also bringing home to the same home, it might well be forgiven the old man if, through all his compassion, he felt a sensation of indescribable, hopeless pain.

But, happily, ere they reached their journey's end, Charlotte's small strength broke down. He had not looked at her for a good while, and then he saw that she had quietly leaned her head in the corner of the fly, and fainted. And when the carriage stopped at the Parsonage gate, and he tried to help her out, she, equally quietly, dropped down on the damp doorsteps, and had to be carried off at once up stairs, and put to bed by Jane like a baby.

It was a strange, sad coming home of Keith's wife, but it was the best thing that could have happened. And, after an hour of great uneasiness, spent in wandering up and down the house, and lingering outside the long-vacant "guest-chamber," where the sick girl lay, Mr. Garland was astonished to find how entirely he had forgotten every thing except anxiety and compassion for her.

"Well?" said he, eagerly, to Jane, as she came out of the room.

Jane cast down her eyes, determined not to meet her master's.

"She's better, sir—she's only tired like—she'll be all right to-morrow."

"I am glad to hear it. She has had a long journey; and it was hard parting with her husband, of course."

"Of course," echoed Jane, and made no farther remark or inquiry.

Mr. Garland was going into his study, but, struck by the tone, and more by the after silence, he turned back. He felt how much depended upon Jane, who had had sole control of the house for twenty years, and who, though sharp at times, was not a bad woman in her way.

"You'll be very good to her," said he, half appealingly.

Jane was still silent.

Then Mr. Garland perceived his mistake. He said, looking full at her, and assuming the parson's "high" tone, which, gentle as he was, all the parish were a little afraid of—

"My daughter-in-law is only sixteen—too young to take the management of my house. Besides, she has yet to finish her education. Therefore, Jane, you will keep your place as housekeeper, and all will go on as usual—for the present. But I trust to you to see that she has every comfort, and that all proper attention and respect is invariably paid to Mrs. Keith Garland."

Jane lifted her eyes at last, inquisitively and sharply, and fixed them on her master. In them he saw—and hardly knew whether he was glad or sorry to see—that she was fully aware of every thing.

Mr. Garland had expected this—at least he thought he had, and that he had prepared himself for it, as being a result inevitable in a country parish, where every body knows every body's business; for, let Mrs. Love be as kindly silent as she might, she could not chain the tongues either of the farm-servants or the neighbors. Of course Jane knew—every body knew—the whole story by this time. But when he met this cruel fact blank and plain; when his old servant looked him in the face, not with disrespect certainly, but with a sort of half-pitying, half-angry amazement, without one word of sympathy or regret for Keith's departure, or of curiosity over Keith's young wife, the parson felt it hard.

He said nothing—what was there to say? He had

borne much sorrow, but the first shame of his life was come upon him now.

"Be the young woman to stop here, sir?"

"My son's wife will certainly stop here," replied Mr. Garland, with a dignity that silenced Jane. And then feeling that—cruel as the explanation was—it was his duty, both as a man and a clergyman, to explain himself sufficiently, even to his own servant, so that neither she nor any one would mistake him, or suppose that he glossed over wickedness, paltered between right and wrong, he said, "Jane, you must never again speak in that tone of Mr. Keith's wife. It was a marriage without my knowledge or consent, but it was the right and best thing under the circumstances. They are both very sorry, and God may have forgiven them; I have, Jane," he added, almost entreatingly, for he felt how critical the position was; "don't judge her, only be kind to her."

Jane looked as if she doubted the evidence of eyes and ears—looked at her master until big tears gathered and fell. She wiped them off with her apron, and said, in a husky voice,

"Well, I never seed such a man as you—never! Yes, I'll do it, sir. I'll be kind to her, but it's only for your sake, mind that, master. May the good Lord reward you, Mr. Garland!"

And Jane went hastily away, more overcome than she had ever been seen since the day when she stood with Keith, a new-born baby, in her arms, weeping her heart out beside her dear mistress's coffin.

Mr. Garland went slowly up stairs, not into his study, but his own bedroom. He was very weary, and yet composed. The worst was over; there was nobody else to be spoken to, or to speak to him, on this subject. And Keith was gone. He had suffered as much as he could suffer, and felt strangely at rest.

If any eyes had watched him—but there were none to watch, at least none visible to mortal ken—they might have seen the old man shut his door, seat himself in his arm-chair by the window, and, undrawing the curtain, gaze out upon the church and church-yard, where, cradled in moonlight, the white grave-stones slept. He sat a long time, and then went quietly to bed, his last conscious thought being, with a sense of repugnance tinged with involuntary tenderness, that now, for the first time for so many years, there slept under the Parsonage roof another Mrs. Garland.

CHAPTER VI.

In spite of Jane's confident assertion that her patient would be all right to-morrow, it was several weeks before the expectant village, or indeed any body except Jane and her master, saw Mrs. Keith Garland.

Though only a servant, poor Charlotte had a heart in her bosom; her power of self-control was very great for one so young; but, after the need for calmness was over, she "fretted above a bit," as Jane expressed it, for her husband. Instead of rising from her bed, and parading before all Immeridge her honors and glories as Parson Garland's daughter, the poor thing turned her face to the wall; did nothing but weep all day long, and fell into a sort of low fever, or "waste," which, had it been done out of policy, was the wisest thing she could have done at that crisis. For old Jane's kindly nature was touched by the mere act of tending her; she forgot all that Master Keith's wife was or had been, and thought of her only as a poor sick child, who depended upon her—Jane, for every thing; so that between these two women, who otherwise might have become naturally antagonistic, the one obtruding and the other resenting their painfully false position, there grew up a true and not unnatural bond, which contributed very much to the peace of the Parsonage household.

The parson, too, in the daily half-hour visit which he compelled himself to pay to his daughter-in-law's room, talking to her about trivial things, or perhaps, as was his habit in sick-rooms, reading to her a few verses out of the Bible, became familiarized to the pale face that he found lying on the pillow, or propped upright in the easy-chair by the fire. Its prettiness pleased his eye; its silent smile as he entered moved his heart; he felt glad this poor young creature had not been left a castaway upon the cruel world.

By degrees his duty-visit ceased to be a trouble and a task: he found himself looking forward to it with some slight interest, wondering what he should talk to her about that day, and what she would say in return. Not that she ever said much; she seemed to have an instinct that it was safer to be silent, or perhaps, in the long confidential hours which she and Jane necessarily spent together, she got to know more of her father-in-law than he suspected, or than she ever would have done had they been thrown together very much at first; so, either from prudence or timidity, she rarely did more than smile her welcome, and pay to the old man the tender flattery of a mute listener. Still, she supplied him with an interest, an object of thought and care; he scarcely knew how it was, but the Parsonage felt less empty; and even the small domestic fact of having to send up to the invalid her portion from his daily meals made them seem a little less selfishly solitary.

For his life outside, it went on just in its ordinary round. His parishioners were none of them of that rank who could take upon themselves the liberty of intimacy;

nobody questioned him even about his son, and not a soul in the smallest way adverted to his son's wife. Sometimes he was glad of this, and then again he involuntarily resented it, and it inclined him the more compassionately to the poor pale girl, who lay so quiet in the little room up stairs, harming nobody, and of scarcely more importance to any body than if she already lay "under the mools."

Thus things went on, and seemed as if they might go on forever, until the quiet of the Parsonage was stirred by an event—a momentous event always—the first letter from over the sea.

Keith wrote to his father at some length, very explicitly and satisfactorily; but to his wife was only a small note, inclosed in the other. Mr. Garland sent it up stairs at once, and followed it himself half an hour after, with his own letter in his hand; for, amid all his pleasure in the long loving letter, which had a tone of thoughtfulness and manliness quite new, the old man was touched with slight compunction that Keith's confidences were all to his father. The thing was inevitable, and yet it was not as things should be. As he walked up stairs to his daughter-in-law's room, Mr. Garland could not help sighing.

Charlotte turned toward him with her customary smile, but this time it was not quite natural; she had evidently been in tears.

"Is not this good news?" said the old man, cheerily, and gave her his letter. Hers was lying open on her lap; it seemed to consist of only half a dozen lines, written in large copper-plate hand, as you would write to a child. The parson felt almost sorry when he looked at his own long letter. "You see, Charlotte, all the business facts come to me; but would you care to read them? Perhaps you do not feel strong enough?"

"Oh yes; but—I can't. Please, sir, I haven't learnt to read written hand."

Mr. Garland might have felt, for the hundredth time, that bitter sense of incongruity in this wife with whom unfortunate Keith had burdened himself for life, had it not been for Charlotte's burning blush, which showed her own painful consciousness of the same.

"Never mind," he said, kindly, "I will read it to you. But your own letter."

"I couldn't read it, and I thought you might not like my asking Jane to. Oh, sir, is he quite well? Has nothing happened to him? Is he glad he went?" added she, eagerly, while her lips quivered, and, despite all her efforts to prevent it, the tears came streaming down.

"My dear," said the parson, deeply touched, "keep quiet, or we shall have you as ill as ever again. Keep quiet, and you shall hear every word he says—you have a right; he is your husband."

"Yes, yes!" And for a minute the poor girl's eyes brightened with love; the rare unbought treasure which heaven can light up in a beggar's heart or in a queen's, but which once kindled, nothing earthly will ever quench—and Mr. Garland saw it.

He silently extended his hand and held hers while he read aloud Keith's letter. When he had done so, and talked it over a little, explaining any thing that he thought she was not likely to understand, he asked, hesitatingly, if he should read the other one.

"Mine! Oh yes—if you would be so kind." She had sat folding and fingering it, and now she gave it up with a sad, lingering look. Poor Charlotte!

"You must not mind my seeing it, even if it is a love-letter," said the parson, half apologetically. But there was no need; all the world might have read every line of Keith's first letter to his young wife:

"DEAR CHARLOTTE,—You will be glad to hear I am safe landed at Halifax, and shall shortly be on my way to the back woods of Canada. My father will tell you where they are, and all about them if you care to hear. I shall have to work hard, chiefly at farming work, which you know all about, though I hear farming is rather different there from what it is in Old England. Still I can learn—and you will learn too, when I can fetch you or send for you. I hope you will be a good girl till then, and take care of your health, so as to get thoroughly strong, for health is very much wanted out here. I hope to have mine, perhaps better than in England; for other things it is of course a very great change.

"I write this large, hoping you may contrive to read it. Perhaps by-and-by you might manage to learn to write. Be as cheerful as you can, and be always dutiful and obedient to my dear father.

"Your affectionate husband,

"M. K. GARLAND."

Nothing more than this—and there scarcely could

have been less; yet Charlotte seemed satisfied with the letter, and asked Mr. Garland to read it over again to her.

"Then I shall learn it by heart," said she, simply; and the old man felt it hard to meet the touching patience of her eyes. Sinful as she was, she had been sinned against likewise. The wrong, for which no man can ever fully atone, had been done, and done by his son, to this poor servant-girl.

He staid with her much beyond his customary half hour, sometimes talking, sometimes sitting silent, pondering—not the questions of sin and forgiveness; he left that to heaven alone—but wondering whether, contrary to all his theories and habits, he was being taught how, in heaven's sight, nothing is "common or unclean"—whether, by rare chance, Nature might not have put sense and intelligence under that broad, low forehead; sensitiveness and refinement in the always sweet-tempered, flexile mouth—whether, in short, though she was not born one, it might not be possible in time to make something like "a lady" out of Charlotte Garland.

At last he said, "Charlotte, when you are stronger, you and I must have a word or two of serious talk. No, don't look frightened. It is not to scold you; the only fault I mean to find is that you will not get well fast enough."

"Would you like me to get well, sir? I have sometimes thought—well, it has been put into my mind—that —that—"

"Speak out—always speak out."

"That you would rather—I know it would be better

—Oh, sir, you know—you can't help knowing—that it would be a deal easier for him if I died."

This outburst—and, alas! it was not altogether without foundation—quite overwhelmed Mr. Garland. Its very truth made it more difficult to answer. Nor had he expected it, though he had before noticed, with some surprise, that in this coarse, unlettered girl lurked the true principle of feminine devotedness—the faculty of seeing all things as they affected "him," and not herself at all.

"My dear," said he, gently, "you must not talk thus. Every thing that is past is past; we must make the best of it. Instead of dying, suppose you were to come down stairs and make tea for me to-night?"

Charlotte looked amazed. "Do you really want me? Would you really like me to come?"

For once in his life the parson told an untruth—or half a truth, disguising the rest—and answered briefly, "Yes, my dear." But he forgave himself when he saw how Charlotte's whole countenance brightened up.

"Then I'll do it at once—this very night, sir. I can. I felt quite strong enough to come down stairs, only there was nothing to come down for."

"How so?"

Charlotte hung her head. "Jane said I was not to help her in the kitchen, and there is no other work I am fit to do. Besides, I should only have been in your way —I know that."

Mr. Garland avoided answering the last half of her sentence. "You seem to have a grand notion of work, Charlotte," said he.

"I was brought up to it—it comes natural to the likes 'o we;" and then recognizing her provincialisms, out of which she had struggled very much of late, at least whenever she talked with her father-in-law, the girl suddenly blushed—Charlotte's vivid, scarlet blush.

"By 'us' you mean the people you were among before my son married you," said the parson, determined to shirk nothing, though he spoke both kindly and familiarly. "No doubt as Mrs. Love's servant you worked hard enough, but there is no reason why an emigrant's wife, and"—he paused—"a clergyman's daughter, should not work too, though in rather a different way; and that is what I wanted to speak to you about. Shall I?"

"Yes, please, sir."

"Would you not like to learn something? Learn to write, that you may answer Keith's letters; to read books, that you may be a companion to him when he comes home. The Bible speaks—I read it to you only yesterday—of the wife being 'a help-meet' for the husband."

"What does that mean?" asked Charlotte, humbly.

The parson thought a minute, and then, trying to put his thoughts into as simple language as possible, retranslating himself as if it were for a child, he explained to her his own beliefs about marriage—his faith, and also his experience; how, though the man was the head of the woman, the woman ought to be the heart and right hand of the man—able to help him in his difficulties, to sympathize with him in all his aims, to comfort him in all his troubles. That outward differences or incongruities might exist, or might be got over in time; but that this inner union must be, else the marriage was a total failure from beginning to end. And whether from the excessively simple way in which he put it—all divinest truths are the most simple and most clear—or from a tender earnestness of manner which supplied what his words failed in, he saw that, somehow or other, Charlotte understood him. When he ended she looked up wistfully in his face.

"I know it's all true, sir. I knew I wasn't a fit wife for him—but do you think I might grow to be?"

That doctrine of growth is one of the saving truths of life. When we reject it—when we judge people harshly by what they were once, or hopelessly in looking forward to what they may be, we often make terrible mistakes. We are far harder upon one another than God ever is upon us. We forget that in His divine plan—so far as we can see it—all existence appears to be an eternal progress, an ever-advancing development—unless, as sometimes happens, the tide runs backward, and then the only future is infinite retrogression. Looking at our life—or lives—to come, after what seems to be the system of this one, we can imagine a just and merciful Being making possible to His creatures not only eternal life, but eternal death—never eternal punishment.

But this is too solemn a sermon to come from such a very simple text as Charlotte Garland.

If any one had seen her three months—well, say six, for they slipped away so fast that nobody counted them—from the day when she was brought home to Immeridge, she would scarcely have been recognized. It is true, she was at the most impressible season of a woman's life, when new habits are formed and old ones effaced with a rapidity incredible to those who have not seen such things. Besides—and the more her father-in-law perceived this, the more patient he grew with her—she was in addition to his own, under the teaching of the great master, Love.

Without a doubt Charlotte was deeply attached to her husband. Perhaps something naturally refined in her had made her fancy a gentleman rather than a plowboy, and sorrow developed this fancy into the real love, which nothing can imitate and nothing destroy. Cold as Keith was, and neglectful — for, after the first letter, he rarely wrote again, but contented himself with sending messages to his wife through his father—unquestionably the poor wife loved him. Love guided the pen in her clumsy fingers over dozens of blurred copy-books; Love wakened her with the lark, to pore over old spelling-books and Reading-made-easy's — relics of the last Mrs. Garland's governess-days — for hours before any one in the Parsonage was stirring. Love — and perhaps affection also, as for two hours daily she "said her lessons" in the study like a child—softened her rough provincial tones, and made her try to speak good English, and to move about, not in her old floundering way, but with the subdued quiet which she knew the parson liked. And he knew that she knew he liked it, and why he did so; for once, when the kitchen-door was left open, he overheard her saying in a deprecatory, grieved way, "Please, Jane, I wish you would always tell me when I do these sort of things. I must be so unlike any thing he has ever been used to. And, oh! couldn't you tell me something more about poor Mrs. Garland?"

Nevertheless, human nature is human nature, and many a time the old leaven of servanthood would reappear. It was evidently a sore restraint to her to sit still in the parlor instead of being busy with Jane in the kitchen. At her lessons, though she learned easily and fast—as quick brains, left fallow till quite past childhood, very often do learn, which was a great mercy to the parson — still she was often stupid through sheer awe and timidity, and her manner, when frightened, assumed that painful subserviency which annoyed Mr. Garland more than any thing.

Their life together was not easy; but things were less dreadful than the good man expected them to be; and sometimes he thought—when he had time to think about it at all — that he was scarcely so unhappy as his son's miserable marriage ought to have made him. It had pleased God to take away his life's hope; to end all his dreams for his boy's future; to put endurance for happiness, and a burden for a delight; and yet — and yet— he was conscious of many pleasures left. He could still enjoy the spring sunshine, and watch the cliff swallows return to their old nests from over unknown seas, and the primroses people in multitudes the little dell below Immeridge village, with scarcely less interest than he had done, season after season, when the seasons' change formed the only epochs in his monotonous days.

Then, too, during their Sunday walks, begun through a painful sense of duty to the solitary girl, and also to lessen the weariness of their sitting looking at one another in the Parsonage parlor throughout the whole blank Sabbath evening, he gradually took pleasure in showing her all these country things, and talking about them, and in watching their effect in the pretty face, which, though healthy enough now, never again offended his taste with the coarse Blowsabella beauty of Valley Farm. That mysterious impress which the mind makes upon the body, altering, refining, and sometimes altogether transforming, began to be very perceptible in Charlotte. Her features deepened in expression; her slender figure acquired that grace of motion which is as important as grace of form, and her gentle, even temper lent to her voice, even though it did speak bad English, a certain musical tone (*timbre*, as the French call it, and no other word is quite equivalent), which made grammatical errors pardonable. Not that she was in any way like Moore's low-born heroine, of whom he wrote so enthusiastically—

> "Has the pearl less whiteness
> Because of its birth?
> Hath the violet less brightness
> For growing near earth?"

Thomas Dean's child was neither a pearl nor a violet, but merely a very pretty young woman, whom Nature had accidentally gifted with qualities, physical and mental, which would have made her noticeable in any rank of life, and which, being cultivated, bade fair to lift her out of her own. One occasionally sees such persons—ladies'-maids, who have more of "the lady" in them than their mistresses; and graceful gentlewomen, whom, meeting in society, one hears with astonishment were once barefooted mill-girls, whom some honest, romantic master educated and married. And though such cases are but remarkable exceptions to a most wise and righteous law, and the truth yet remains that the most insane act a young man can commit is an unequal marriage, still there is another truth behind it—that in this, as in every phase of human experience, exceptional cases will arise sometimes upon which we dare not sit in judgment, if only because they are exceptional.

Nobody sat in judgment upon this case — at least not openly, probably because there was nobody to do it. Except Valley Farm, where, with a certain instinctive hesitation, Mrs. Keith Garland did not attempt to go, nor did her father-in-law desire it at present, there was not a house in the parish likely to criticise the parson or the parson's daughter so loudly as to reach their ears, for Immeridge village had the true English respect for its betters. And the Hall — which might have been found a difficulty, and, indeed, Mr. Garland looked forward with a vague dread to the squire's return — was shut up this year since, instead of returning, Mr. Crux died, and the family property devolved to a cousin — a barrister in London.

So, after the first hard stares in church, some finger-pointings as she left it, and, when she casually walked abroad in the village, visible hesitations between a broad laugh in the face of "Lotty Dean," or a decent courtesy to Parson Garland's daughter — after all these things, which Charlotte herself did not seem to perceive, and the parson shut his eyes to, while Jane, that faithful servant, fulfilled a servant's true duty of holding her tongue entirely on her master's affairs, gossip ceased to trouble itself about Mrs. Keith Garland. Time went on, and it was already a year since that dreary day when Mrs. Love had come into Mr. Garland's study, and, as he thought, destroyed his peace forever with her terrible tale. Only a little year, and all things had smoothed down, as they do so wonderfully, when we cease to fight against Providence, but simply do our best, and let Providence fight for us.

CHAPTER VI.

It was early spring—Easter week, indeed—and Mr. Garland sat writing his Easter sermon with his study window open, inhaling the odor of bursting sweet-brier leaves and of double Russian violets: there was a bed of these just underneath, sprung from a single root which Mrs. Garland had planted; and in this sheltered nook, under the mild southern climate, they had flourished so as to overspread the whole border. The parson could generally pick one or two every week all winter through: he put them in a wine-glass on the desk, when, however faded they looked, Jane never ventured to touch them; nobody did. Even in spring, when the violets became plentiful, nobody quite liked to gather them from this bed; so they bloomed and withered in peace, pouring their scent in at the study window like a fragrant cloud of invisible love.

The old man often stopped in his writing to drink it in, delighting himself in it, as he did in all delightsome things. Perhaps if heaven had made him very rich, or very prosperous, or very happy, in this world's happiness, he might have been something of a Sybarite, and therefore it was better that things were as they were—at least he often thought so. Still he felt, and thanked God for it, that even to old age he had kept the keen sense of enjoyment, especially in Nature's luxuries. Thus spring was just as delicious to him now as the spring-days of his youth, perhaps affecting him with a higher and more chastened delight; for then it had brought visions of things never to be, and now it stirred up in him no earthly longings at all, but a peaceful looking forward to what the return of spring mysteriously foreshadows— "the resurrection of the body, and the life everlasting."

He was alone, for, Charlotte's daily lessons being over, she had gone as usual into the garden, where she was very fond of working, and where her labors had of late almost superseded his own. It was good for her, since it gave her plenty of active, open-air occupation—occupation with her hands; for Charlotte had one great deficiency in the making of a lady, or, at least, a fine lady— she hated being idle. And it was very difficult to find her enough to do. She could not study all day long, and though she now read fluently enough to enjoy books, still she liked best story-books, novels, and such like, which did not abound in the parson's library. Though she did some house-duties, she was not the house-mistress, Mr. Garland thinking it wisest, during the two years she would be with him, not to put her above his faithful Jane. Nor had he as yet given her any parish work, neither Sunday-school teaching, she being only a learner herself, nor district-visiting, where her former equals might naturally resent her coming among them in a different character. His conscience soon told him that, for the present, the very difficult position of Keith's wife was made least difficult by her being kept in a state of comparative isolation—shut up within the Parsonage domains like Eve within the garden of Eden. Often when he watched her moving about as now, and saw what a pretty creature she daily grew, he felt thankful that he had had the power and the will so to shelter her, and glad that her secluded life left no chance for any tempting devil of the world to do harm to Keith's girl-wife, so mournfully neglected. Alas! the parson felt it was so; that more and more was poor Charlotte felt to be a burden by the young husband whose love had been the mere selfishness of passionate youth, not true love at all.

Keith's letters came, very long, dutiful, and loving, to his father, but sending only a line or two, or a message, to his wife; and though he had plunged bravely and heartily into his new life, and was prospering well, never reverting to his return home or to Charlotte's joining him in Canada. The parson's heart grew sad and sore, nay, a little angry. He did not love his daughter-in-law; love with him was a plant of very slow growth; but he liked her with the tender liking that a good man can not but feel toward a creature wholly dependent on him, and who never consciously offends him in word or deed. There was no romantic affection shown on either side, but she was a good girl, and he had the strongest sense of pity for her and responsibility toward her. He did not now feel his work done and wish to die. He prayed rather to be kept sound in body and vigorous in mind for a few years longer, that he might work on, or live to see the dark future unfold itself.

He said nothing to his son of either his angers or misgivings; he knew that compelled love is more fatal than hate; but he wearied himself with plans to keep Charlotte from fretting. She did look sad and grave sometimes when Keith's letters came; and, above all, he tried to keep her fully employed.

"I wonder," he thought, "how young women in general employ their time—those three Misses Crux, for instance; for the new squire and his family had appeared at church the Sunday previous, and the parson had called at the Hall, as in duty bound, on the Monday morning.

He compared Charlotte, as she moved about the lilac bushes in her gray merino gown and straw hat, with these stylish London damsels, in good looks, and in a certain simplicity of costume, which, after considerable struggles, she had attained to; he fancied Keith's wife had rather the advantage. But he sighed when he thought of the nameless graces of ladyhood, to his delicate perceptions so indispensable; the quiet dignity of speech and mien, the repose of perfect self-possession, the noble simplicity which, however perfect it may appear to others, always sees for itself an ideal beyond any thing it now is, or can ever attain to. Alas! all these things would, he feared, be hopelessly wanting in Mrs. Keith Garland.

But this Monday morning, while his perplexed mind was turning over all the ways and means for her improvement, he was summoned to the parlor, where was the overwhelming apparition of the very ladies he had been uneasily meditating upon as forming such a contrast to his daughter-in-law.

Their personality did not improve upon nearer view,

for Mr. Garland was a gentleman of the old school, completely unused to the lively, not to say fast style of modern young ladies. The three Misses Crux, with their voluminous draperies, their masculine jackets, and tiny hats, upon which a whole bird with glass eyes sat and stared at beholders, were no nearer his ideal woman than Charlotte was. Very incongruous they looked in the old-fashioned room, its decorations unaltered for twenty years, where they poked about, admired the old china, the fading embroidery, the valuable antique engravings, seeming determined, with their mother, a mild and unimpressive person, to make themselves as much at home as if they had been Mr. Garland's neighbors all their lives.

"What a charming house!"

"The very picture of a country parsonage!"

"And you live alone here, Mr. Garland? A charming old bachelor life. Oh no! I remember now you are not a bachelor. But what a sweet, quiet life it must be!"

"It is very quiet," said he, answering all the three girls at once, for they all spoke at once, and wondering what he should say to them next; but they soon saved him that trouble.

"We shall find the Hall quiet too after London, for papa means to live here all the year round."

"Oh, indeed!" replied the parson, with a slight shiver of apprehension, he hardly knew of what or why.

"And we hope, Mr. Garland, that the Parsonage and the Hall will prove the best of neighbors, for all other neighbors are so far off. You must dine with us—

musn't he, mamma? — at least once a week, if only out of charity."

"You are very kind;" for, under the rough demonstrativeness, he could perceive a certain frank kindliness for which he was not ungrateful.

"Come, then, what day will you give us? Next Sunday?"

"I have never in my life dined out on Sunday. Not that I condemn others for doing so, but still it is not my liking nor my habit," said the parson, gently.

"I beg pardon, I forgot; Sunday is so usual a visiting day with us in London; but perhaps in the country it is different. What week-day, then? Fix your own day, and we will send the carriage for you at seven."

Mr. Garland's hesitating reply was stopped by an exclamation from the youngest and manliest Miss Crux, who had placed herself at the window, with her hands in her jacket pockets, and her mouth looking as if it would excessively like to whistle.

"Bless me, if there isn't the prettiest girl I ever set eyes on! Your daughter, Mr. Garland?"

"No, my daughter-in-law."

"Is she married—that young thing actually married? And where's her husband?"

"My son is in Canada; he will return shortly, and meantime has left his wife with me. She is, as you say, very young, only just past seventeen. May I offer you some cake and wine, Miss—Miss—"

"Beatrice is my name — otherwise Bea — sometimes degenerating into B," said the young lady, archly, though the parson's manner would have "shut up," to use her own phraseology, any less forward damsel. "But tell me more about your daughter; for, though I am ugly myself, I do like pretty girls. It's lucky you keep her close here, or every young fellow that saw her would be falling in love with her. I'm half in love with her myself—I vow I am," added this feminine "young fellow," on whom the old man looked with undisguised amazement, as she stood tossing her short, curly hair, and rubbing her hands, evidently enjoying his bewilderment.

"Bea, for shame! You are so ridiculous," observed at last the silent mother. "My dear sir, I hope you will let us have the pleasure of being introduced to Mrs. Garland."

"Mrs. Keith Garland," corrected the parson, slightly wincing, and then stopped, puzzled what to reply to this request.

Here was a conjuncture which he had never foreseen —never even thought about. To receive Charlotte under his own roof—to bear with her—to like her if he could—at any rate, to put up with her, and to be kind to her—that he had undertaken—and accomplished; but to introduce her into society as his son's wife, either forcing her upon his friends with all her antecedents openly acknowledged, or bringing her in surreptitiously, with her previous history concealed—as for Keith's sake, he felt bound to conceal it if possible—this was a position which had never before suggested itself to his simple mind. A most critical position too, full either way of great difficulties, and yet he must decide instantly, and his decision might affect the poor girl's whole future life.

He trembled; he felt himself visibly tremble before all these inquisitive women, who might know—how much or how little he could not possibly divine; but no! their manner showed that they knew nothing. Ought he to tell them?

While he asked himself this question, his difficulty was summarily solved.

Charlotte, who had been at the other end of the garden, gathering flowers to replenish the beau-pot in the grate, came in, ignorant of visitors, and suddenly opened the parlor door. Bareheaded, her hat hanging down behind, her hands full of daffodils and flowering currant blossoms, yellow and red, her cheeks and lips rosy with health, her eyes smiling over the one delight of her simple life—her successful horticulture—

"She stood—a sight to make an old man young."

Seeing the room full of ladies, she drew back in the extremest confusion.

There was no alternative now. "Come in, my dear," said the parson, rising. "Mrs. Crux, this is my daughter-in-law—Mrs. Keith Garland."

Involuntary Charlotte began her courtesy, but stopped and turned it into a bend, as Jane had tutored her—a gesture not exactly awkward, but so painfully shy and uncomfortable that Mr. Garland, out of pure pity, bade her "take her flowers away, and come back again presently." So, without her having once opened her lips, the door closed again upon that charming vision.

"Really, Mr. Garland," said the youngest Miss Crux, "your daughter-in-law is the very prettiest person I ever saw—a regular country belle. I say, girls, it's lucky for us that she's off the course."

"Eh?" said the puzzled parson.

"Lucky, I mean, that her name's scratched off the books of the matrimonial race—that she's already Mrs. Keith Garland."

The parson made no answer; indeed, he was sore perplexed. Like many another man, large of heart and yet very sensitive, he could meet nobly and grapple bravely with a grand moral difficulty, but the petty puzzles of daily and social life were quite too much for him. He needed a woman to save him from them or help him through them—such a woman as the wife he had lost, or the imaginary daughter who never came. For this daughter, well seeing he could do nothing, he attempted nothing, but waited in trepidation for her reappearance, determined to let things take their course, and act on the spur of the moment as best he could. However, Charlotte never reappeared.

The Crux party, after prolonging their visit to the utmost limit that politeness allowed, let fall some suggestions about hoping to see her again; but no effort being made by the host to gratify their curiosity, they departed, merely leaving "kind compliments to young Mrs. Garland." However, the same evening, before the parson and his daughter had met or spoken together, there strode up the Parsonage garden a tall footman in livery, bearing an elegant missive—nay, two missives from the Hall, addressed respectively to "Rev. Mr." and "Mrs. Keith Garland."

Charlotte took them herself to the study. She was in

the habit of waiting upon him there with letters or messages, and presented both to Mr. Garland.

"Open yours, my dear," said he, and watched her while she read, which she did slowly and carefully, first looking surprised and then exceedingly delighted, for it was an invitation to dinner at Cruxham Hall.

"Is the man waiting? Tell him we will send an answer presently, or to-morrow morning, and then give me my tea, if you please, Charlotte," for he wanted to fortify himself and gain time before he decided.

Charlotte went away without speaking—she rarely did speak first to her father-in-law on any subject—and sat silent all the while he drank his tea, and read, or pretended to read, his three days old "Times."

Poor man! he was making up his mind, and it was to him a very troublesome business. He wished, as ever, to see the right, honestly and plainly, and then do it. By the sudden gleam of pleasure in Charlotte's eyes, he perceived—what had not struck him before—that this lonely life, shut up in a country parsonage with only an old man for company, and lessons for recreation, debarred from the amusements of the class she sprang from, and not joining, nor capable of joining, in those of that to which she now belonged, was not the best sort of life for a young girl of seventeen—active, energetic, lively, pretty; and looking at her, more and more he perceived how excessively pretty she was.

Nor, as she presided at the tea-table, did Mr. Garland notice any thing in her, either as to appearance or behavior, so very different from ordinary young ladies of her age. In truth, though the old man would never have thought of this, it was impossible for any one, with common instincts or observation, to sit at the board and share the daily society of such a thorough gentleman as Parson Garland without acquiring in degree the outward manners of a lady. He noticed, as he had never done before, the great change in her; nor was his hesitation caused by the fear that as a companion she would be any personal annoyance to him, or would commit solecisms of good-breeding at the Hall dining-table any more than in the Parsonage parlor.

Still, the question remained—the vital question. Had he any right to inflict upon the Cruxes, who were probably acting in the dark, or upon other neighbors who might not be in the dark, association with one from whom they were sure to shrink, although they might endure her a while out of respect to his cloth and to him? She was his daughter-in-law; but still she was once a common servant-girl, and—alas! alas! if that had been all!

"Charlotte," said he, after watching her from behind his newspaper, trying to criticise her with the equal eye of a stranger, the result of which criticism was an amazement, mingled with solemn thankfulness, that so little of her antecedent history was written in her face: a face —was it looking into his face that it had grown so? —gentle, modest, simple, and sweet. "Charlotte, my dear, what do you think about this invitation to Cruxham?"

"Me, sir?"

"I think we ought to decline it."

"Very well, sir. You know best."

She spoke meekly, but a shadow of disappointment

crept over the pretty face. It was natural. She was only seventeen.

"I really do not see how we can go. You have no proper dress." And then, ashamed of the flimsy excuse, the good man added, "Besides, to speak truth, Charlotte, as I always do, and I speak it not to hurt you, because you have too much good sense not to see the thing as plain as I do—you have never been used to that kind of society, and I doubt whether you would enjoy it, or feel at home in it."

"Perhaps not," with a little sigh, which prevented Mr. Garland from putting more harshly the other side of the matter, that the Hall society might not welcome her.

"But what do you wish yourself? Tell me plainly."

"I hardly know. Yes I do," continued Charlotte, plucking up courage. "I hope it isn't wrong, but I should rather like to go. I have sometimes thought how nice it would be to meet people like the people in the books I read—real ladies and gentlemen, who are so good, and so beautiful, and so kind. I dearly like to read about them. How delicious it must be to live always among them!"

"Poor little girl," said the parson to himself. Simple as he was, he was not quite so simple as she.

"But, Charlotte, grand people are not always 'real ladies and gentlemen;' and they sometimes do very unkind things. They might be unkind to you. I am afraid they would be. Would you feel hurt by that?"

"I don't know. But, if I could still admire them, would it much matter what they thought of me?"

The parson heard, and marveled at poor Charlotte's instinctive leaping at that truth, the foundation of all hero-worship, all human devotedness, ay, even of religious faith —"I love, I admire, I adore," without reference to self at all. Equally he felt surprised at what a year had effected in this girl—this mind once blank almost as white paper, simply by keeping it white, removing from it all bad influences, and letting the unconscious influence of daily companionship with nature, and books that were pure and true as nature do the rest.

While, roused out of her ordinary silence, she thus spoke, there was such longing in Charlotte's eyes, such an eager stretching out into "fresh fields and pastures new;" not the girlish craving for excitement, but the aspiration of a mind that was slowly opening, like the petals of a rose, to the mysteries of life, about which she was still as ignorant as a baby. Ay, in spite of all that had been, he was certain she was ignorant—and innocent too, in a very great degree. Such things, though rare, are possible.

Another idea occurred to him. What if his Quixotic education of his son's wife, shutting her out from all chance of harm, and filling her with ideal views of life, had lasted long enough, and it would be wiser to let her come into contact with human beings more real and tangible than the heroes and heroines of her story-books? And she had been so good ever since she came to Immeridge, so patient under Keith's neglect, so obedient to Keith's father, it was hard to deprive her of a little pleasure, the first for which she had ever seemed to crave.

"But, my dear, if we did go, what dress have you?"

"I could manage that," interrupted she, eagerly. "In every book I read, the young girls always go to their first party in white muslin, and I could make myself a white muslin dress in two days. And I have still a whole pound and more of the money he last sent me—that would buy it, and ribbons too. Oh, it would be so delicious!"

The parson smiled. His judgment slumbered—he had not the heart to say her no. So he took that first step which always costs so much—took it unwillingly, but without much calculation of consequences, saying to himself that it was "only once in a way," and that no harm could come.

The same evening, two responsive notes, one written to dictation, and in Charlotte's very best hand, which now was at least as good as that of most school-girls, were sent up to the Hall by Jane's small assistant in the kitchen, who also posted a written order to the nearest market town for white muslin and pink ribbon. Then the parson put the matter from his mind. The die was cast.

When, on the appointed day and hour, he handed his daughter from the Parsonage door into the Hall carriage, it must be owned he was not ashamed of her. Her fresh and simple dress was very neatly made; up to the throat and down to the wrists, for Charlotte did not seem to know that while women of the lower classes like their best gowns to be an extra covering, women of higher rank do just the contrary. She went, like Tennyson's Lady Clare, perhaps copied from that original, for Mr. Garland had often seen her reading the book,

"With a single rose in her hair,"

gathered from the rose-tree which, by greatest care, she had made to bloom in the parlor as if in a hothouse.

And though she had no gloves on, having apparently no idea that they were ever worn indoors, her hands had grown white and shapely, not unlike a lady's hand, even though quite unadorned—except by the one plain gold ring. She fingered it nervously. Poor Charlotte! was she thinking of her husband?

Mr. Garland did not ask. In truth, he dared not reason about that or any thing else. He only told her "she looked very nice," at which she blushed into brighter beauty, and relapsed into silence. His mind misgave him, as it had done more than once that day; but it was too late to draw back.

Besides, why should he? He was doing nothing wrong. If Charlotte were good enough for the Parsonage, she certainly was for the Hall. At worst, in taking her there, he was only going counter to social prejudices; but he infringed no moral law or sense of right. The Cruxes probably knew every thing about her by this time, or, if they did not, would soon learn, and then it would be at their own option to continue the acquaintance.

Thus he argued with himself, and palliated one of the few weak things, and the only uncandid thing he had ever done in his life, determined that, if done at all, it should be done without shrinking. Yet even while doing it a sharp pain came across him; a sense of the inevitable price that all sin must pay — to be paid, alas! not only by the sinner, but by those belonging to him. Oh, if Keith had ever thought of that!

When, mustering his courage, Mr. Garland walked into the splendid drawing-room with Charlotte on his arm, he could not help a certain relief at finding only strangers there—the Crux family, and some guests staying at the Hall.

"We asked several of your neighbors—I suppose every body is one's neighbor here, within ten miles—asked them specially to meet you and your daughter," said Mrs. Crux, apologetically, "but, unfortunately, they were all engaged."

"Well, it's their loss," added Miss Beatrice, as she took hold of Charlotte with both hands, stared hard and admiringly into her blushing face, then gave her a resonant kiss, remarking, "I beg your pardon, my dear, but I really couldn't help it."

Mrs. Keith Garland was then introduced to old Mr. Crux, a stout and bland gentleman; to young Mr. Crux, a thin, small, fashionable youth, drawling in voice and lazy in manner; and to various other people, the family or the visitors. They all talked so much and so fast that she could easily hold her tongue. She retreated behind her usual shelter of sweet, smiling looks, and almost total silence, even when she was paid the compliment of being taken down to dinner by the host himself, probably under some misty notion that she was still a bride.

The Cruxes had brought their easy London manners to their country dinner-table, in the dazzle of which it would have been easy for a more awkward person than Keith's wife to have passed muster, and been only commented upon as "very quiet." Quiet she was, her voice being rarely heard save in monosyllables; but her sweet looks spoke for her, and her excessive modesty and gentleness disarmed criticism, even if criticism had been attempted by these gay, metropolitan pleasure-seekers, who were accustomed to take people as they saw them, without inquiring much into their antecedents. Charlotte was treated with great civility by both ladies and gentlemen; and it never seemed to occur to either that she was other than she seemed — an unobtrusive, pretty, silent girl, very shy, and very oddly dressed; but then that was not surprising, considering that, as she herself said in answer to Miss Bea's question, she had spent all her life in these parts. Probably she was the daughter of some other country parson, who might not have been nearly as "nice" as the old parson of Immeridge.

Nevertheless, for lack of other entertainment, the youngest Miss Crux seemed determined to patronize the country damsel in the most alarming manner. She kept her under her wing all the evening, treating her much as an admiring young man treats a charming young lady; that is, in these modern days, when young men deport themselves not as humble knights and devoted swains, but as if they thought they did the young lady great honor by falling in love with her. She planned rides, walks, picnics on the sea-shore, and other amusements, with the bewildered Charlotte, finally parting from her with every demonstration of the most ardent friendship.

Of all this the parson noticed very little. Having seen his daughter-in-law fairly afloat, treated kindly, and looking happy, he devoted himself with his usual courtesy to spend the evening as pleasantly as might be, though wishing in his heart that he was safe beside his own study fire. He had lost the habit of society, as people do when they grow old in long seclusion.

And as they drove home — still in the Hall carriage, for undoubtedly these Cruxes were very good-natured — he was so thoroughly wearied that instead of talking to his daughter he fell fast asleep. All he did was on bidding her good-night to hope she had enjoyed herself, and her looks answered the question at once.

"So," thought the old man, still very sleepy, "the evening is safe over, and no harm has come of it. I have been civil to my neighbors, I have pleased poor Charlotte, and there is an end of it all."

CHAPTER VII.

THE good parson was mistaken in his reckoning. That dinner of Cruxham Hall turned to be not an end, but a beginning; which, like the beginning of strife, was "as the letting out of water." For henceforward the Crux family, headed by Miss Beatrice, who governed them all, bore down in a torrent upon the peaceful Parsonage, and swept away Charlotte with them in a flood of friendship.

This state of things came about so imperceptibly that Mr. Garland had no chance of taking any preventive measures against it, even had he been so inclined. Before a week was over it was too late. That easy and almost inevitable intimacy, which comes about in the country when people live close enough to be meeting daily, and can not choose but meet, was fairly established between the Hall and the Parsonage.

Charlotte seemed to like it—passively, if not actively. She submitted to be led about by the ardent Miss Beatrice as sweetly and silently as any pet lamb. For now, as always, her silence was her safeguard. And, to tell the truth, the fashionable Misses Crux were not gentlewomen enough to tell that she was none. They patronized her—and she was the meekest possible person to patronize—they fell into a *furore* about her, and showed her off to their guests as "the parson's pretty daughter;" they laughed at her *gaucheries* and mispronunciations, which they set down merely to "country ways." In short, being used in their wide London experiences to catch strange creatures, and amuse themselves with them while the novelty lasted, they caught Charlotte, and tried to tame her, and play with her, and make entertainment out of her, very much as if she had been a squirrel, a bird, a guinea-pig, or any other temporary pet, which could serve to while away a dull hour, especially in the winter.

They were forever sending for, or fetching her to the Hall; taking her drives, walks, picnics on the shore, and sketching parties inland, all of which enjoyments they made her believe would be incomplete without the pretty face of the parson's daughter. Also because, except herself, they had no other companions; the old families of the neighborhood seeming rather to ignore, or at least taking time to investigate, the new Cruxes of Cruxham Hall.

So two or three weeks rolled by; and this vehement friendship, though carried on under Mr. Garland's very eyes, was scarcely noticed by him, or noticed only because he saw Charlotte looked especially bright and happy whenever she told him—as, if questioned, she invariably did—that she had been with the young people of the Hall.

"You seem to like those Cruxes?" said he, one afternoon, when he left her, waiting in the garden, with her bonnet on, for an appointed walk with Miss Beatrice.

"Yes," she answered, in her usual gentle and undemonstrative way. Certainly Charlotte was not a passionate person, which was, perhaps, all the better for Keith, or would be one day. "Yes, I like them; they are very kind to me."

So the parson thought he would let matters drift on. It might have been wrong, or at least foolish, but it was a weakness belonging to his character not to take decisive steps unless absolutely driven to them.

Besides, this soft spring weather made him feel feeble, and conscious of his feebleness—gave him a solemn sense of how his years were narrowing down to months and weeks, which could not be very many, and might be very few. As he looked at the green leaves budding, all his longing was that, by the time they fell, Keith, taking advantage of the long holiday of a Canadian winter, might come over, as was his duty, to see his wife, and, finding her so changed, might fall in love over again with a new Charlotte, in which case their permanent residence in America, which, as his father saw with pain, Keith now drearily planned as the only future open to a young man whose wife was no better than a farm-servant, might never come about. They might settle in England—perhaps even near Immeridge—Keith finding work of some sort to help them, or help to keep them, till by-and-by he succeeded to his mother's little income, a safe certainty which could not, in the course of nature, be very distant now.

But as the old man thought of these things, calmly planning for and providing against the time when he too should be numbered among the innumerable multitude

"Who have passed through the body and gone,"

leaving their place free for a new generation, he felt no regret, rather a deep content, the purest content of all, the divine unselfishness of parenthood. If he could only see his child—nay, his children—for those whom marriage had joined together he did not dare even in thought put asunder—see them safe and happy together, how cheerfully would he say *Nunc dimittis* and go home! Thankful, above all, for one thing, that neither Keith nor Charlotte would ever have to remember of their father one word, one act of harshness or unkindness.

He strolled leisurely back to the Parsonage and went into his study, tired, indeed, but so peaceful that he was half annoyed when Jane came abruptly in to tell him there was a visitor in the parlor.

"One of the Cruxes, I suppose?"

"Young Mr. Crux; and he's been a sitting there with Mrs. Keith for the last half hour." Jane said this with an air which implied that she was not entirely pleased at the circumstance.

Neither was Jane's master. Unworldly and unsuspicious as the parson was, he had a certain amount of common sense. He had reconciled himself to the Crux avalanche, seeing it was of a purely feminine character, the male members of the family spending most of their time in London. But he saw at once that it would never do for a young man like Mr. Charles Crux to be hanging about the Parsonage, and holding *tête-à-têtes* with Keith's wife. Weary as he was, he went immediately into the parlor.

Nobody was there. The visitor had disappeared, and he heard his daughter-in-law's steps overhead in her own room. There must have been some mistake, he thought; so he waited till he could ask Charlotte about it.

When she came down to tea he observed her sharply. She was pale—a little paler than ordinary, he thought—but she was her usual gentle, composed self; and when he questioned her she answered without the slightest hesitation or confusedness of manner.

"Yes, sir, I had a visitor—Mr. Charles Crux."

"What did he come for?"

"He said, to bring an apology for his sister."

"She did not come, then?"

"No."

"And how long did the young man stay?"

"Half an hour."

It was cruel to suspect her; besides, from the depth of his soul, Mr. Garland hated suspicion. Very often, it is the dormant evil in our own hearts which we are most ready to attribute to others. To continue his catechism would be, he felt, almost an insult, so he passed the matter over, merely saying,

"Another time, my dear, send word by Jane that I am not at home. Gentlemen's visits should always be paid to the gentleman of the family."

Charlotte was silent.

Their tea-hour went by peacefully as usual, she sitting half hidden behind the urn, and Mr. Garland occupied with his book, when Jane came in with two letters, one for each of them.

"From the Hall, of course! They make a great fuss over you, Charlotte," said the parson, smiling. But when he opened his own note, the smile vanished.

Mrs. Crux, who was used to write him the most cordial and long-winded of notes on every conceivable parish matter, "presented her compliments, and requested the honor of half an hour's private conversation with the Reverend William Garland."

The parson dropped the letter on his lap. A tremor ran through him; Mrs. Crux must have discovered all.

Jane was waiting, with her sharp eyes fixed first on one and then on the other; but Charlotte sat immovable, with her letter lying unopened beside her.

"Say to Mrs. Crux—no, stop!—I will write my message."

And he wrote slowly, that it might look like his steadiest handwriting, though still it had the pathetic feebleness of his seventy years:

"The Reverend William Garland will not fail to wait upon Mrs. Crux immediately."

And then he turned his attention to his daughter-in-law.

She still sat in her place at the tea-table; but her color had quite faded out, and she was trembling perceptibly.

"Have you read your letter, Charlotte?"

"No, sir."

"Will you do so, then?"

For he felt it must be penetrated at once—faced at once—this something which had surely happened; doubtless that which he ought to have foreseen would sooner or later inevitably happen—the discovery of all particulars concerning his son's unfortunate marriage.

"It is my fault—oh that I had been wiser!" thought he, with a pang of bitter humiliation—even dread.

But the next minute he felt himself blush, not for the shame, but the cowardice. What could the Cruxes accuse him of? He had done what he thought was right; in a most sore emergency he had acted as he believed a parent should act before God and man, in taking under the shelter of his roof his son's wife, who had led there for more than a year and a half a life as blameless and harmless as that of a child.

He watched her reading her letter. It was not a pleasant letter, evidently, for her cheeks were burning and her eyes glowed with a flash—an actual flame, which he had never seen lighted in them before.

"Who writes to you, my dear?"

"Miss Beatrice."

"What does she say? May I read?"

Charlotte passed the letter across without a word.

The parson, accustomed to ladies' letters—precise, elegant, feminine, formal—of half a century ago, was altogether puzzled by this one, with its scrawling masculine hand and its eccentric phraseology:

"DEAR LITTLE FELLOW,—I can't come to you to-day; the maternal parent forbids. Not that I mind *her*, but she'd tell the governor, and there'd be a row. Indeed, there has been a precious row at home. Some county people called, and talked a heap of nonsense about you. But you were really married—weren't you, my dear? Anyhow—never mind—you're a jolly little soul, and I'm a fellow that thinks for myself on this and all subjects. So I told the maternal parent, and said I meant to stick by you. And Charley backed me up, which wasn't much good, as he's rather a loose fish, is Charley. Don't you stand any of his nonsense, by-the-by.

"I can't get out to-day, but I'll meet you to-morrow, by hook or by crook. Hang it! this grand blow-up is rather fun than otherwise—nearly as good as having an elopement for myself. Never you care, there's a dear little soul, I'll stand by you. Yours ever, B. CRUX."

Mr. Garland read the letter—twice over, indeed, before he could properly take it in—then laid it on the table beside him, and pressed his hand over his eyes, trying to realize the position in which he stood, what he had done, and what he ought to do. Above all, what he should say, and how he should say it—to Charlotte.

Pleasant and kindly as their intercourse had grown, there had never been between the parson and his daughter-in-law the least approach toward intimacy. She was far too much afraid of him still; and on his side he shrank with a repugnance, even yet unconquered, from the occasional coarseness, though more of habit than of innate nature, which he could not fail to see in her, and which, in his ultra refinement, he perhaps saw plainer than most people. Except in the necessary civilities of domestic life, and the daily lessons, they rarely talked much, for he did not exactly know what to say; and her replies, though sensible and to the point, were always as brief as possible.

But now he felt that the ice must be broken; that, somehow or other, confidence must be established between them before they met and breasted mutually the impending storm.

For, in whatever shape it might come, he never thought of leaving her to breast it alone—this poor defenseless girl, left with the mere name of a husband to protect her—the mere memory of his love, and that a selfish love—to keep her heart faithful and warm. However Keith might act, it never once occurred to Keith's father to cast her off; not even to preserve untarnished his own good name, though well he knew that it was in peril. He could easily imagine all that might be said about him and of his conduct—for there is hardly any conduct which will not bear two interpretations, and no story that can not be told in two different, often totally different ways. Besides, his own conscience told him that in one point he had been weak to a fault. He had no right, without telling Mrs. Crux the whole story, to allow his daughter-in-law to visit at Cruxham Hall.

Still, whatever she was or had been, she was now his daughter-in-law, his son's lawful wife, sheltered by the sanctity and irrevocableness of marriage ties—ay, even such a marriage as this had been. As he looked at her, so young, so helpless, and with an air of innocence difficult to believe in, and yet not impossible, for the facts of daily life sometimes show it possible for a girl, even with Charlotte's antecedent history, to have instincts of virtue strong enough afterward to retrieve herself, and become an honest wife—as he looked, every chivalrous feeling in the old man's nature rose up to defend her. He felt thankful that there was even an old man left to stand between the poor girl and harm.

He opened the conversation at once.

"Thank you, my dear, for permitting me to read your

letter. It is not a pretty letter for a young lady to write. Do you understand to what Miss Beatrice refers?"

"I think I do. *He* told me."

"He? Who?"

"That—that *villain!*"

The fierce emphasis of her words, accompanied by such a glare in the soft eyes, such a clench of the hand, told Mr. Garland all—perhaps more than the truth. He rose in much agitation.

"Do you mean Mr. Charles Crux? for it can not be any body else. Has he dared— Tell me what he has been saying to you."

Still she was silent. The hot blood flooded her face; she seemed bursting with indignation, grief, and even a sort of terror; but she did not reply.

"Charlotte, you *must* tell me. Remember, I am your father."

Then Charlotte broke down. She hid her face in her hands, and her whole frame shook with the wildness of her weeping.

Mr. Garland stood by, attempting to do nothing—in truth, because he did not know what to do. At last he laid his hand on her shoulder, and she looked up.

"Let me hear every thing. I ought to hear it, Charlotte."

"I didn't mean to tell you, for it would only vex you, sir; besides, I knew I could take care of myself. But he is a villain! You must never let him inside these doors again. And I will never go to the Hall—never! And when you go out you will take me with you—oh, please do, sir! for he has met me once or twice, and said silly things to me, though he never insulted me till to-day."

"Did he insult you?" asked the parson between his teeth.

Charlotte hesitated. She had spoken rapidly and vehemently, but now she hesitated.

"What did he say? Speak out! Don't be afraid."

"I am not afraid, sir. He told me just what his sister hints at in this letter—that after thinking I was a young lady born, they found out I was only a servant—and—and other things; that his mother was very angry, and his sisters would never be allowed to see me again."

"I expected it. Any more?"

"Then he spoke—as I thought nobody would dare to speak to a married woman. He said my husband didn't care for me, and would never come back to me—and I had better go away with him—*him!*"

"And what did you answer?"

Charlotte sprang from her seat. If the parson had still doubts concerning her, he could have none now.

"Answer? What was I likely to answer but one thing—that I hated him! Besides, I was married. If I had not hated him, still I was married."

"And then?" said Mr. Garland—astonished, almost awed at the passion she showed.

"He laughed at me, such a horrid laugh, and I sprang to the door; he tried to hold it, but I pushed him away—I could have killed him almost—and I ran away up to my room, locked myself in, and—I don't remember any thing more, sir."

"My poor girl!"

The parson held out his hand—his steadfast, blameless right hand, which had never failed a friend nor injured an enemy—held it out to the forlorn creature, who, her momentary excitement gone, had sunk down shame-stricken beside him. And, as soon as she had courage to lift her eyes, Charlotte saw him looking at her, with the only look that has power to draw sinners up out of hell and into heaven—the true father's look, full of infinite pity, infinite forgiveness.

"Oh, I'll be good, I'll be good!" she cried, in the accent and the very words of a child. "Only take care of me, please, sir! Nobody ever did take care of me, or teach me. I didn't even know how wicked I had been—not then, but I do now. It's no wonder people should treat me thus; and yet they shouldn't—they shouldn't—for they were taught better, and I never was!"

"Ay, that's true!" said Mr. Garland. And thinking of the young man, the cowardly libertine who had stolen into the Parsonage that day—of the young girl, no older than Charlotte, who had written such a flippant, worse than flippant letter—his heart burned with anger, and the poor sinner who still knelt weeping at his feet showed like a saint beside them.

Still he made no attempt to justify her, either to his own mind or to herself. No pity, however deep, led him to palliate her sin, or to allow that it might be softened by extenuating circumstances till it came to be no sin at all.

It was sin. Its very consequences proved it to be. Who could doubt this, looking at that pretty creature, who might have been almost like Wordsworth's *Lucy*—

"The sweetest thing that ever grew
Beside a cottage door"—

who had already a marriage-ring on her finger, and was awaiting a settled married home, with all outward circumstances combining to make her happy? Yet there she crouched, hiding her face like the unhappiest, guiltiest woman living. "Conviction of sin" (to use that phrase so awfully true, but which canting religionists often twist into a hypocritical lie) had come upon her—whether gradually or suddenly, who could tell?—and the secret shame, the hidden pollution, was worse to bear than any outward contumely.

Nor could he help her—this good man, this minister of God, who knew what God's Word says. He knew, too, what the hard world would say, and that it has reason in its hardness; for without the strict law of purity to bind society together, families and communities would all fall to pieces, drifting into wild anarchy and hopeless confusion.

"Charlotte," he said, very kindly, but firmly, "try and calm yourself if you can. It is a very serious position of affairs. We must look at all things quietly."

"Yes, sir."

She rose and resumed her seat. As he, and Jane too, had long since found out, Mrs. Keith Garland was no weak girl, to lay all her burdens upon other people. She could bear them herself, silently, too, if need be; and in this instance, perhaps, the very sharpness of her anguish made her strong. Her sobbing ceased, and she sat in patient expectation.

"Here is Mrs. Crux's letter to me," said Mr. Garland.

"There can be no doubt she had heard what I supposed she knew already, but which, had I been wiser, I should have told her myself before I took you with me to the Hall."

"Did it disgrace you, taking me? If I had known it, I would never have wished to go."

"I believe that. It was my fault. I ought to have seen things clearer, and met them—as we must endeavor to meet them now. Can you, Charlotte?"

She looked at him inquiringly.

"I mean—can you bear me to speak to you plainly, as a father may speak—about things that hitherto I have left between you and that Father who knows you much better than I ever can."

Charlotte bent her head. "Thank you. Please speak." Yet still Mr. Garland hesitated. It seemed so like trampling on a poor half-fledged or broken-winged bird.

"I answered Mrs. Crux that I would go and see her to-night, and so I shall. She has some right to be angry. She was kept in ignorance of facts she ought to have known before I took you to her house. You must be aware, my poor Charlotte, that many mothers would not like their daughters to associate with you—that is, until they knew you as well as I do; then, I hope—I am sure they would feel differently."

Charlotte looked up with a sudden gleam in her sad face, but the parson did not see it. He went on, speaking, as it seemed, more to himself than to her.

"Our past, in one sense, is wholly irrevocable. Whether it be sin or only sorrow, we can not blot it out; it must remain as it is forever. But we can cover it over, conquer it, atone for it. And the present, upon which depends the future, lies wholly in our own hands. My poor girl, don't despair. If I can forgive you, be sure God will, and then it matters little whether the world forgives you or not."

Thus talked he, arguing less with her than with his own mind the strait in which he found himself—this upright, pure-hearted old man—against whom not a breath of reproach had been raised till now.

"What does it matter?" he repeated, as he thought of all that would be said to him and of him — many falsehoods, no doubt, but still grounded on the bitter truth that could not be denied, which he never should attempt to deny. "God is my Judge, not man. I will not be afraid. What harm can my neighbors do me?"

"Harm to you?" said Charlotte, anxiously. "Will people blame you? What for? Because you were good to me?"

"I am afraid they will, my dear! But, as I said, it does not matter. Give me my hat and stick; it is time I should be going to the Hall."

"Stop a minute, please; just tell me. What do you think will happen through their finding out this?"

"Nothing very terrible," replied the parson, with a faint smile; "only you and I are likely to be left alone together. Nobody will come to the Parsonage, and nobody will ask us any where. We shall be 'sent to Coventry,' in short."

"And why? Because of me?"

The parson was silent.

"Tell me, oh, please do!" and Charlotte's voice was hoarse and trembling; "when my husband comes home, shall I be a disgrace also to him? Will his friends take no notice of him because of me?"

Mr. Garland was sorely troubled. It was such a cruel truth to tell, and yet it was the truth, and she might have to learn it some day, perhaps from far unkinder lips than his own. Would it not be better to make her understand it now — the inevitable punishment that all sin brings — which in degree they both must bear all their life long — she and Keith — but especially she? Would it not be safer to make her recognize it, and be brave under it?

"Charlotte, I will not tell you what is untrue. It would have been far better for my son, and I myself should have been far happier, if he had married a girl in his own station—married with my consent, openly, honorably, as an honest man and gentleman ought to marry. But we can not alter what is past. I accepted his wife simply because she was his wife. Since then I have learned — yes," holding out his hand — "I have learned to—to like her; she is a very good and dear girl to me. And if the world should look down upon Keith on account of his wife, never mind! Let his wife love him all the more—nobly, faithfully, patiently; let her prove herself such a good wife to him that the world will be ashamed of its harsh judgment. And whether it is or not, there is only one Judge she need tremble before, and He is a Father likewise."

Charlotte leaned forward eagerly, but scarcely seemed to comprehend his words.

"Yes, that is all good and all right, but it will never be. I shall not have strength to do it. I had much better do the other thing that I was thinking of."

"What other thing?"

"To run away and hide myself—die if I could—because if I died he would be free to marry again. He would soon forget me—every body would forget me—and I should cease to do any body any harm! Oh! I wish—I wish I could die!" cried she, breaking, for the first time, into a cry of actual despair.

"Charlotte!" she started, recalled to herself by the stern reproof of his tone. "To die, or even wish to die, before the Father calls us, is unchristian cowardice. And it is our own fault always if we do our fellow-creatures harm. It will be your own fault if, from this time, you are any thing but a blessing both to me and to your husband. We will talk no more now. I am going up to the Hall. Sit quiet here till I come back."

She obeyed without resistance, waiting upon him silently, in her usual humble and mindful way, to which he had grown so accustomed that he scarcely noticed how much she did for him. But now, while she was mechanically brushing his coat and smoothing out his gloves, it suddenly came into Mr. Garland's mind—what if she should carry out her intention and do something desperate—as from former experience, and from the expression of the dull, heavy, stony eyes, and the little resolute mouth, he knew she was quite capable of doing.

"Charlotte," he said, looking back ere he closed the door, "mind, I shall want you when I come back. Remember, whether any body else wants you or not, I do."

Charlotte turned away and burst into tears.

CHAPTER VIII.

MR. GARLAND walked slowly from his own gate up to the Hall, which was not more than half a mile from the Parsonage. It was a clear starry night—light enough for him easily to find his way; so he hid his lantern under a bush and went on without it, to give himself more freedom for meditation. As he did so, he thought how often we purblind mortal creatures set up our petty lanterns, carry them so carefully and hug them so close that they make us believe all the rest of the world, within a yard of our own feet, lies in blackest darkness, and obscure for us altogether the broad light of God's heaven, which, whether in daylight or darkness, seen or unseen, arches immovably above us all.

The night sky, in its clear darkness, so thickly sown with stars, comforted the parson more than words can tell; for it showed him the large Infinite in contradistinction to his little finite woes, and it reminded him of that other life in the prospect of which he daily walked, and which made all perplexing things in this life grow level, simple, and plain.

Before reaching the Hall—for, though it was so short a distance, he had proceeded slowly and with unusual feebleness—Mr. Garland made up his mind, that is, his conscience, as to how he ought to act. For the exact words he should say to Mrs. Crux, not knowing what she would say to him, nor what tone she meant to take toward him, he left them undecided, believing with a child-like simplicity of faith that now, as in the apostles' time, when a man has the right and the truth in his heart, there is, under every emergency, a Divine spirit not far from him, which tells him what to say.

The light from the drawing-room windows shone in a broad stream a long way across the park, but it did not look so cheerful as usual in the eyes of the old man, who was entering, for the first time in his life, this house—nay, any house—where he had the slightest doubt of his welcome—a welcome combined of the reverence due to his cloth, the respect won by his personal character, and the warm regard which even strangers soon came to feel for one so gentle, unobtrusive, large-minded, and sincere. He had been so long accustomed to this universal respect, that the possibility of the contrary affected him with a new and very painful feeling. He had need to look up more than once to that quiet heaven which soothed all mortal troubles, and dwarfed all mortal cares, before he could nerve his hand to pull the resonant door-bell at Cruxham Hall.

"Dinner is over, I conclude?" he said to the footman on entering. "Is your mistress in the drawing-room? Can I see her?"

And he was mechanically walking forward when the man opened the door of the study—a small room close at hand, where every body was shown; that is, every body who came on business, and was not considered fit to be admitted into the family circle.

"Mrs. Crux said, sir, that when you came you was to be asked in here."

"Very well; tell her I am waiting."

It was a trivial thing, but it vexed Mr. Garland more than he liked to own. It was the feather which showed which way the wind blew—a bitter, biting wind it might prove to be, and he was an old man. Why could he not have gone down to his grave in peace?

Many fathers bring discredit on their sons—that is, externally, though in righteous judgment no child ought ever to be contemned for the misdeeds of a parent; but the reverse scarcely holds. It is a much sadder thing for a father to suffer for the ill-doings of a son, especially as he himself is seldom held quite guiltless of the same. For the second time Mr. Garland asked himself bitterly, as he knew the world at large would ask (and in many cases justifiably too), whether he had not himself been somewhat to blame in this dark shadow which had fallen upon his old age?

He sat down wearily in the great arm-chair whence for so many years the old Squire Crux had administered justice, and Mr. Garland, who was also a county magistrate, had sometimes been called upon to assist him in difficult poaching or affiliation cases—the usual rural offenses, and almost the only ones that ever occurred at Immeridge. He remembered the very last one, and how he had judged it—not harshly, thank God! How little he then thought that in a few months the same kind of sin might have been laid by his neighbors at, or at least near to, his own stainless door.

After keeping him waiting many minutes—this, too,

was something new, and he noted it with sensitive pain —Mrs. Crux appeared.

She was in her dinner-dress, the richness of which gave her a kind of adventitious dignity, as it often did; the fat, weak, good-natured woman was one of those who take great courage from their clothes. As she closed the door behind her, and stood in the centre of the floor, all in a rustle of silk, she tried hard to look stately, distant, and commanding, but signally failed. The parson in his shabby coat, for he had forgotten to change it, was decidedly the more self-possessed of the two. He rose, bowed, but did not offer to shake hands, nor did she. Nevertheless, it was he who had to open the matter.

"You sent for me, madam, that we might have a little conversation on a subject which you did not name, but which I can easily guess, from a letter written by your daughter to my daughter-in-law."

"Beatrice has written? Oh, dear me, what shall I do with her," cried the mother, nervously; but Mr. Garland took no notice of the exclamation.

"It is about my daughter-in-law, is it not, that you wish to speak to me?"

"It is—it is! Oh, Mr. Garland, how could you do it —you, a clergyman of the Church of England, and a gentleman of such credit in the county? I declare, I was so shocked, so scandalized, I could hardly believe my ears when Lady Jones told me."

"What did she tell? Will you repeat the story exactly, and I will tell you if it is true, or how much of it is true."

But neither accuracy nor directness were special qualities of Mrs. Crux, especially when, as now, she was obviously puzzled and distressed.

"Such a pretty girl — such a sweet, modest-looking girl. I could not have believed it possible. And you to have her residing with you, and even to bring her here to associate with my daughters! Mr. Garland, I am astonished at you. You ought to be ashamed of yourself."

"Madam," he answered, with a touching, sad humility, "I am ashamed of myself, but it is not for the reason you suppose. It is because I had not the courage to state to you all the sad circumstances of my son's marriage, and then leave it to yourself to judge how far the acquaintance you so wished was either suitable or desirable. Not that I had any doubt of my daughter-in-law, or of your daughters taking any harm from association with her, but that, in her sad position, all acquaintanceships or friendships ought to be begun with open eyes on both sides. Mrs. Crux, I was to blame. I beg your pardon."

The lady was disarmed; she could not but be, at such gentle dignity. She looked sorry, and answered half apologetically,

"Well, on that principle, Mr. Garland, it's little enough you know about us, though at least our position in society is unquestionable. But it is quite different with Mrs. Keith Garland, who I hear was a common servant-girl, at some farm near here where your son used to visit, and where, like all those sort of persons, she made a bait of her pretty face, and cunningly entrapped the poor boy to marry her."

"Stop a minute," said Mr. Garland. "She did not entrap him. The error was my son's as much as hers. He felt bound in honor to marry her."

"Why? Goodness gracious, Mr. Garland, you don't mean to tell me—" She stopped aghast.

The old man blushed painfully, agonizingly, all over his face. He saw at once that in his roused sense of justice he had betrayed more than even Mrs. Crux had heard—the worst, the saddest thing of all, compared to which Charlotte's being a servant-girl had seemed to him a light evil—so light that he had naturally concluded Mrs. Crux knew the whole story, and that the violent, almost insulting measures she had taken were on this account. For the moment he paused, repenting, but it was too late now. Besides, had he not come determined to explain, and to face the whole truth; why should he dread it now?

"Mrs. Crux, I do not in the least wish to deceive you: as a mother of daughters you have a right to every explanation, and I came here to give it. I should have done so long ago, only I thought Immeridge gossip must already have told you what is so painful for me to tell to a stranger. Still, I ought not to feel pained, for my daughter-in-law's daily life speaks for itself as to what she is now; so simple and humble, so good and true, that I have almost forgotten she was ever—"

The sentence died on the parson's lips, for the cruel truth had never been put into words before. Still, he must utter it.

"She was, I grieve to say, not only a poor illiterate servant-girl, but—my son seduced her before he married her."

"What!" cried the lady, starting back in undisguised horror. "And you were so misguided, so insane, as to let him marry her?"

"Madam," said the parson, as he too drew back a step, "I am not accountable for the marriage, since I was unaware of it till it was over. But the one thing which inclined me to forgive my son was that he did marry her."

Mrs. Crux regarded him with the blankest astonishment. "I never heard of such a thing. That is—of course, such things happen every day; we mothers of sons know that they must happen. It's a sad, sad matter, but we can't help it; we can only shut our eyes to it, and hope the poor lads will learn better by-and-by. But to view the case in this way—to act as you have done—I protest, Mr. Garland, it appears to me actual madness. What would the world say of you?"

"I have never once asked myself that question."

And then, as they stood together—the old man and the elderly woman—for Mrs. Crux was over sixty, though she dressed like a girl in her teens—they mutually investigated one another, with as much success as if they were gazing out of two different worlds. As in truth they were—the world of shams, and the world of realities.

"I am very tired—will you excuse my sitting down?" said the parson, gently; she had never yet asked him to be seated. "But I shall not detain you long; and after to-night the Parsonage will intrude upon the Hall no more. It never would have done so, save for the persistent attentions of your family, which I wish I had prevented earlier, for more reasons than this."

Mr. Garland suddenly paused, for again he had been

led on to say too much. After mature deliberation, he had resolved—out of his dislike to any dis-peace, and because no good could come from the revelation—to be silent respecting Mr. Charles Crux and his insolence. But the poor mother, made sadly wise, was also quickly suspicious; for she said uneasily,

"Please explain; I insist on your explaining any other reason."

"I would rather not, for it is one of those things which are best not even named. And it can never occur again; for, by my daughter-in-law's express wish, I shall keep my door closed henceforward to every member of your family."

"Mr. Garland, surely—I saw Charley was a little smitten—but surely he has not been such a fool as to—"

"I do not know what you call a fool," replied Mr. Garland, indignantly, "but I should give your son a much harder name."

"Oh, you mistake," said the mother, a little frightened. "Young men are always taken by a pretty face. Charley likes flirting, especially with married women. He means no harm—and every body does it."

"Which makes it no harm, I suppose," said the parson, bitterly. "But I, and happily my daughter-in-law, think otherwise. Since you have mentioned the subject, which it appears you were not quite ignorant of, will you say to Mr. Charles Crux that if he ever dares to cross my threshold again—though I am an old man, I have a strong right hand yet—and—there might be a horsewhip in it! I beg your pardon, madam," added he, suddenly stopping, and reining in the passion which shook him, old as he was. "In truth, I forbear to speak, because I am more sorry for you, as being mother to your son, than I am for myself, as the father of mine."

"Why, what difference is there between them? Or between your conduct and mine?"

"All the difference between plastering over a foul ulcer, and opening it boldly tc the light; ugly, indeed, and a grievous wound, but a wound that, by God's mercy, may be cleansed and healed. All the difference between the sinner who hides and hugs his sin, thinking nothing of it, if only it can escape punishment, and the sinner who repents and forsakes his sin, and so becomes clean again, and fit to enter the kingdom of heaven—always so near at hand to all of us. Where, please God, I hope yet to see my poor boy, and that poor girl Charlotte too —ay, madam, even in this world."

Mr. Garland spoke as he had never meant to speak; but the words were forced into him and from him. They fell on deaf ears, a heart too narrow to understand them.

Nevertheless, the lady moved uneasily, and regarded Mr. Garland with a puzzled air. "You talk in a very odd way; but I suppose, you being a clergyman, it is all right—only please do not confound Mr. Keith Garland with Mr. Charles Crux. What your son may be I can not tell, but my son is quite correct in conduct always. He goes to church with his family—you might have seen him every Sunday. He visits where his sisters visit—and I can assure you we are exceedingly particular in our society. Beatrice is the only one who takes up with doubtful people; she laughed at this dreadful business—I mean at Mrs. Keith Garland's having been a servant. And even if she were told every thing, very likely she would not care for that either; young people are getting such very queer notions nowadays. Oh, you don't know what a mother's anxieties are, Mr. Garland," cried the poor woman, appealingly, and glancing at the door, as if she expected every minute to have their interview burst in upon.

"Pray give yourself no anxiety on our account," said Mr. Garland, rising. "I have said all you wished to hear, and all that I had to say; now let me assure you that this visit of mine will be the last communication between the Hall and the Parsonage."

Mrs. Crux looked infinitely relieved. "It is best, a great deal the best—thank you, Mr. Garland. And yet"—her good-nature overcoming her, or else being touched in spite of herself by the picture of the solitary, feeble old man going out into the dark to meet the obloquy which Mrs. Crux felt certain must inevitably rest on every body who was "dropped" by Cruxham Hall—"I don't wish to do an unkind thing. Perhaps, since nobody knows, you might still come here—coming by yourself, of course."

"Thank you; but it is quite impossible. You felt it necessary to protect and to uphold the dignity of your daughters—excuse me if I feel the same regarding mine. All acquaintance must henceforth cease between our two households."

"But as to Beatrice," said Mrs. Crux, who, like most weak women, when she saw a thing absolutely done, usually began to wish it undone—"what am I to say to

Beatrice? She has taken such a fancy to young Mrs. Garland."

"Let her find another protégée, and she will soon forget my Charlotte."

"*My* Charlotte!" The word slipped out unawares—he was startled at it himself—but he did not retract it. And all the way home he thought of her tenderly—as good men do think, even of those that have caused them woe, when they themselves have had the strength not to requite pang for pang, and evil for evil. It is a true saying, that those against whom our hearts harden most are not those who have wronged us, but those whom we have wronged.

Steadily and bravely, though without an atom of love in his heart, Mr. Garland had done his duty to his daughter-in-law; steadily and bravely he had fought for her now—the poor girl—simply because she was a poor, defenseless girl. Now, when she was wholly thrown upon his pity and care; when not a door but his own was likely to be open to her; when even her husband neglected her, and shrank from coming back to England because it was coming back to her; the old man, who had in him that knightly nature which instinctively takes the weaker side—the good old man felt almost an affection for Charlotte.

When he saw by the glimmer from his study-window that she was still waiting there, and heard the front door open almost before he had fastened the clinking latch of the garden gate, a sensation approaching pleasure came over him.

"Well, my dear, I have returned safe, you see," said

he, cheerily. "It is all well over. We shall see no more of the Cruxes. You and I must be content with one another's company. I can. Can you?"

Charlotte looked up and smiled—a smile the brightness of which was soon accounted for, as well as the indifference with which she omitted all questions concerning the interview that had just before seemed so momentous to them both.

"Look here, sir," said she, drawing a letter from her apron pocket. "This came directly after you had gone. What can it mean? For, do you see, it is not by the ordinary Canadian mail; the postmark is London, and there is an English stamp upon it."

"Poor little soul, how well she loves him!" thought Mr. Garland, as Charlotte came hovering about his chair with a trembling eagerness of manner, and a brightness of expectation in her look. "You thought, my dear, that Keith might be in England, but it is not so. He dates as usual, you see; this is merely sent by private hand, and posted in London."

"Yes, I understand." And Charlotte sat down patiently, the light in her eyes quite gone. Patiently too, without a word of interruption or comment, she listened while, as was customary, her father-in-law read aloud her husband's letter.

It was chiefly to say—what Keith had hinted by the last mail, that he should find it impossible to come home this next winter—when his two years of absence would expire. Equally impracticable—as he explained with greater length than perspicuity of argument—was it for him to send for his wife to Canada. Not that he was too poor to have her—indeed, he inclosed a very handsome sum of money to defray her maintenance and her own personal wants; but his very prosperity seemed to make a barrier between them.

"We enjoy some little civilization, even out here," he wrote; "the few people I have as neighbors are tolerably well educated. And besides, in the lonely life of a Canadian farm, a man wants not only a wife, but a companion. I think, father, it would not be a twelvemonth wasted, either for her sake or mine, if for a year at least you would send Charlotte to some good boarding-school, or hire a governess to live in the village—you might not like a strange lady living at the Parsonage. I must say, I should like my wife to get a little education. It would be very valuable out here; and if I ever should return and settle in England— But we will leave that an open question for time to decide."

Thus summarily, with a briefness that showed how indifferent he was to it, Keith dismissed the subject, and went on to other things.

The father's heart was very sad—more than sad—angry. And yet Keith's conduct was hardly unnatural; the more so as, with a feeling that it was best to leave Time's workings to work themselves out without any interference on his part, Mr. Garland had carefully abstained from writing much about Charlotte. He wished now he had done a little differently; he determined by the next mail to speak his mind out plainly and clearly; but, in the mean time, there Keith's will was, given with a hard determination which seemed to have grown upon him of late, and his young wife must obey.

She never seemed to have any thought of disobeying. She sat passively, with her eyes cast down, and a dull, hopeless shadow creeping over the face, that ten minutes before had almost startled the old man with its exceeding brightness. She listened to the letter's end, the part about herself being a very small portion of it; the rest being filled up with statements of Keith's affairs, which seemed very flourishing—and long essays on American politics, into which he seemed to have thrown himself with the ardor of one who has set aside, conscientiously perhaps, a young man's temptations to pleasure and amusement, and plunged desperately into the pursuits of middle age. In short, he seemed, even at this early age, to have substituted ambition for love, and exchanged his heart for his brains. Throughout all the reading of his son's letter, Mr. Garland saw, and felt when he did not see, the poor little face of his son's wife, so quiet, so uncomplaining, that how much she thought he could not tell—he was half afraid to conjecture. But she spoke not a single word.

"My dear," he said at last, "should you like to have a governess?"

"Oh yes. Any thing you please—any thing he pleases."

"Charlotte," the parson spoke almost apologetically, "your husband does not quite know, but I shall explain to him next mail, how well you and I have got on together, in studies and every thing; how greatly you are improving—as a girl of your age has infinite capacities for doing. Above all, what a good, dear girl you invariably are to me."

"Am I?" She looked up with those great dark eyes of hers, and in them he saw, as he had never seen it revealed before, the real womanly soul; quick to feel, yet strong to endure; long-suffering to almost the last limit of patience, yet having its pride too—its own righteous, feminine pride, which on occasion could assert itself—not aggressively, but with a certain dignified reticence, more pathetic than the loudest complaints.

Though she was not his ideal of womanhood, and was wholly unlike the wife he had adored, the daughter he had imagined—quite a different type of character indeed, still the parson was forced to acknowledge that it was not an unbeautiful character. As it developed itself, he did more than merely like—he began, in degree, actually to respect Charlotte.

He attempted neither to question her nor to draw out her feelings, so closely, so bravely restrained; but, simply giving her the letter to read over again at her leisure, asked her to light his candle for him, and he would go to bed; he felt very weary to-night.

"So the boy will not be back for another year at least," thought he, sighing; "and my years are growing so few."

Though he did not put the thought into words, Charlotte heard the sigh, and saw the expression of the sad old face.

"It is as I expected, you see," said she, in a low voice. "He will not come home because of me. Oh sir"—and humbly, very humbly and tenderly she laid her hand upon Mr. Garland's—"please forgive me. I am so sorry—for *you*."

"Never mind—never mind, my daughter."

And the desolate old man did what he had never in his life done to any woman—except one; he took her in his arms and kissed her.

CHAPTER X.

MUCH is said and written upon the mournfulness of broken friendships—a subject almost too sad to write about; for such are like the hewing down of a tree—a sharp axe and a rash hand will destroy in an hour a whole life's growth, and what no second lifetime can ever make grow again. And thinking thus of all shattered things, how easy it is to destroy and how difficult to retrieve, there is a certain sadness in contemplating even a broken acquaintanceship.

It was not likely that a sensitive man like Mr. Garland could see with indifference the Crux family sitting beneath him in the Hall pew Sunday after Sunday, listening with civil attention to his sermons, but regarding him as no longer their friend—only their clergyman; and the service over, sweeping silently out of the narrow church, where every body knew every body and noticed every body, to their carriage, omitting entirely the customary greeting at the church-door or the church-yard gate. It was painful, too, to meet them in his walks, which he never took alone now, and for him and Charlotte to have to pass without recognition, or tacitly to alter their path so as to escape meeting at all. At last these chance rencontres began to be looked forward to with such a sense of dread and discomfort that all the pleasure of the parson's walks was taken away. He gradually seceded from the places he best liked—the shore, the cliff, and the downs, restricting his rambles daily, till after a few weeks he rarely stirred beyond the boundary of his own garden.

His daughter-in-law, too, seemed to have no wish to go farther. Since the day on which these two momentous events had happened—the interview with Mrs. Crux, and Keith's unexpected letter—a great change had come over poor Charlotte. Not in any tangible shape; she complained of nothing; she went about her daily avocations as usual, and betrayed neither by word nor act any thing that was passing in her mind; but the whole expression of her countenance altered. It grew sad, wistful, wan, and pale; there was a dreary hopelessness, at times even a sort of despair in it; the remorse of the roused conscience; the agony of the blank, lost future; the cruel awakening to a knowledge of happiness that might have been. At least so Mr. Garland read her looks—nor marveled; for he knew that all this must come; he could hardly have wished it not to come.

Every man's sin *will* find him out, and he must pay its penalty in a certain amount of inevitable suffering, from which the utmost pity can not, and should not, save him. Doubtless the Cruxes were very hard when they drew their own not spotless robes round them, and would not so much as look at poor Charlotte; but their stained garments did not make Charlotte clean. And when, as they passed her by, the parson saw her face flush up, then settle into its customary sad patience, however much he grieved for her, still he dared not speak. He could say with his Divine Master, "Go, and sin no more." He could even believe, from the bottom of his thankful heart, "Thy sins are forgiven thee;" but he could not say that the sin was no sin, or that the ultimate result would be the same as if it had never happened. He could not look at that poor little face—so young still; she was only nineteen even now—with all its lines sharpened by mental pain; with its sweet smile darkened, and its sad eyes drooping; no longer able to face the world with the bright, clear gaze of conscious innocence—he could not see all this without acknowledging the just, righteous, inevitable law of God, which can never be broken with impunity.

And what of the other sinner—still closer to the old man's heart—who ought to have borne equally with Charlotte the burden that they had laid upon themselves?

How Keith felt, or how much he suffered, neither his wife nor his father had any means of knowing. The one letter in which the parson had told about the Cruxes, and spoken his mind on many painful things; which had cost him much, for it is hard to write such sad, reproachful letters across the seas, in the long ignorance of how they may reach, and whether happier letters may ever follow them—this letter Keith never received. It went down to the bottom of the Atlantic with a wrecked mail-steamer.

"I must write it over again," said Mr. Garland, when he found out this. But he delayed and delayed, and meantime Keith went farther West on a trapping expedition, and for several weeks it was useless to write, as no letters would find him. And then came one—the restlessness, bitterness, and hopelessness of which grieved his father to the heart.

In it he only referred to his wife so far as to take for granted that his commands had been obeyed; that she was now at school, or busy with her education under a governess. But it was not so. At first Mr. Garland had tried to fulfill his son's wishes; but no lady could be found willing to bury herself at Immeridge except at a salary higher than even Keith's liberal remittances made possible. Besides—and Mr. Garland, when he showed her the letters, felt how bitter they must be to Charlotte—more than one governess made painfully pertinacious and rather suspicious inquiries as to the "curious circumstance" of an adult pupil being a married lady, living apart from her husband. It was one of the sharp inevitables of the position, but not the less hard to bear.

Then Mr. Garland suggested a boarding-school; but here, for the first time in her life, Charlotte evinced a decided will of her own, and offered steady, though not violent resistance. The reason she gave for this was brief and simple, but quite unanswerable.

"I am a married woman now; I could not possibly become a school-girl, or go among school-girls."

It was only too true—true in a deeper sense than she put forward; and her father-in-law acknowledged this. The poor thing could never be a girl any more; the door of girlhood was shut behind her; and for the happy pride, the contented dignity which comes to any one, be she ever so young, when she finds herself a married woman, taken quite out of herself and made to live for another, perhaps for many others, in the sweet self-abnegation of matronhood—alas! this blessedness had not come, and, in one sense, never could come, to poor Charlotte.

Not since the day when she first came to him had Mr. Garland pitied her so intensely, or mourned over her with such a hopeless regret as he did now. And yet he could not do any thing to make her happier or brighter, or take out of her heart the sting that he saw was there, piercing daily deeper and deeper the more as her nature developed. He knew it must be so. She, like himself, like every mortal soul, must be taught to accept and endure the inevitable.

So the days passed on—the long, bright, weary summer days—the heat of which made the parson feel how feeble and old he was growing; too feeble to struggle against the hard present, or to fight his way out of it into a better future; a future not for himself—he had long ceased to think of himself—but for these, his children.

"My working days are done, I think," said he, sadly, one day when he and Charlotte had been busy together in the garden. For he now kept her about him as much as he could, from pure compassion, and to prevent her from falling into those long reveries in which he had sometimes found her, when the dull expression of her eyes, and the heavy, listless drop of her once active hands, made his heart bleed. "Come here, my dear; do help me. I never had so much trouble in training this creeper. I can not lift up my right arm at all."

He spoke almost in a querulous tone, for he felt ill and unlike himself. Charlotte came quickly. The only brightness that ever dawned in her sad face was when she was doing something for Mr. Garland.

"Don't work at all—I'll do it," she said. "Pray, sir, give me the hammer and nails, and be idle a while. Let me fetch you your garden-chair."

This was a rough but comfortably-constructed piece of workmanship, the joint invention of Charlotte and the Immeridge carpenter, in the days when her simple daily occupations had been enough to fill her life, before the bitterness that came with the awakening soul had entered into it. Some of her old cheerfulness returned as she brought the chair and settled the old man tenderly in his favorite seat.

"There, now, I am sure you will be comfortable. What is wrong with your arm, sir? May I rub it? Jane lets me rub her rheumatic shoulder sometimes."

"But this is not pain—it is numbness. I felt it when I woke this morning."

"Perhaps you had been lying upon it, and your arm had gone to sleep, as children call it."

"Perhaps. And yet, if so, it ought to have been quite well by now."

"It will be well presently," was the soothing answer, as Charlotte, now fairly roused out of herself, knelt down beside Mr. Garland and began chafing the delicately-shaped right hand—he had once been conceited about the beauty of his hand, or his wife had been for him. It was still delicate, still unwithered; but the fingers seemed dropping together in a helpless way, and when Charlotte laid it on the chair-arm, it remained there passive and motionless.

The old man shook his head. "It is of no use rubbing, my dear. I can not feel your fingers."

Charlotte redoubled her energies. "Oh, but you must feel them—you will feel them. My rubbing always does Jane good, she says. You are sure to be better by-and-by."

"But suppose," Mr. Garland replied, after a long pause and in a low tone, which had a certain concealed dread beneath its quietness, "suppose, Charlotte, that this should not be rheumatism. There is another complaint which old people have sometimes."

"What is that?"

"It is in our family too," said Mr. Garland, musing. "I know my grandfather died of paralysis."

Charlotte looked up.

"What is that? At least I half know, but not quite. Please tell me."

"It is no pain—don't look so frightened, my poor girl—no pain at all. And it does not kill people—not suddenly. But sometimes it makes them helpless—totally helpless for years before they die. O my God, my God!"—and the old man lost all his courage and groaned aloud—"save me from that! Take me—take me at once! but oh, save me from being a trouble and a burden to any body."

"A trouble? a burden? Oh, Mr. Garland!" And Charlotte seized the poor numb right hand, pressed it to her bosom like a baby, kissed it, fondled it, sobbed over it, and expended on it such a passion of emotion, that the parson's thoughts were turned from his own uneasy apprehensions into watching her, and wondering at the wealth of love that lay buried in that poor heart.

"Do not, my child, do not cry so bitterly. I should

not have said this. I had no idea you cared for me so much."

"I have nobody else to care for—nobody that cares for my caring—in the wide world."

He could not contradict her—he knew she spoke the truth. But he said, what was also the truth, and every day when he saw the depths of sweetness, and patience, and womanly wisdom that sorrow was drawing out of her, and expressing visibly in her face, he himself believed it more and more. "No one but me to care for? It may not be always so, Charlotte. God's mercy is as infinite as our need. Wait and hope."

Whether it was that this sudden and unwonted emotion stirred up the old man's vital forces into strength enough to shake off the impending ill, or whether this had been only a slight forewarning, he certainly grew better under his daughter's care, and for some days was even brighter than ordinary. But it was only a temporary wave of the gradually ebbing tide, which left the sands barer than before.

Very soon there fell upon Mr. Garland's green old age that most trying phase of life's decline—often only a phase, and not necessarily implying life's close, in which the body begins to fail faster than the still youthful and active mind, producing an irritable restlessness most painful both to the sufferer and to the standers-by. The more he needed care, the less he seemed to like being taken care of. He felt it hard to resign one by one his independent ways, and sink into, not an elderly, but a really old man; becoming, as he said, like Saint Peter, who, when he was young, "girded himself," but when old was to have "another to gird him, and lead him in the way he would not." If at this crisis he had been left only to Jane, and had not had about him a younger woman, gentle, sweet-tempered, and gifted naturally with that infinite patience which is, or ought to be, at once the duty and delight of all youth to show to all old age, things would have gone rather hard with Parson Garland.

Perhaps he was aware of this, perhaps not; for the narrowing powers of fading life dim the perceptions of even the best of people; but he was conscious of feeling great comfort in Charlotte. A change, sudden and bright, had come upon her ever since the day that he had told her of his fear of paralysis. She lost her listless, solitary ways, and began to devote herself daily and hourly to him, and him alone. Not that she troubled him with unnecessary watching or too patent anxiety, but she was always at hand when wanted; she never thwarted him; she bore with all his little crotchets, even when, as he acknowledged to himself, they were very unreasonable. And sometimes, in the long, sleepless night that succeeded many a restless day, the old man used to lie thinking, with a wondering gratefulness both to her and toward heaven, of the sweet temper that was never ruffled, the young face that tried so hard to be always pleasant and sunshiny when in his sight, the attentive hands that were ever ready to do enough, and never too much, for the innumerable wants of his selfish, or he thought it selfish, old age.

"God is very good to me, more than I deserve," he ofttimes said in his heart; "and if I wait, surely in His own time He will be good to these my children."

But, although the tie between him and his daughter-in-law grew closer every day, Mr. Garland, with the shrinking delicacy which was a part of his nature, never attempted to lift the veil which Charlotte still persistently drew over the relations between herself and her husband, and her own feelings toward him. The old man would have been ashamed to pry into what she evidently desired to conceal. All his life he had borne his own burdens, troubling no one; he could understand and respect another's doing the same. Charlotte's total reticence and silent endurance touched him deeper than the most pathetic complaints or most unreserved confidence.

So they lived together, these strangely-assorted companions, who yet in their deepest hearts were so curiously assimilated as to become better company to each other every day. Contentedly they spent the life of almost total solitude which circumstances had forced upon them, for the Crux influence had leavened the neighborhood, which indeed, without much malice aforethought on their part, it was sure to do; and those few county families who were in the habit of driving over to Immeridge at intervals, just to acknowledge the existence of, and pay a passing respect to, the Reverend William Garland, gradually ceased their visits to the Parsonage. He had not wanted them when they came, but he noticed their absence, and was sure that Charlotte noticed it too, for she often looked at him in a strange, wistful way, as if she wished to say something to him, and could not. Heaven had punished her, as Heaven does sometimes, not directly, but vicariously. In a heart so full of love as hers (often did the parson recall Keith's almost complaining words, "She is so very fond of me"), that others should suffer through her fault was of all retributions the sharpest, and likely to work out the most lasting result on her character.

It did so presently in a manner unforeseen. Seeing Mr. Garland had no one left him but herself, Charlotte shook off her depression, and learned to be cheerful for his sake. She tried to make herself every thing that pleased him, and his being the sole influence that ever approached her, it was almost omnipotent of its kind. When two people of opposite dispositions are thus thrown constantly together, they either end by absolute dislike and disunion, or they grow into the most touching likeness in unlikeness, which often harmonizes better than absolute similarity.

Ere many months, the parson's daughter-in-law had become to his failing age almost more than a daughter of his own; for, as he said sometimes, his own daughter would certainly have gone away and left him, to marry some strange youth, while his son's wife was safely bound to him forever. And he to her was not only as dear as a natural born father, but was also—what, alas! all fathers in the flesh are not—her ideal of every thing that a man should be. She became to him a perfect slave, as women like to be, though in that happiest bondage where affection is the only forger of the chains. But the title he himself gave her was his "right hand!"

Ere long this became only too true a name.

One day, as he was writing his sermon, Charlotte sitting sewing at the study window, for he was so constantly needing her help in little things that he liked to have her within call, the pen dropped from Mr. Garland's fingers. The same numbness which he had once complained of came on again; his right hand fell helplessly by his side, and he never used it more.

This was not discovered immediately; as before, the affection was at first considered temporary, and all remedies were tried. Simple household remedies only; for Mr. Garland did not feel ill; he suffered no pain; and it was only on Charlotte's earnest entreaty that he allowed medical help to be sent for.

But when this was done, and the doctor looked grave, and said, on being questioned, that it was really "a stroke" —as the country people call it—and that the natural use would in all human probability never return to that poor, nerveless right hand, the blow fell lighter than might have been expected. Most likely because the parson himself bore it so well. Now that his secret dread for months—and he owned now how heavy it had been—had come upon him, the reality seemed less dreadful than the fear. He met his misfortune with a wonderful calmness and fortitude. His irritability ceased; he faced courageously the local bodily infirmity, thanking God that it was only local, and did not affect either his faculties or his speech. He made his arrangements for future helplessness with a touching patience, reminding Charlotte, who hovered about him in pale silence, and Jane, who broke into loud outbursts of lamentation at every word, how the doctor had said that he might yet live to be ninety, and die of some other disease after all.

"And if not," added he, "if the burden that I myself feel heaviest is to be the especial burden that God will have me bear—(you will often find it so in life, Charlotte)—still, I will take it up and bear it. I have received good from His hands all my days, and He will help me in what seems like evil."

"You speak like a saint almost," said Charlotte, softly.

"She was a saint who taught me."

"Some day—if you should ever think I deserve to hear—will you tell me about her?"

It was said so humbly, with such a world of reverence and tenderness in the imploring eyes, that the parson was startled. Never before had he even mentioned to his daughter-in-law this one woman whom he had so adored; a woman and wife like herself, yet who always seemed a being of another creation from poor Charlotte. But now, in the strange changes that time had made, through the mysterious influence by which his memory of the wife he had lost had guided his conduct toward the daughter he had so unexpectedly and regretfully found, Mr. Garland recognized, amid all differences, the common womanhood of these two—Mary and Charlotte Garland. Ay, though one had lived and died white as snow, and the other was smirched with sin; though one was all that was charming in ladyhood, and the other— Well, things had gone hard with poor Charlotte! Still, still, there was in both of them the root and centre of all lovableness in woman —the strong self-abnegation, the divine humility of Love.

"Charlotte," said the parson—and he tried to see her with the eyes with which his Mary would have regarded this girl, her son's wife—eyes searching as a mother's should be, yet withal unfailingly tender, pitiful, generous, and just: "Charlotte, would you really like to hear about your husband's mother—the noblest woman that ever breathed?"

"Should I?" Charlotte's face answered the question.

So, forgetting every thing else, forgetting even that this was the first sad night when he was made fully conscious of his infirmity, and of the fact that it would last during the remainder of his life, Mr. Garland sat down by his study fire, and began talking with his daughter-in-law quietly and cheerfully, and with an open confidence that he had never shown her before. And she listened with all her heart in her eyes, and yet with a touch of sadness, like one who was hearing of a far-off paradise, of which, for her, the door was forever closed—about the days of his youth, studious and solitary; his long but never weary courtship-years; of his one happy twelve-month of married life, and his dear dead wife, Mary Garland.

M

CHAPTER XI.

BY the next Sunday all Immeridge had learned the heavy affliction—as many would have said, till his placid face forbade them to call it so—which had befallen the parson. There was scarcely one of his flock present who did not follow him with compassionate eyes as he walked slowly up the pulpit stairs, his right arm hidden under the sleeve of his gown, and began to turn over the leaves of the prayer-book with his left hand. And when, giving out the hymn, in his nervousness and slight awkwardness he dropped the book, and it narrowly escaped the clerk's head, and was solemnly picked up and handed back to him by the beadle, not even a mischievous child smiled; the congregation were all far more inclined to weep.

After service was over, many hung about the church-yard, as if they wished to see or speak to the parson. But Mr. Garland remained in the vestry for a considerable time, no one being admitted but his daughter-in-law. Then, taking her arm and walking feebly, he was seen to cross the church-yard the accustomed way, and re-enter his garden gate.

If any of his neighbors had ever said a word against him, they were all silent now—silent and sorry. They gathered in knots round the church door and the lane leading to it, every body talking with sympathy and respect of "poor Mr. Garland."

Next morning, to the extreme amazement of the little household, once more the tall footman from the Hall appeared at the Parsonage with a message: kind inquiries after Mr. Garland's health, and begging his acceptance of a basket of hot-house grapes and a brace of partridges.

"What shall we do, Charlotte?" said the parson, who looked pleased: it was not in human nature that he should not be somewhat pleased. "It is unneighborly and unchristian to refuse their peace-offering, and yet I can not bear to take it. I never wish to have any thing more to do with the people at the Hall."

"No," replied Charlotte, with the sad gravity which always came over her when the Cruxes were named—of her own accord she never named them at all.

"What would you like done, my dear? You shall decide."

She thought a minute, and then said, "Send a friendly message back, but do not accept their present. Say the grapes would be welcome to old Molly Carr, or to some other sick person down the village, whom Mrs. Crux used so often to send things to."

"Yes, that will do. You have a wise little head, child," said the parson, affectionately.

He went himself and delivered the message to the servant, making it as kindly and courteous as possible; then he and his daughter-in-law sat together for a good while in silence, he reading and she working, as was their habit after breakfast.

"And now, my dear, let us put aside all unpleasant things, and make ourselves busy — usefully busy, this sunshiny morning. I like the sunshine. Oh, thank God that he has left me the sight of my eyes!" said the parson, sighing. "But come, we'll have no sadness and no complaining; for I might be much worse off. Charlotte, you will have to be really my right hand now. How does your writing progress? it is long since you showed me your copy-book. What if I were to begin and dictate to you my next Sunday's sermon?"

"Only try me, and you will see how I will do it," answered Charlotte, brightly.

"Very well. But first there are all my letters to write. Look how many lie in the box marked 'unanswered.'"

There was an accumulation of four or five, which he turned over uneasily. "Ah! I neglected them, and now it is too late."

"Could not I—"

"No, you couldn't, child," with some slight irritability. "They are business letters; a woman's writing would look odd, especially— Oh, if I had but my son beside me! If Keith would only come home." He once more sighed bitterly, then saw Charlotte's face, and stopped.

"My dear, you must not mind me if I say sharp or foolish things sometimes. I do not mean it. You will bear with an old man, I know."

"Oh, Mr. Garland!"

She came to his side and began caressing, in her own tender way, the powerless hand, which, by an ingenious arrangement of his coat-sleeve, she had tied up so that its helplessness might inconvenience him as little as possible. A slight caress, not much; he was not used to affectionate demonstrations; but these touched him. He put his other hand on her head.

"You are very good to me, Charlotte. I think you must be fond of me—a little."

She laughed—the loving little laugh which supplies all words—and then placed herself beside him, with pen and paper all arranged.

"I am quite ready now, sir. But"—with a slight hesitation—"there is one letter which, perhaps, to make quite sure, had best be written first. Do you remember to-morrow is the Canadian mail?"

"Ah! true, true! Poor Keith! He will never again see his old father's handwriting."

It was a small thing, but one of those small things which, causing us fully to realize any loss, cut very deep sometimes. The parson leaned back in his chair, and the rare tears of old age stole through his shut eyelids.

"Never mind—never mind!" said he at last, drawing his fingers across his eyes. It must be so some time or other. We go on taking care of our children, and fancying no one can do it but ourselves, till God removes them from us, or us from them, as if just to show us that He is sufficient to take care of them. And in this matter—why, Keith will hardly miss my letters. You can so easily put down all I want to say, Charlotte, my dear. So begin at once.

"What shall I write?"

"Let us see. 'My dear Keith.' But that will puzzle him. Put at the top 'Dictated.' No, stop! My dear, why should not you yourself write to your husband?"

"He has never asked me."

That was true, though the omission had grown so familiar that the parson had of late not even remarked it. Since the first few illiterate scrawls, which, with almost an exaggerated dread of their effect on a young man educated and scholarly, Mr. Garland had forwarded, Keith had never asked his wife to write to him, nor—carefully regular as were his messages to her—had he taken the slightest notice of her continued silence. In truth, in this and in all other things, except mere surface matters, he had sheathed himself up in such an armor of reserve, that of the real Keith Garland, the man who now was, they knew absolutely nothing; though they felt—most certainly his father did—that he was a person very different from the boy who went out to Canada two years and a half ago.

"Supposing he has not asked you to write; still, why should you not do it?"

"I can not tell; only I think it would be better not." And Charlotte's firm-set mouth showed that she did not wish to say any more. Nor did her father-in-law attempt to urge her. It was with him both principle and practice that no third hand—not even a parent's—can safely touch, under almost any circumstances, the bond between husband and wife.

"Well," said he, sighing, "do as you think best, Charlotte. And now let me write my letter—that is, dictate it. Put at the top that it is dictated, and then he will understand."

So they sat together a long two hours; for Mr. Garland was restless and awkward, unaccustomed to any pen but his own, and nervously anxious over the wording of the letter. His patient secretary tore up more than one sheet to please him, and began again; he seemed so fearful of saying either too much or too little.

"You see, my dear, I wish to be careful. If we alarm Keith too much about me, he may come home at once, and I would not have him do that against his will, or to the injury of his future prospects. Yet if we left him quite in ignorance, and any thing did happen to me—"

Charlotte looked up alarmed. "But the doctor said—"

"He said what was quite true, that I may live ten years and never have another attack. But if one did come—there was no need to tell me this, for I knew it—things might prove very serious."

"What would happen? How would the stroke affect you? Do not be afraid to tell me all you know."

Charlotte spoke with composure, fixing her eyes steadily on the old man's face as she did so, though she had turned very pale.

"I will tell you, my dear, for you are not a coward, and it is right you should know; it is right I should have somebody about me who does know. If I were to have another 'stroke,' as people call it, I might lose my speech, the use of my limbs, my mind even. Oh Charlotte," as with a touching appeal he took hold of her hand, "it is great weakness in me—great want of faith and trust; but sometimes I feel frightened at the future, and I wish my dear boy would come home."

"What hinders his coming home? Is it—is it me?"

The old man was sorely perplexed. It was one of

those questions so hard plainly to answer, so impossible wholly to deny. He met it as alone this good man could meet any thing—by the plain truth.

"Yes, my child," he said, keeping her hand, and speaking tenderly, for he felt so exceedingly sorry for her, "it may be, in some degree, on account of you. This is the penalty that people must pay who make hasty or ill-assorted marriages, or, indeed, do any thing that is wrong; they must go through a certain term of probation, and bear a certain amount of suffering. You have suffered, my poor Charlotte?"

"Oh, I have—I have!"

"And, I doubt not, so has Keith. He may dread coming home, and finding you only what he left you, which was very different from himself, and equally different from what you now are. Still, not knowing this, he may shrink—most men do—after the first impulse of passion is over, from spending his whole life with a woman who was not his deliberate choice."

"Yes, I understand."

"Ah! my dear, I did not mean to hurt you. It was as hard for you as it was for him. We may learn from our mistakes, and make the best of them, and they may come right in time; but we must suffer for them. Marriage is an awful thing, and its very irrevocableness—the 'till death us do part,' which to some is the dearest comfort, to others becomes the most galling bondage."

The parson had gone on speaking, more in his moralizing, absent way than with any special reference to her, but his words struck home.

Charlotte drew her hands softly away from him, and

folded them together with a determination desperate in its very gentleness.

"Mr. Garland, will you tell me one thing? Can married people be parted—legally—except by death?"

"It ought not to be, my dear, but I believe it is done sometimes. I have heard of a Court in London where people can get separated from one another so as even to be free to marry again. But we old-fashioned people do not like such divorces. We will not speak about them, Charlotte. We were speaking about you and your husband. He may dislike the thought of coming home now; but if he once came, I hope, I feel sure, things would be quite different. Still, let us neither compel him nor urge him—it is best not. Forgive me if, just for my own selfish sake, I can't help wishing my boy would come home."

"He will come home. Do not be uneasy; he is sure to come home."

And then, recurring to the letter, Charlotte kept the old man's wandering attention fixed upon it till it was finished. Afterward she said, to her father-in-law's great but carefully concealed surprise,

"And now, if you could spare me for an hour, I should like to go and write myself to my husband."

"That is well—that is excellent," cried Mr. Garland, much delighted. "Do write to him—as long a letter as ever you can. He will be very glad of it."

"Will he?"

"Only, Charlotte, please, tell him no more about me than we have said already. You will promise that? You comprehend my reasons?"

"Yes," said Charlotte, as she rose, slowly and dreamily, and gathered up the ink and paper.

"But why go away? Why not write here? I would not interrupt you; and my good little scholar writes so well now that I have not the slightest intention of looking over or correcting her letters—never again, I assure you."

"Oh no!" and Charlotte smiled, not one of her old childish smiles, but the exceedingly sad one which had come in their stead. "But, indeed, I had rather be alone. I am very stupid, you know, sir. You forget, it is not easy for me to write a letter, and it ought to be a pretty letter—ought it not? when it is written to my husband?"

"Certainly — certainly. Off with you, and do your very best. Ah! my dear, you'll be such a clever girl by the time your husband comes home!"

Charlotte smiled again, but this time the smile was not merely sad—it was broken-hearted.

After she was gone, Mr. Garland sat in anxious meditation—at least, as anxious as his failing age, upon which all cares now began to fall slightly deadened, allowed him to feel. Much he regretted that with the weak putting off of a painful thing, which was the peculiarity of his character, he had so long delayed rewriting that missing epistle about the Cruxes and Charlotte. How could it be done now? Never, at first he feared; for it was impossible Keith's wife could write it, and no other hand could he use to indite so private a letter.

"If I could but do it myself. I have heard of people who learned to write with their left hand," thought the parson; and, taking up a pen, he began to try — a proceeding which needs trying in order to discover how very difficult it is. Discomfited entirely by pen and ink, he attempted a lead-pencil, and with much effort, and many an ache of the feeble old hand and wrist, succeeded, after an hour's hard practice, in legibly signing his name. Then, quite worn out, he stretched himself in his arm-chair and wished for Charlotte.

"What a long time she has been away—far more than an hour!" And then he smiled, with an amused wonder, to think how much he missed her.

"If I find her so necessary, surely her husband will, when he has learned all her usefulness, all her goodness. Oh yes, it will be all right by-and-by, when Keith comes home."

And so it was with a cheerful countenance that he met his daughter, showed her how he had been amusing himself in her absence, and exacted her approbation of his left-handed performances.

"I am so clever I shall be able to write with my own hand next mail, I think. But we will not tell Keith now. We will just give him a surprise."

And the idea of this, and the relief to his mind that it brought, pleased Mr. Garland so much, that he went on talking quite gayly all the time Charlotte was inclosing, addressing, and sealing her letter, which she made no attempt to offer for his perusal. Nor did he desire it.

He never noticed, also, that all the time she scarcely spoke; and that, after she had given Jane the letter to post—Canadian letters were not trusted to any body but themselves or Jane—she came and knelt beside him, ostensibly to warm her hands at the fire. She was shaking like a person in an ague.

"How very cold you are! How could you stay up so long in that chilly room, you foolish girl! you never think of yourself at all."

"Oh no. It isn't worth while."

Mr. Garland regarded her uneasily as she crouched on the rug, her face to the fire-light, which seemed to cheer her no more than the moon upon a snow-field. But he thought of his letter, which he would certainly be able to write by next mail—ay, he would, if he accomplished it at the rate of a line a day, and became comforted concerning Charlotte.

After the mail had gone, the parson's mind was so relieved that his bodily health began to recruit itself a little. His helpless hand was at least no worse, and he began to get accustomed to the loss of it, and to do without it, awkwardly and drearily at first, but soon very uncomplainingly. The trouble it gave him to do the most ordinary things, and the time they took in doing, occupied the hours, and prevented his feeling so bitterly the lack of his daily writing. He dictated to Charlotte whatever was absolutely necessary, and he set himself to work, with the diligence of a shool-boy, to learn to write with his left hand. In short, Providence was tempering the wind to him, poor old man! in many ways, so as to make him slip easily and painlessly into that world where he would awake and be young again; or be—whatsoever God would have him to be, in the unknown country, where he had but two desires, to find Him and his wife Mary.

Still, he had much enjoyment of his present existence. It happened to be an especially lovely spring, and he and his daughter-in-law spent hours daily in wandering about the cliffs and downs, looking at the sunshiny sea which was settling itself down in peace after its winter storms, or else penetrating inland, and hunting for wild-flowers in those woody nooks which make this part of the country, so near the coast, a perfect treasure-house for all who love nature. And he tried, not vainly, to put into Charlotte that simple but intense delight which he himself took in all natural things, thereby giving her an education, both of mind and heart, which is worth much book-learning, especially to a woman.

Their walks were made pleasanter by the lifting off of the Crux incubus. With the extraordinary infatuation of the "fashionable" world, this gay metropolitan family had discovered that living any where out of London in spring-time was absolutely unendurable. So they migrated back to their old haunts, leaving the Hall, for the time being, deserted, and the roads about Immeridge safe and free. They had never again called at the Parsonage, but they had sent at least twice a week to inquire for Mr. Garland; and once, in passing him and Charlotte, they driving in their handsomest barouche down a hilly road where to stop and speak was conveniently impossible, Mrs. Crux had bowed, whether to one or both remained questionable, but it was a most undoubted and condescending bow.

"Our friends certainly mean to take us up again, by slow degrees," said the parson, a little amused. He had returned the salutation distantly, but courteously, as a parson should, whose duty, more even than most men, is to live in charity with all; but he did not wish to have his motives or intentions mistaken. "I have no desire," he continued, "to have any intimacy with the Cruxes. You will find, Charlotte, throughout life, which is not long enough for any needless pain, that 'marry in haste and repent at leisure' is as true of friendship as it is of love. We should be quite sure our friends suit us before we join hands, otherwise they either cumber us or drop from us, like ill-fitting clothes, or they cling to us and destroy us, like the poisoned shirt of Dejanira—did you ever hear of Dejanira?"

And then he told her the story—as he did many another story, out of his endless learning—partly to amuse himself, and partly from the feeling that every sort of knowledge might one day be valuable to her.

"But to return to the Cruxes," continued he; "I do not regret their civilities, though more than civility is neither possible nor desirable. Still, if they are polite, we will be polite too, if only on Keith's account. It is bad for a man not to be on good terms with his neighbors."

And then the parson began to talk—as he never could help talking—more and more every day, of the chances pro and con of Keith's return, and what would happen when he did return; whether he would go out again to Canada, or whether, since he had been so successful, and shown such remarkable capabilities for success in farming, he would not turn his attention to it in England, and perhaps settle near Immeridge, to the infinite comfort of his father's declining days.

"And, if he has a real pleasant home—if his wife makes it as pleasant as she has made mine—why then—"

He turned and saw Charlotte's face—it was deathly white.

"Please don't!" she gasped. "Oh, please don't, Mr. Garland."

He said no more, for he saw she could not bear it; but he thought with deep thankfulness how devotedly Keith's poor little wife must love him still.

And the love might be not unneeded. For several times, when in his weary want of something to do, he had amused himself by re-reading, in regular succession, his son's letters, Mr. Garland was struck by an undefined and yet clearly perceptible change in them. There seemed a harshness, a hardness growing over Keith, mingled with a reckless indifference, a complete avoidance of all reference to the future, which, the more he pondered it over, the more alarmed his father. But there was nothing to be done—nothing but to write that letter, which he penned painfully, a few lines every day, telling his son the whole history of himself and Charlotte; how he had grown week by week, and month by month, to pity her, to like her, to esteem her, to love her.

Yes, he did really love her. He had long suspected this, now he felt sure of it. Into the lonely, self-contained, but infinitely tender heart, where no woman, save one, had ever dwelt, crept this new relationship, full of all the delicacy and chivalry which such a man was sure to have toward any woman, by whatever tie connected with him, uniting at once the grave protection of fatherhood with the clinging dependence that his now feeble age made natural to him. Ay, in this strange and mysteriously bitter way, the last way he had ever contemplated or expected, the parson had found his "daughter" —found her simply by doing a father's duty, in the inevitable circumstances under which he had been called upon to act.

He felt great peace as he sat in his garden-chair with Charlotte busy near him, or sitting sewing at his side. She was one of those women who, without any obnoxiously demonstrative industry, are never seen idle. Day by day he admired her more and more, and was convinced that Keith would do the same, until the true tender love, ay, and reverence, which every husband should bear to his wife, would surely come. He felt so certain that all would be right soon, very soon—perhaps even during his lifetime. He spent hours in planning out and dreaming over the future; and so absorbed was he in these fancies and speculations, that he forgot to take much present notice of Charlotte.

When Jane suggested, as she did once, that Mrs. Keith Garland was looking excessively thin and worn, he still scarcely heeded it, or set it down to the hot weather, or to a natural suspense concerning her husband's return; but, as she never opened the subject of her own accord, he did not like to question her; and she, being always so very unobtrusive and uncommunicative regarding herself and her feelings, doing all her duties, and especially those which concerned Mr. Garland, with the most affectionate and sedulous care, he did not discover, as perhaps indeed only a woman would, that this poor woman, so young still, went about like a person stunned—who does every thing in a sort of dream, waiting with terror for the moment of awakening.

Only once or twice, when unable to resist talking of his hopes, and longing for some confirmation of them from another's heart than his own, Mr. Garland asked her seriously what she thought of the probabilities of Keith's return, Charlotte answered decidedly,

"Oh yes, he will come—be quite sure your son will come home."

And, in the delight of this expectation, the old man forgot to notice that she said, as she always did now, "your son," never "my husband."

CHAPTER XII.

THE following mail brought Keith's never-failing letter, written, of course, in ignorance of the sad tidings now speeding to him across the seas. Nor would they probably reach him in time to be answered by the return mail, for he spoke of an intended business journey down South, which would occupy the few days between the receiving and answering of letters; so he prepared his father for having none at all this time.

"The first time he will ever have missed writing," said the parson, trying to shake off a certain dreary feeling which Keith's letter left behind—the letter, written with that unconsciousness of all that was happening at home, and read, unknowing what might have happened to the writer since, two things which throw such an indefinite but unsurmountable sadness over even the cheeriest and pleasantest "foreign correspondence."

This was not an especially cheerful letter as to its tone, though its contents were good news. Keith explained to his father, who tried to explain to Charlotte—and the old man and the girl were about equally obtuse in comprehending it—some business transaction by which he hoped to realize a considerable sum. "Perhaps I may turn out a rich man yet," wrote he, with a slight tone of triumph. "I have certainly done very well so far; in a worldly point of view, that forced march to Canada was the best thing that ever happened to me. Besides, I like the climate; I have no dislike to the country; in truth, nothing should induce me to leave it. I would not care ever to see Old England again, if coming over (he did not say "coming home") were not my only means of getting a sight of my dear old father."

Always his father, never his wife. Charlotte listened—a little paler, a little stiller than before, if that were possible—but she neither questioned nor complained of any thing. Once only, as she was hanging over her father-in-law's chair, arranging his cushions for his afternoon nap, he talking the while of Keith—for, indeed, the subject never failed him—she said gently, when he asked what she thought about the matter,

"Oh yes, your son will come home. Make yourself quite easy; he is sure to come home—not immediately, perhaps, but by-and-by."

The old man looked up with a touching eagerness. "Do you really think so, Charlotte? Before winter?"

"Yes, before winter," said Charlotte, as she turned away.

The following mail brought no letter, for which, however, they were prepared. Nevertheless, the blank seemed to make the parson rather restless for some hours, till he consoled himself by reflecting that the journey down South, while it hindered Keith's receiving his letters, saved him temporarily from the pain of the news they brought, and lessened by a few days his suspense till the next mail came in. And that next mail would bring him the all-important letter, so long delayed, but which the father had duly finished, left-handed, accomplishing it line by line, with a tender persistency, in spite of all sorts of remonstrances from Charlotte, who would not see why he should be so earnest about it.

"Suppose it should never reach him," said she, when, in compliance with Mr. Garland's desire, she inclosed and forwarded it, declining to write herself this time. "Suppose," and she watched her father-in-law stealthily but eagerly, "suppose he should even now be on his way home?"

"Oh no, that is quite impossible," replied the parson, sighing. How impossible he did not like to say; for, judging his son by himself, by most men, he felt that nothing except the strongest sense of duty could conquer the repugnance a man would feel to coming home under Keith's circumstances—to a wife whom he neither respected nor loved, but only pitied. But that momentous letter would set every thing right. He had written it with the utmost tact and tenderness of which he was capable, placing every thing before his son in the plainest light, and yet doing it delicately, as should be done by the father of a grown-up son, who has no longer any right to interfere in that son's affairs farther than to suggest and advise. Yes, this letter would surely make all right. So he had sent it off in spite of Charlotte, and with an amused resistance to her arguments, and his heart followed it with prayers.

Thus, after the first few hours, he ceased to be disappointed at the absence of Keith's letter, and after waiting another half day, and hearing accidentally that other American letters had come all safe—the housekeper at Cruxham Hall had also a son in Canada—the parson and his daughter settled their minds calmly to wait on until the next mail.

It was a bright summer morning, and Mr. Garland sat enjoying it in his garden—alone, too, a thing which rarely happened. But, fancying he saw a certain restlessness and trouble in Charlotte's look, he had made occupation for her by sending her away on a long expedition, to visit a sick person at the other end of the parish.

For, since his increasing feebleness, this duty also—so natural under most circumstances to a parson's daughter—visiting the sick, had gradually slipped into Charlotte's hands. He hardly knew how it had come about, whether it was his suggestion or her own that she should undertake it, but she had undertaken it, and she fulfilled it well. Nor had there come any of the difficulties which he had once anticipated; for the whole parish was so anxious about him, and so touched with tenderness concerning him, that they would have received gladly and gratefully any body who came from the parson. The ice once broken by mutual sympathy, Charlotte—the new Charlotte, who was so strangely different from Lotty Dean—slowly made her way into the folks' hearts, especially by the exceeding kindness which she showed toward old people and children. Soon, though she said nothing about it herself, others said—and it reached the parson's ears with a strange thrill, half pleasure, half pain—that Immeridge parish had never been so well looked after since the days of the first Mrs. Garland.

Mr. Garland watched his son's wife as she walked across the garden with her basket in hand, stepping lightly, in her brown Holland morning-dress and jacket, and simple straw hat, under which her abundant hair no longer curled; the parson, with his classic taste, had made her twist it smoothly up, in Greek grace and matronly decorousness, round the well-shaped head. She was a pretty sight; to one who loved physical beauty, a perpetual daily pleasure; but he hardly knew whether it made him most sad or most glad to see—and he had seen it especially this morning—in her face that without which all faces, and all characters, are imperfect, the beauty of suffering.

The old man's gaze followed her with great tenderness, and when she was out of sight he involuntarily took out his watch, to reckon how many hours she was likely to be away from him. If any one had told him this two years and a half ago—if he could have believed that this brief time would have made so great a change, not only in his feelings toward her, but in herself! And yet, at her impressionable time of life, it was not impossible; least of all, considering the many strong influences at work within her and around her, not the least of which, though he was the last person to suspect it, was Mr. Garland's own.

Still he acknowledged to himself that, whatever she had been, she was a sweet, good woman now; that he dearly loved her, and had rational grounds for loving her, all of which her husband might find out soon.

"And it is a melancholy fact," thought the parson, smiling to himself; "but if that boy comes back and falls in love with his wife over again, and wants to carry her away with him, as of course he must, I wonder what in the wide world I shall do without Charlotte!"

But he left that, as he had long since learned to leave all difficulties that concerned his own lot, and tried to leave those that concerned others, in wiser hands than his own, and occupied himself, as old age will when its decline is sweet and calm, unselfish and pure, in the trivial pleasures about him—trivial, and yet not so, for they all came to him like messages from the Giver of every good thing—the sunshine and soft airs, the scent of the flowers, the humming of bees and flutterings of white butterflies, and, above all, the songs of innumerable birds, so tame that they came hopping and picking up food almost at the parson's feet. He loved them all, he enjoyed them all, as he felt he should do to the very last. In spite of sorrow he had had a happy life, and he trusted in God to give him a happy and a peaceful death; blessed it was sure to be, since it took him home to Mary.

And so, in this sleepy warmth of sunshine, and lulled by the buzz of insects and the incessant warble of birds, the old man's senses became confused, his head dropped upon his bosom, and he fell into a sound slumber. In his sleep he had a curious dream, which he did not fully recall till some hours after his waking; but when he did, it made upon him the impression of being less a dream than a vision, so clear and distinct was it—so like reality.

He thought he was sitting exactly where he did sit, and in his own garden-chair, thinking much the same thoughts, and conscious of much the same things around him as really was the case that morning, when, suddenly, and as naturally and as little to his surprise as if he had seen her but yesterday, his wife, Mary, crossed the lawn toward him. He noticed her very dress, which was white —one of her favorite spotted muslin gowns, such as were still laid up in lavender in the old chest of drawers; and her own garden basket was in her hand, full of flowers. She came and stood right in front of him, gazing at him steadily with those pure, limpid, candid eyes of hers —eyes which looked as young as ever, though he had grown quite old. But he never considered that, nor any thing else, except the mere delight of seeing her. He forgot even Keith, for she looked exactly as she used to do before Keith was born or thought of—before her days of weakness and weariness came upon her—until she said, in a soft, tender voice, "William, where is my son?"

After that the dream fell into confusion. He had a troubled sense of seeking every where for Keith, and not being able to find him; of seeing him by glimpses at different ages and in various well-remembered forms, till at last there came a great fellow, with heavy footsteps and a bearded face, whom his father could scarcely recognize; but Mary did at once, and welcomed smiling. And then again her husband saw her standing still on the Parsonage lawn, but not alone—surrounded by a little troop of children, in whose faces he beheld, mysteriously reproduced, both her face and his own. "Oh yes," she said, as if in answer to his dumb questionings, for he struggled vainly to speak, "yes, all these are mine. I never saw them, never had them in my arms, but I did not die childless—and all these are my children!" When Mr. Garland stretched out his arms to clasp her and them, the dream melted away, and it was no longer that bright picture of Mary and the little ones, but his son Keith standing gloomy and alone, and looking as sad as he had done that hazy winter morning at Euston Square terminus, when the father's heart had felt well-nigh broken, and it seemed as if the hopes of both their lives were forever gone.

"Keith! Keith!" he cried, trying to burst through the dumbness of the dream, and speak to his son. With the effort he woke, and recognized where he was—alone in the sunshiny garden. He called Jane, who in Charlotte's rare absences never kept far out of reach, but she was some time in coming to him.

"Jane," said the parson, rubbing his eyes, "I must have been asleep very long. Is she come back yet—my daughter, I mean?"

"No, sir; but—but—"

Jane's voice was abrupt and husky, and she kept glancing at the open front door.

"Won't you come in, sir? I've got a piece of good news for you. You'll take it quietly, though, I knows you will, for it's a bit of very good news." Nevertheless, Jane sobbed a little.

The parson turned round slowly, calmly, with the preternatural instinct of what has happened, or is about to happen, which sick people sometimes show.

"Jane," he said, looking her full in the face, "I know what it is. My son is come home!"

* * * * * *

Keith and his father sat together under the veranda. The first half hour of their meeting had passed safely over, and they had settled down side by side, talking of ordinary things with a quietness and self-restraint which both purposely maintained as much as possible. But there was no fear. People seldom die of joy—as seldom, thank God! of sorrow.

Already Mr. Garland was listening, cheerfully and naturally, as though his son had been at home a long time, to Keith's account—given briefly and succinctly—of how, on receiving his letters, he found he had still two days' time to catch the return mail and come home; how some accidental delays had prevented his starting for Immeridge till the night before; how he had left his luggage at the nearest station, and walked ten miles across the country to the Parsonage gate, where, looking in, he saw his father asleep, and would not disturb him till he waked of his own accord.

He did not tell, nor did Jane, till long after, how Keith had appeared before her in her kitchen, looking "like a ghost from the grave," and "took on terrible bad;" till, finding things less dreadful than he had at first supposed, he suffered himself to be comforted, and soothed, and fed by the good old woman, who three-and-twenty years ago had dressed him in his first clothes, and loved him ever since, with a patience that he had often tried, but never came to the end of; for Keith, faulty as he was, had the art of making people fond of him. Perhaps because of another simple art—he also could love most deeply and faithfully, as was plain to be seen in every feature of the brown, rough face, whenever he looked at his old father.

Yes, they were very happy, no doubt of that. Was it a punishment—poor girl! it was her last—that in the first moments of their reunion both father and son entirely forgot Charlotte? It was not till the church clock struck twelve, and she was to be home to dinner at one, that the parson, with a sting of compunction, remembered his son's wife, after whom his son had never once inquired.

"My boy," said he, "some one besides myself will be very glad you are come home."

"You mean my wife," replied Keith, with a sudden hardening both of countenance and manner.

"You do not ask after her, so I conclude Jane has already told you all about her."

"Jane said she was well."

"And nothing more?"

"Nothing more. Was there any thing to be told?"

The question was put with a sudden suspiciousness, but alas! not with the quick anxiety of love. And on receiving his father's negative, Keith relapsed into his former gravity of behavior, intimating a determination to bear his lot like a man, however hard it might be, but at the same time resolved to say, and to be said to, as little about it as possible.

This, and several other slight but significant indications of character which had cropped out even in the first half hour, convinced Mr. Garland of the great change that circumstances had brought about even in so young a man. He felt, too, what parents are often fatally slow to see, that without any lessening, perhaps even with deepening affection, there had, in the natural course of things, grown up between them, father and son as they were, the reserve inevitable between man and man, however closely allied; so much so, that, in his own shrinking delicacy, the parson found it difficult to open the subject nearest to his heart.

"Keith," said he, at last, "I do not want to meddle in your affairs; you are of an age to judge and act for yourself now. Still, your father can never cease thinking about you. And before she comes in, which she will presently, for she is always very punctual, may I speak to you a few words about your wife?"

"Certainly, father."

Yet the few words would not come. It was, after all, the son—the less sensitive and most demonstrative nature of the two—who first broke the painful silence.

"Father," said Keith, turning his head away, and taking up the old man's stick to make little holes in the gravel-walk while he spoke, "I had best make a clean breast of it to you, and at once. I know now that my marriage was a terrible mistake—a mistake, the consequence of—no, the just punishment of— Oh, father, father! heavily I sinned, and heavily have I been punished!"

While speaking he turned white, even through his tanned cheeks. Whatever the punishment was to which he referred, or whatever special form his remorse had taken, unquestionably both had been sharp and sore.

The parson did not attempt inquiries or consolations, still less reproofs. He only laid his hand on his son's shoulder, saying, "My poor boy!"

"Yes," Keith repeated, "I have been punished. Not in outward things; I have had plenty of external prosperity. I have often thought of two lines of poetry I used to say at school, about

"'Satan now is wiser than of yore,
And tempts by making rich, not making poor.'

That was the way he tried it with me—eh, father? And he very nearly had me—but not quite."

"You have been successful, then, as regards money. You ought to be thankful for that," said the father, gravely.

"Oh, of course, very thankful. Never was there such a run of good fortune. It got to be quite a proverb, 'As lucky as Garland!' Why, I have made enough to start afresh in England—to set up a pleasant little home of my own, to which I might bring some sweet, charming English girl—English *lady*," with a sarcastic accent on the word—"a fit companion for me, a fit daughter for you—such a woman, in short, as my mother was. Oh, father!" and Keith dropped his head with something very like a groan, "it is a fatal thing for a man if, when he chooses a wife, he can not, or dare not, measure her by what he remembers of his mother."

The parson was silent. He knew his son spoke the truth, none the less true because Heaven had mercifully made things lighter to him than he deserved. And though henceforward his burden would be lifted off, still what it had been the father could imagine, though even he might never thoroughly know. Still, as he looked on his boy's face, he saw written on it many a line that was not there before, and was certain that these years—the most critical years of a young man's life, had not passed without leaving their mark—that bitter, searing brand upon him—possibly forever.

Neither then nor afterward did Keith make to his father any special revelations of the manner in which he had been "punished," whether by conscience-stings alone, and that vague, dark dread of the future which he was sure to feel, or by meeting, as many an honest-meaning and yet most miserable man has met, and been man enough to fly from, conscious that her very goodness and sweetness is to him as poisonous as the hot breath from the open pit of hell, some ideal woman who is, alas! *not* the woman he has married. Such things do happen, and if this or any thing like it had happened to Keith Garland, even though the temptation was conquered and the struggle past, his torment must have been sharp enough to teach him lessons such as his old father had not learnt—nor ever needed to learn—in all his seventy years.

Still, something of this Mr. Garland dimly divined, and regarded his son with the sort of awe which parents feel when they see that their dealings are not the only dealings with their children; that for each successive generation, and each individual of it, Providence has a separate education of its own. There was a kind of respect, as well as tenderness, in the old man's voice as he took his boy's hand, saying gently,

"Yes, Keith, you speak truly; I can not deny it. It would have been far happier for us all if your wife had been more like your mother."

There was a long, long silence—a silence due in one man to the memory of what was lost, in the other to the thought of what might have been. It was scarcely unnatural; in one sense it was even right; for it is not our merit, but God's mercy, which creates peace out of pain, and oftentimes changes resignation into actual happiness, till we count among our best blessings the things which once were our sharpest woes.

"My son," said the parson at length, "we will now set the past forever behind us, and look forward to your future. Therein I see many reasons not to grieve, but to rejoice."

"Rejoice! over a man who comes home to a wife that writes him such a letter as this?" and Keith took out of his pocket-book the small note which Mr. Garland had seen Charlotte inclose with his own dictated letter, two mails back.

"What does she say? I did not read it."

"Of course not. She had doubtless her own reasons for keeping it back from you. Now, father, do not look alarmed. I shall not act rashly; I am not going to take her at her word; indeed, I could not do it if I wished. No, I'll not be hard to her. I took my burden on myself, and I'll bear it like a man; but, just read the letter."

And he again applied himself, in angry agitation, to destroying the garden-walk, while his father read, slowly and with difficulty, for it was ill written, and startled him painfully at first, the poor little scrap which Charlotte had penned to her husband.

"Dear husband" (and then "husband" was crossed out and "Dear sir" put instead)—"If I may make bold to say it, you ought to come home to your father. He is breaking his heart for you, and nothing will ever comfort him but the sight of you. Please come at once.

"I take this opportunity of saying what I ought to

have said a good while ago, that ours having been such an unsuitable and unfortunate marriage, I will not be a trouble and a burden to you any more, but as soon as you come to the Parsonage I will leave it. Also since—as your father tells me—there is a place in London where people unhappily married can get rid of one another, so as to be free to marry again; if you wish to get rid of me, so as to be able to marry somebody else more suitable for you, do it; I shall not object. I would never have let you marry me had I seen things as I do now, or had I ever known your father. I remain your obedient wife,

"CHARLOTTE GARLAND."

"Poor little soul!" said Mr. Garland, tenderly, as he finished the letter.

"Then you did not know any thing about this?"

"Certainly not. She hid it all from me—the only thing she ever has hid, I think, since she came to live with me. How she must have suffered before she could have written such a letter—poor, patient, loving little soul!"

"Loving?"

"Yes. Don't you see—but how could you?—that this is just the sort of thing she would do? She loves you so well that she will not even let you see her love, lest it should seem to be an additional claim on you."

"But she wants to get free from me."

The parson smiled. "She wants to set *you* free, which is quite a different thing. She thinks of nobody but you—or perhaps of me a little, sometimes. She is the most unselfish woman I ever knew—except one. And to think that she had hidden this secret in her heart all these weeks, and kept telling me you were sure to come home, when she expected to lose you as soon as ever you came—lose you that I might gain you! My poor little daughter!"

Keith looked amazed.

"Yes, she is my daughter; she has become such to me, and such she will always remain. Keith," added the old man, solemnly, "however you may act toward your wife, I know how I shall act toward my daughter."

"What do you mean, father?"

"I mean that though I took her into my house out of pure duty, she has grown to be the greatest blessing in it, and she shall never leave it unless she leaves it for yours. Will you hear how things came about?"

Then Mr. Garland began and told his son, from beginning to end, what he had written in the letters which Keith never received—the history of himself and Charlotte. Just the bare history; not dwelling, as indeed he was not likely to dwell, for in his great humility he scarcely saw it himself, on the one fact, the root of all, that it had been this simple doing of a parent's duty under sharpest pain which brought about the whole.

Still, whether he saw it or not, his son saw it clear and plain, and recognized, with an emotion that almost overwhelmed him then, but which afterward taught him a lesson which he in his turn acted out to his children, that not only had his sin been covered and healed, but the best gift of his existence had been brought to him by his father's hand.

The parson's story was hardly concluded, and the silence with which his son listened to it throughout had not been broken by a single word, when they heard from behind the syringa bushes the click of the garden gate.

Keith sprang up, violently agitated. So was Mr. Garland; for it seemed as if the happiness or misery, for life, of these his children, trembled in the balance, and hung on the chance of the next few minutes. He could not speak a word—he only prayed.

"Father, is that my wife?"

"Yes."

Both father and son held their breaths while unconscious Charlotte walked up the garden-path to the elm-tree under which the parson usually sat, and missing him there, came slowly on toward the house. Her step was weary—she had walked a good many miles, and her downcast face was very pale and sad; still, in spite of this, nothing fairer, nothing sweeter, nothing more truly womanly could a young man's eyes find to rest on than Charlotte Garland.

Either the creepers of the veranda hid the two figures more completely than they were aware, or else Charlotte was so absorbed in thought as to take little notice of outward things, for she came quite close to them before she perceived her father and her husband.

When she did, her recognition was instantaneous. But even then—like herself, poor girl!—she had self-control enough to make no "scene," to startle nobody and trouble nobody. She neither fainted nor screamed, but stood there, deadly pale, and steadying herself by the pillars of the veranda—still, she stood quiet, gazing at them, attempting neither to move nor speak.

"Charlotte," Mr. Garland said, touching her dress to draw her nearer to him, at which her eyes turned to his happy face—the old man who had found his son again—and she feebly smiled. "You see, my dear, you were right after all. He has come home."

"Lotty," said Keith, speaking in a low, almost in a humble tone, as he rose from his seat and came over to her side, "Lotty, dear, haven't you a word for your husband?"

She looked up—looked in his face—first, as if she could hardly believe that it was himself; then with a piteous inquiry, as though trying to read in his countenance her sentence of life or death.

"Lotty, forgive me; I am your husband."

He opened his arms wide and took her into them, and she sobbed her heart out upon his breast.

* * * * * *

Keith fell in love with his wife all over again, as his father had foreseen, and in the true, and rational, and righteous way; not suddenly—which was, indeed, hardly to be expected—but with the steady, progressive affection which is built up day by day in the heart of a man who continually finds in the woman to whom he has bound himself for life something fresh to love, something more worthy of his loving. For love never stands still; it must inevitably be either growing or decaying—especially the love of marriage.

As to Charlotte's love for her husband, it scarcely needs to be spoken of. It was of that kind which, put into the heart of almost any woman, is a blessing and a safeguard to herself all her lifetime, and, abiding in the heart of a good woman, constitutes the strength, the hope, often the very salvation of two lives.

Of her sin—of both their sin—what shall we say—what dare we say? except that He may have forgiven it, as He did to one who "loved much."

Enough of these. And of the old man—the good father—whose days were nearly done?

Mr. Garland lingered on, in a serene old age, for fully ten years more. He lived to see about him, as he had seen in his dream, wonderful new faces, wherein he caught strange glimpses of other faces old and dear; likenesses such as grandfathers and grandmothers delight to trace, in which the vanished generation seems revived again. One of Keith's children—the first—was, as not seldom happens, both in features and character, so exact a reproduction of her father's mother, that even as a little baby the parson would hold her on his lap for hours, almost believing he was young again, and that she was his own "little daughter" who never came. But the grandchild did come, and she grew to be the very darling of the parson's heart. Of course she was called Mary.

When at last, after the brief two days' illness—which was the only suffering sent to take him home—Mr. Garland lay, conscious and content, in full possession of all his faculties, and knowing his time was come—lay with his white head resting on his long solitary pillow, those about him thought that his last word, like his last smile, was meant for this little granddaughter.

But Charlotte, matron and mother, who had yet found leisure from her many duties to be the parson's daughter still, and who stood silently behind him, fulfilling to the end all those tender offices which, during his latter years, had smoothed down every care, and kept every trouble away from him—Charlotte knew better.

"Stand aside, Mary," she whispered softly to her little girl, "he is thinking of dear grandmamma."

That evening the blind was drawn down at Mr. Garland's bedroom window. No one sat there now; no one looked out in the twilight upon the church and churchyard, keeping watch as it were—as he had kept watch for more than thirty years.

By the next Sunday there was a new face in the pulpit of Immeridge Church, and a new voice—which, though it was a stranger's, often faltered with emotion—preached the funeral sermon; eulogizing, as funeral sermons do, that long, yet outwardly uneventful life, the real beauty of which was known only to God.

After the service the congregation went in little groups to look at the date newly filled up on the white headstone, and to talk in whispers of "the parson"—and of his dear wife, whom only one or two people now living in the parish ever remembered to have seen. But, though every one loved him and missed him, no one grieved—no one could grieve, not even his own children; for the long separation was ended, and Mary Garland's husband slept by her side.

THE END.

Abbott's Young Christian Series. Very greatly improved and enlarged. Numerous Engravings. The Volumes sold separately. Complete in 4 vols., 12mo, Cloth, $1 75 each:

The Young Christian; The Corner-Stone; The Way to do Good; Hoaryhead and M'Donner.

Aikin's Evenings at Home; or, The Juvenile Budget Opened. By Dr. AIKIN and Mrs. BARBAULD. With 34 Engravings by ADAMS. 12mo, Cloth, $1 50.

Child's History of England. By CHARLES DICKENS. 2 vols., 16mo, Cloth, $2 00.

Child's History of the United States. By JOHN BONNER. 3 vols., 16mo, Cloth, $3 75.

Child's History of Rome. By JOHN BONNER. With Illustrations. 2 vols., 16mo, Cloth, $2 50.

Child's History of Greece. By JOHN BONNER. With Illustrations. 16mo, Cloth, $2 50.

Edgar's Boyhood of Great Men. By JOHN G. EDGAR. With Illustrations. 16mo, Cloth, $1 20.

Edgar's Footprints of Famous Men. By JOHN G. EDGAR. With Illustrations. 16mo, Cloth, $1 20.

Edgar's History for Boys; or, Annals of the Nations of Modern Europe. By JOHN G. EDGAR. Illustrations. 16mo, Cloth, $1 20.

Edgar's Sea-Kings and Naval Heroes. A Book for Boys. By JOHN G. EDGAR. Illustrated by C. Keene and E. K. Johnson. 16mo, Cloth, $1 20.

Edgar's Wars of the Roses. By JOHN G. EDGAR. Illustrations. 16mo, Cloth, $1 20.

Nineteen Beautiful Years; or, Sketches of a Girl's Life. Written by her Sister. With an Introduction by Rev. R. S. FOSTER, D.D. 16mo, Cloth, $1 00.

Harper's Boys' and Girls' Library. 32 Volumes. Numerous Engravings. 18mo, Cloth. Sold separately at 75 cents a Volume:

Lives of the Apostles and Early Martyrs.
The Swiss Family Robinson. 2 vols.
Sunday Evenings. Comprising Scripture Stories. 3 vols.
Mrs. Hofland's Son of a Genius.
Thatcher's Indian Traits. 2 vols.
Thatcher's Tales of the American Revolution.
Miss Eliza Robins's Tales from American History. 3 vols.
Mrs. Hofland's Young Crusoe; or, The Shipwrecked Boy.
Perils of the Sea.
Lives of Distinguished Females.
Mrs. Phelps's Caroline Westerley.
Mrs. Hughs's Ornaments Discovered.
The Clergyman's Orphan; the Infidel Reclaimed.
Uncle Philip's Natural History.
Uncle Philip's Evidences of Christianity.
Uncle Philip's History of Virginia.
Uncle Philip's American Forest.
Uncle Philip's History of New York. 2 vols.
Uncle Philip's Whale Fishery and the Polar Seas. 2 vols.
Uncle Philip's History of the Lost Colonies of Greenland.
Uncle Philip's History of Massachusetts. 2 vols.
Uncle Philip's History of New Hampshire. 2 vols.

Harper's Fireside Library: expressly adapted to the Domestic Circle, Sunday-Schools, &c. Cloth, Seventy-five Cents each:

Alden's Alice Gordon.
Alden's Lawyer's Daughter.
Alden's Young Schoolmistress.
Burdett's Arthur Martin.
The Dying Robin.
Ellen Herbert; or, Family Changes.
Mayhew's Good Genius that turned every thing into Gold.
William the Cottager.
Mayhew's Magic of Kindness.

Harper's Story Books. Narratives, Biographies, and Tales for the Young. By JACOB ABBOTT. With more than 1000 beautiful Engravings.

"HARPER'S STORY BOOKS" can be obtained complete in Twelve Volumes, each one containing Three Stories, at the price of $21 00; or in Thirty-six Thin Volumes, each containing One Story, at the price of $32 40. The volumes sold separately.

Vol. I. Bruno; Willie and the Mortgage; The Strait Gate. Vol. II. The Little Louvre; Prank; Emma. Vol. III. Virginia; Timboo and Joliba; Timboo and Fanny. Vol. IV. The Harper Establishment; Franklin; The Studio. Vol. V. The Story of Ancient History; The Story of English History; The Story of American History. Vol. VI. John True; Elfred; The Museum. Vol. VII. The Engineer; Rambles among the Alps; The Three Gold Dollars. Vol. VIII. The Gibraltar Gallery; The Alcove; Dialogues. Vol. IX. The Great Elm; Aunt Margaret; Vernon. Vol. X. Carl and Jocko; Lapstone; Orkney the Peacemaker. Vol. XI. Judge Justin; Minigo; Jasper. Vol. XII. Congo; Viola; Little Paul.

Some of the Story Books are written particularly for Girls, and some for Boys; and the different volumes are adapted to various ages, so that the Series forms a complete Library of Story Books for Children of the Family and the Sunday-School.

Miss Mulock's Our Year. A Child's Book in Prose and Verse. Illustrated by Clarence Dobell. 16mo, Cloth, gilt edges, $1 00.

Children's Picture-Books. Square 4to, about 300 pages each, beautifully printed on Tinted Paper, with many Illustrations by Weir, Steinle, Overbeck, Veit, Schnorr, Harvey, &c., bound in Cloth, gilt, $1 50 a volume; or the Series complete in neat case, $7 50:

The Children's Bible Picture-Book; The Children's Picture Fable-Book; The Children's Picture-Book of Quadrupeds, and other Mammalia; The Children's Picture-Book of the Sagacity of Animals; The Children's Picture-Book of Birds.

Mayhew's Boyhood of Martin Luther; or, The Sufferings of the Little Beggar-Boy who afterward became the Great German Reformer. By HENRY MAYHEW. Beautifully illustrated. 16mo, Cloth. $1 25.

Mayhew's Peasant-Boy Philosopher. The Story of the Peasant-Boy Philosopher; or, "A Child gathering Pebbles on the Sea-Shore." (Founded on the Early Life of Ferguson, the Shepherd-Boy Astronomer, and intended to show how a Poor Lad became acquainted with the Principles of Natural Science.) By HENRY MAYHEW. Illustrations. 16mo, Cloth, $1 25.

Mayhew's Wonders of Science; or, Young Humphrey Davy (the Cornish Apothecary's Boy, who taught himself Natural Philosophy, and eventually became President of the Royal Society). The Life of a Wonderful Boy written for Boys. By HENRY MAYHEW. Illustrations. 16mo, Cloth, $1 25.

Mayhew's Young Benjamin Franklin; or, The Right Road through Life? A Story to show how Young Benjamin Learned the Principles which Raised him from a Printer's Boy to the First Embassador of the American Republic. A Boy's Book on a Boy's own Subject. By HENRY MAYHEW. With Illustrations by John Gilbert. 16mo, Cloth, $1 25.

Mr. Wind and Madam Rain. By PAUL DE MUSSET. Translated by EMILY MAKEPEACE. Illustrated by Charles Bennett. Square 4to, Cloth, 75 cents.

Mrs. Mortimer's Reading without Tears; or, A Pleasant Mode of Learning to Read. Beautifully Illustrated. Small 4to, Cloth, 75 cents.

Mrs. Mortimer's Reading without Tears, Part II. Beautifully Illustrated. Small 4to, Cloth. (*Just Ready.*)

Mrs. Mortimer's Lines Left Out; or, Some of the Histories left out in "Line upon Line." The First Part relates Events in the Times of the Patriarchs and the Judges. By the Author of "Line upon Line," "Reading without Tears," "More about Jesus," "Streaks of Light,&c. With Illustrations. 16mo, Cloth, 75 cents.

Mrs. Mortimer's More about Jesus. With Illustrations and a Map. By the author of "Peep of Day," "Reading without Tears," &c. 16mo, Cloth, 75 cents.

Mrs. Mortimer's Streaks of Light; or Fifty-two Facts from the Bible for Fifty-two Sundays of the Year. By the Author of "Reading without Tears," &c. Illustrations. 16mo, Cloth, gilt, 75 cents.

Harry's Ladder to Learning. With 250 Illustrations. Square 4to, Cloth, 75 cents.

Harry's Summer in Ashcroft. Illustrations. Square 4to, Cloth, 75 cents.

Kingston's Fred Markham in Russia; or, The Boy Travellers in the Land of the Czar. By W. H. G. KINGSTON. Profusely and elegantly illustrated. Small 4to, Cloth, gilt, 75 cents.

Reid's Odd People. Being a Popular Description of Singular Races of Men. By Captain MAYNE REID. With Illustrations. 16mo, Cloth, 75 cents.

Reuben Davidger. The Adventures of Reuben Davidger, Seventeen Years and Four Months Captive among the Dyaks of Borneo. By JAMES GREENWOOD. With Engravings. 8vo, Cloth, $1 75.

Seymour's Self-Made Men. By CHARLES C. B. SEYMOUR. Many Portraits. 12mo, 588 pages, Cloth, $1 75.

Smiles's Self-Help: with Illustrations of Character and Conduct. By Samuel Smiles. 12mo, Cloth, $1 25.

Thackeray's Rose and the Ring; or, The History of Prince Giglio and Prince Bulbo. A Fireside Pantomime for Great and Small Children. By Mr. M. A. TITMARSH. Numerous Illustrations. Small 4to, Cloth, $1 00.

Wood's Homes without Hands: Being a Description of the Habitations of Animals, classed according to their Principle of Construction. By J. G. WOOD, M.A., F.L.S., Author of "Illustrated Natural History." With about 140 Illustrations, engraved on Wood by G. Pearson, from Original Designs made by F. W. Keyl and E. A. Smith, under the Author's Superintendence. 8vo, Cloth, Beveled, $4 50.

"They do honor to American Literature, and would do honor to the Literature of any Country in the World."

THE RISE OF THE DUTCH REPUBLIC.

A History.

BY JOHN LOTHROP MOTLEY.

New Edition. With a Portrait of WILLIAM OF ORANGE. 3 vols. 8vo, Muslin, $9 00.

We regard this work as the best contribution to modern history that has yet been made by an American.—*Methodist Quarterly Review.*

The "History of the Dutch Republic" is a great gift to us; but the heart and earnestness that beat through all its pages are greater, for they give us most timely inspiration to vindicate the true ideas of our country, and to compose an able history of our own.—*Christian Examiner* (Boston).

This work bears on its face the evidences of scholarship and research. The arrangement is clear and effective; the style energetic, lively, and often brilliant. * * * Mr. Motley's instructive volumes will, we trust, have a circulation commensurate with their interest and value.—*Protestant Episcopal Quarterly Review.*

To the illustration of this most interesting period Mr. Motley has brought the matured powers of a vigorous and brilliant mind, and the abundant fruits of patient and judicious study and deep reflection. The result is, one of the most important contributions to historical literature that have been made in this country.—*North American Review.*

We would conclude this notice by earnestly recommending our readers to procure for themselves this truly great and admirable work, by the production of which the auther has conferred no less honor upon his country than he has won praise and fame for himself, and than which, we can assure them, they can find nothing more attractive or interesting within the compass of modern literature. —*Evangelical Review.*

It is not often that we have the pleasure of commending to the attention of the lover of books a work of such extraordinary aud unexceptionable excellence as this one.—*Universalist Quarterly Review.*

There are an elevation and a classic polish in these volumes, and a felicity of grouping and of portraiture, which invest the subject with the attractions of a living and stirring episode in the grand historic drama.—*Southern Methodist Quarterly Review.*

The author writes with a genial glow and love of his subject.—*Presbyterian Quarterly Review.*

Mr. Motley is a sturdy Republican and a hearty Protestant. His style is lively and picturesque, and his work is an honor and an important accession to our national literature.—*Church Review.*

Mr. Motley's work is an important one, the result of profound research, sincere convictions, sound principles, and manly sentiments; and even those who are most familiar with the history of the period will find in it a fresh and vivid addition to their previous knowledge. It does honor to American literature, and would do honor to the literature of any country in the world.—*Edinburgh Review.*

A serious chasm in English historical literature has been (by this book) very remarkably filled. * * * A history as complete as industry and genius can make it now lies before us, of the first twenty years of the revolt of the United Provinces. * * * All the essentials of a great writer Mr. Motley eminently possesses. His mind is broad, his industry unwearied. In power of dramatic description no modern historian, except, perhaps, Mr. Carlyle, surpasses him, and in analysis of character he is elaborate and distinct.—*Westminster Review.*

It is a work of real historical value, the result of accurate criticism, written in a liberal spirit, and from first to last deeply interesting.—*Athenæum.*

The style is excellent, clear, vivid, eloquent; and the industry with which original sources have been investigated, and through which new light has been shed over perplexed incidents and characters, entitles Mr. Motley to a high rank in the literature of an age peculiarly rich in history.—*North British Review.*

It abounds in new information, and, as a first work, commands a very cordial recognition, not merely of the promise it gives, but of the extent and importance of the labor actually performed on it.—*London Examiner.*

Mr. Motley's "History" is a work of which any country might be proud.—*Press* (London).

Mr. Motley's History will be a standard book of reference in historical literature.—*London Literary Gazette.*

Mr. Motley has searched the whole range of historical documents necessary to the composition of his work.—*London Leader.*

This is really a great work. It belongs to the class of books in which we range our Grotes, Milmans, Merivales, and Macaulays, as the glories of English literature in the department of history. * * * Mr. Motley's gifts as a historical writer are among the highest and rarest.—*Nonconformist* (London).

Mr. Motley's volumes will well repay perusal. * * * For his learning, his liberal tone, and his generous enthusiasm, we heartily commend him, and bid him good speed for the remainer of his interesting and heroic narrative.—*Saturday Review.*

The story is a noble one, and is worthily treated. * * * Mr. Motley has had the patience to unravel, with unfailing perseverance, the thousand intricate plots of the adversaries of the Prince of Orange; but the details and the literal extracts which he has derived from original documents, and transferred to his pages, give a truthful color and a picturesque effect, which are especially charming.—*London Daily News.*

M. Lothrop Motley dans son magnifique tableau de la formation de notre République.—G. Groen Van Prinsterer.

Our accomplished countryman, Mr. J. Lothrop Motley, who, during the last five years, for the better prosecution of his labors, has established his residence in the neighborhood of the scenes of his narrative. No one acquainted with the fine powers of mind possessed by this scholar, and the earnestness with which he has devoted himself to the task, can doubt that he will do full justice to his important but difficult subject.—W. H. Prescott.

The production of such a work as this astonishes, while it gratifies the pride of the American reader.—*N. Y. Observer.*

The "Rise of the Dutch Republic" at once, and by acclamation, takes its place by the "Decline and Fall of the Roman Empire," as a work which, whether for research, substance, or style, will never be superseded.—*N. Y. Albion.*

A work upon which all who read the English language may congratulate themselves.—*New Yorker Handels Zeitung.*

Mr. Motley's place is now (alluding to this book) with Hallam and Lord Mahon, Alison and Macaulay in the Old Country, and with Washington Irving, Prescott, and Bancroft in this.—*N. Y. Times.*

The authority, in the English tongue, for the history of the period and people to which it refers.—*N. Y. Courier and Enquirer.*

This work at once places the author on the list of American historians which has been so signally illustrated by the names of Irving, Prescott, Bancroft, and Hildreth.—*Boston Times.*

The work is a noble one, and a most desirable acquisition to our historical literature.—*Mobile Advertiser.*

Such a work is an honor to its author, to his country, and to the age in which it was written.—*Ohio Farmer.*

www.ingramcontent.com/pod-product-compliance
Lightning Source LLC
LaVergne TN
LVHW020237110826
845151LV00003B/945

9781425531355